LONE KING

KING BROTHERS
BOOK FOUR

K.M. SCOTT

Lone King

Marius

I love my life. I do as I want, when I want, and with whomever I want. It's a good life.

I'm the King brother who's always single, but I'll let you in on a secret. I've been with the same incredible woman for two years. She makes me happier than I ever thought possible. I'm crazy in love with her, like the kind of love I never thought actually existed in real life.

So why doesn't anyone know this? I like to keep things to myself. Anyway, my brothers would have a million questions they'd expect me to answer if they found out, so why would I tell them?

It's not certain how long I can keep things on the down low. The woman I love wants to tell the world, and I have a hard time denying her anything. Except this. So for now, she and I will be happy, and no one will know.

That is, until our secret comes out.

Duck

Like the nickname he gave me? I didn't for a long time, but it's grown on me. Plus, he's so cute when he calls me it.

I'm the woman Marius King loves. Except nobody but he and I know that.

I guess to some people that would be strange. I'm not sure we aren't strange. How we got together wasn't exactly a meet cute, but then again, neither of us is the meet cute kind. How we've been since that first day would likely be considered strange by some too.

That's okay. We don't care. I love him and he loves me, so we're good.

That is, until everyone finds out our secret.

LONE KING PLAYLIST

Lone King Playlist

Dream On-Aerosmith
Wrap It Up-The Fabulous Thunderbirds
Breakaway-Art Garfunkel
Still of the Night-Whitesnake
I Fell In Love With The Devil-Avril Lavigne
All I Want Is You-U2
Midnight Rider-Allman Brothers
Urgent-Foreigner
In The Evening-Led Zeppelin
If Anyone Falls-Stevie Nicks
Don't Dream It's Over-Crowded House
Why Can't This Be Love-Van Halen
Always On My Mind-Willie Nelson

CHAPTER ONE

*M*arius

THEY SAY SAVE THE BEST FOR LAST, SO THAT MUST BE what this is. I guess it's my turn to have my story told. Not that it could ever be the whole story. With how close I play my cards to the vest, how could it?

I learned at a very early age to let few people know what I'm actually doing. Most of my life, I've been the middle King. Two brothers before me and two brothers after me left me being the exact middle of the pack.

So what did that mean? Well, Matthias was the oldest, so he got all the pressure. And Ronan was the youngest, so he had a much easier time compared to the rest of us. Theo was usually a dick. Surprised to finally hear someone say that? Yeah, it's not nice to speak ill of the dead, but did you notice how he treated Ava all those years? Dude actually thought he could dip his wick anywhere he chose and she'd always be waiting for him. Serves him right that Matthias took her for himself. And he wasn't the only brother Theo dicked over. As for Kellen, he's always been the brother who prided himself on being out of control. I'm pretty sure that was an attention seeking ploy since he wasn't cool with simply being the second to youngest King.

Now that leaves only me out of the five of us to have his story told. Unlike my younger brother, I never wanted anyone to know what I was doing. Wild or not, it's best to keep your business on the down low. The less people know, the better.

That means that most people who know my family know next to nothing about me. They can point to my being a photographer or a great pool player. Some mention how they've seen my pics in major publications, which is always nice. But truth be told, they really have no idea who I am.

And I love it that way.

Now that it's time for my story, there are a few things you need to remember or nothing you read after this will make sense. (Like that reference to the beginning of A Christmas Carol? No? Leave the references to the bears? Got it. Let's move on.)

First, I've never hated love. I seem to, especially to my brothers, but no, I do not and never have hated love. Who the hell hates love? Sounds like something a psychopath would say.

What I hated was finding out the first woman I ever loved was a gold digger who only wanted me for my family's money. Imagine someone dating me only for money when there are so many other great benefits. So fuck Maia. I heard she ended up marrying some insurance guy. Good. I hope for nothing more than for her to get what she deserves.

Second, I prefer to keep my business to myself, and that includes hiding things from my brothers. None of them appreciate the kind of life I want to live, so why keep them in the loop? It's enough for them to think I spend my time snapping pictures of beautiful women on beaches and then sleeping with them.

Third, and this one is the most important thing to remember, I've been hiding something big from everyone in the world but the one person who means the most to me.

So, are you ready? Buckle up because this is going to be a wild ride. Just remember those three things because they're going to be important. No, there won't be a quiz after. Don't be a smartass.

Without further ado, it's time for this King brother to get his happily ever after. Let's see how it goes.

CHAPTER TWO

*M*arius

I SWIPE MY HAND ACROSS THE MIRROR TO CLEAR AWAY the fog left over from the steam of the shower and take a good look at my face. It's the same face I've seen all my life. Just a little older now. The question for me today is do I want to shave?

After seeing Ronan with that scraggly ass beard, I thought I'd never want to stop shaving. Leave it to my baby brother to have a good looking woman shave him and he makes no move to have her. Then again, that King has only loved one woman in his entire life, and that's Kate, so I guess it's not surprising he didn't want to get busy with Sabrina.

Oh, little minx thought she had a golden ticket for the gravy train before I came along to ruin her plans. Like I told him, she would have switched her affections to me if she thought she had a chance, but alas, I wasn't available either.

Nobody knows that, though, so let's keep that under our hats for a little while. Everyone can find out in due time about my private life. For now, I want to keep it to myself.

I'd bet a hundred bucks it ran through Sabrina's mind to try something with Matthias too, just like I told him. He naturally assumed I was crazy and had watched too much porn. Sure, I watch porn, and the nanny and single dad is a popular theme, assuming anyone gives a fuck what people do for a living in those movies. That doesn't mean I was wrong about Sabrina.

I reach for my razor and slide a new blade in before I look around for the shaving cream. Nothing seems to be where it should be in this bathroom. Then again, I haven't lived here long, so maybe that's the problem. I just closed on this penthouse a few months ago.

With a face full of shaving cream and a fresh blade in my razor, I set about cleaning myself up. That's what you do when the woman you adore is joining you for dinner.

Ten minutes later, my beard is no more, so I head down to the kitchen to find my phone. I check but don't have any messages, which means she'll be here soon.

I hear the elevator doors open and turn around to see her kicking off her three inch heels from work. Honestly, how does she wear those things? She claims they don't hurt and she loves them, especially the red soles. Why women buy shoes because of the color of the soles will always be a mystery to me, but I do have to admit her legs look incredible in them.

"You're not dressed," she says when she walks into

the kitchen and stops in front of me, that beautiful mouth of hers turned down in a pout. "I thought we were having dinner."

"We are," I say with a smile, happier now that she's here with me. I take a step toward her and stare into those gorgeous green eyes looking up at me since she's almost a foot shorter than I am when she's not wearing her shoes. "How was your day, dear? Tough time at work?"

As she slides her arms around my waist to pull me to her, she groans. "You have no idea. You standing here in nothing but a white towel low on your hips is the best part of my entire day, baby."

I've been with a lot of women, but none of them have ever made me want them more than this woman. It's like she has some kind of hold on me.

Not that I mind. I had no idea love could be something so great until this relationship. We've been together for two years, and I have to say they've been the best two years of my life. It's like I never wanted another woman after the first night with her, and that's saying something considering what my life was like before her.

Leaning down, I kiss her beautiful mouth. "I'll be ready in a couple. It's not like it takes long. I'm a guy. We throw some clothes on and voila! Ready to roll."

Turning out of her hold, I look back and chuckle. "I promise I won't take more than five minutes."

I hear her padding across the floor following me up to the bedroom, so I spin around and walk backwards. "Need something from me?" I joke.

She levels her gaze on my face and stares directly into my eyes with such intensity I know the answer before she says a word. "You know what I need, Marius."

That I do.

"Duck, I think that job of yours is too stressful. You should leave it," I say as she steps into my embrace.

Smiling, she shakes her head. "First of all, I want you to know I don't hate that nickname anymore."

"It's a great nickname, and even better, it's wisdom that you can never go wrong with. When someone's throwing punches around you, duck. Or as you should have that night, just a little duck."

She ignores my concise explanation as to why the nickname I gave her still works and continues. "And second, I can't quit my job, Marius. What will I do then? Hang out here all day?"

I slide my hands down her back to cup her beautiful ass. "I love that idea!"

That gets me an eye roll. "You would."

"What's so wrong about wanting to be with the woman I love more often?" I ask as I dip my head to nuzzle her neck.

She runs her fingernails over the back of my head, making a shiver go down my spine as I pepper her collarbone with kisses. "You'd see me more often if you didn't stay at your brother's every night, you know."

I lift my head and gaze into her eyes as she gives me a look that says she knows she's right. "Fair enough. You know I haven't had much of a choice in the past couple months, don't you?"

Her gaze softens, and she nods her head. "I know. I just wanted to make sure you were seeing things clearly. Sometimes you don't."

This woman challenges me more than anyone else ever has. And I love it. I'll take a woman who speaks her mind any day over those meek and mild types.

"I know, but I had to keep an eye on Ronan."

Trailing her fingertips down over my chest, she smiles and stands on her tiptoes to kiss me on the lips. "I think it's great that you wanted to watch out for him, baby. Honestly. I've never given you a hard time about that, have I?"

"No. In fact, that's just one of the million reasons why I love you."

She looks up at me and smiles. "I understand why you feel so protective about him, Marius. I'm just saying you'd see me more if you were here every night."

"I still think you should quit your job. It stresses you out, Duck. Forget that. Life is too short to be stressed out. Quit that job and we'll travel the world. What do you say?"

Her eyebrows shoot up into her forehead. "So you're going to be sleeping in your own bed here from now on?"

"Soon. I'm still concerned about Ronan, but as soon as I know he's okay, absolutely."

She slides her hand down over my stomach and cups my hard cock through the towel. "Then soon is when I might quit my job."

I know she's right. Ronan is a grown man, so he probably doesn't need me worrying about him. It's just that after finding him bleeding out on his bathroom floor that terrible spring night, I can't help looking out for him.

"This is why I love you, Duck. You're not like other women. You don't yell when you're angry."

She shakes her head at my compliment. "Marius, women yell because they're frustrated. Nine times out of ten, if a woman is yelling, she's tried to get her husband or boyfriend to hear what she's saying too many times to count. Maybe if you men listened to us you wouldn't hear so much yelling."

"Well, whatever the reason is that you don't yell, I like it."

"I don't yell because of my father. Nobody ever yelled at him. He's commanded respect all his life. I decided when I was just a little girl that I wanted to be like him, so I watched and learned. He never gets flustered. He says what's on his mind and goes about his life. If someone has a problem with him, he listens, but if he doesn't think he's wrong, he stands firm. However, if he's wrong, he doesn't wait to apologize. That's why people respect him."

I've always gotten the feeling my Duck is a daddy's girl. She's the only daughter with four brothers, and every time she's mentioned her father, it's in almost adoring terms like right now. Let's hope when we finally let the world know about us that he doesn't hate me because we've been hiding our relationship.

Walking away, she heads for the steps. "You coming, or am I doing this alone again tonight?" she asks with a wicked grin.

The thought of her masturbating while I'm not here to give herself what she needs makes me even more excited, and I quickly move to catch up to her. "No need to go it alone tonight since I'm here and ready to roll."

Reaching back, she takes my hand in hers. "Good. I prefer the real thing. Silicone isn't my groove."

As we climb the stairs to the second floor, I say, "Did I ever happen to mention how sexy I think it is that you're so open about everything?"

She glances back and me and laughs. "One of these days, you're going to have to tell me about the women you were going out with before me because they sound like a bunch of puritans."

I never thought I was spending time with uptight women, but compared to Duck, I guess they were pretty puritanical. Maybe that's why I'm not with them anymore.

"Well, forget them. All I want to think about is you and me and how many times I'm going to make you come before dinner."

When she hits the top of the stairs, she turns around to face me, and I see she's unbuttoned her dress. I do love a woman who's ready for fun.

"By the way, if I knew we were going to get busy before going to the restaurant, I would have worn a different bra and underwear. You're catching me unmatched," she says with a smile.

I stop one step below her and slide my hands over her ribs. Does she really think I care that her bra is black but her underwear are pink?

"Duck, you do know men don't care about matching bras and underwear, right? We're pretty base creatures, so all we care about is what's underneath."

She moans when I unhook her bra and slip my hands under it to cup her breasts. Her skin is petal soft but hot, like she's burning up.

"Do you have a fever, Duck?" I ask as I step up to press a kiss on her forehead. "Feels cool up here, though."

"You know how I am, Marius," she says before walking away toward the bedroom.

I do know how she is, but I worry about her too. She works too many hours, and I'm pretty sure wearing three inch heels five days a week isn't good for her either. I'd love if she'd quit that job and spend her time traveling the world with me. Now that Ronan is doing better, I can return to being the nomad I've always been, just with my Duck at my side.

"You're definitely hot," I tease, and she turns around as she walks into the bedroom.

"Thank you. You're pretty hot yourself," she says and then strips out of her dress, tossing it onto the floor near the closet.

She climbs onto the bed and crooks her finger, beckoning me to her. Still wearing my towel, I stop just before I reach her and toss it aside.

With a smile, she looks down my body. Licking her lips, she says, "Do you know what I love most about you right now?"

I palm my cock and give it a few strokes. "This?"

Duck bites her bottom lip. "No, although I do love that. No, what I love more is how playful you let me be. Nowhere else in this world do I get to be like I am with you."

I climb onto the bed and crawl up next to her. "I want you to be exactly who you want to be all the time. I love you, Duck, and whatever makes you happy makes me happy."

"How did I get so lucky to be with a man like you?" she asks as she pulls me down to kiss her.

Snaking my tongue into her mouth, I tease her for a few seconds before answering, "Well, there I was in Vegas at a pool tournament just enjoying life and you walked into it. The rest they say is history."

"You forgot about my getting punched in the eye, the reason for my nickname," she says while she slides her hands down my back, her fingernails raking over my skin and sending strings of need through my body.

I nuzzle just below her ear and whisper, "I didn't forget. I just thought I'd go with the non-violent version of our getting together."

Her bra and panties need to go, so I strip them off her body quickly and toss them onto the floor. Naked and ready for me, she opens her legs, and I settle in between them.

"So I thought I'd like to be on top tonight," she says with a wicked smile.

I kiss her and roll the two of us over so I'm on my back and she's between my legs. "Your wish is my command, my lady."

She runs her hands up from my hips to my neck, her mouth following as she peppers kisses along the way. When she looks up, she smiles and says, "I love that you are okay with me riding you. Some guys are uncomfortable with that."

The very idea of any man not wanting a woman to ride his cock until she comes is fucking baffling. Who are these men? I can't fathom why any guy would say no to that.

"Now it's my turn to ask about the people you used to

date before me because any guy who would tell you no to being on top is a fucking moron."

Duck lifts herself off me and sets her legs on each side of my body. Slowly, she lowers herself until that beautiful pussy of hers is barely an inch away from my cock.

"I didn't say I dated the best guys. I thought all men loved women riding them, but come to find out, that's not the case."

"Well, I swear I'll never say no to you being on top, Duck," I say as I set my hands on her hips. "I have no problem with a woman being in control. At least sometimes."

Leaning down, she kisses me long and deep, and all I can think about is how much I want to be balls deep inside her right now. Thankfully, she's thinking the same thing.

I look down my body and watch as she slowly takes every inch of me. It's the sexiest fucking thing I've ever seen in my life and feels ten times better than it looks.

"Jesus, you feel incredible."

She rolls her hips and giggles as my eyes roll back into my head. "I love seeing you like this. You're so sensual. It's very sexy."

With a smile, I slide my hands up her body and cup her beautiful breasts. "I could say the same about you."

Her eyelids flutter closed as I play with her, teasing for a few seconds before I push myself up to take one of her dark pink nipples into my mouth. I know how she loves it when I do this. It never fails to get her going.

"Mmmm...God, Marius. I'm not going to last long

with you nibbling on me like that. You know what it does to me."

I lift my hips off the bed and drive into her hard. She's so fucking wet right now, and I swear I'm not going to last very long either with how she feels around my cock.

"That's why I do it. You want to come, don't you?" I ask as she begins riding me in earnest, her long black hair swinging around her.

"Yeah, but I'd like to last a little longer than a few seconds."

"Not to worry. We have all night."

She moans and then asks, "What about dinner?"

I slide my right hand up her body and encircle her neck as she rides me faster and faster. Her eyes get big when I tighten my grip ever so slightly, and I can feel her cunt contract around me.

"Fuck dinner."

Smiling big, she rolls her hips and whimpers. I can feel her pulse race against my fingertips. "I thought that's what you were doing with me."

"Actually, I think this is technically considered you fucking me," I joke.

She stops moving as if she's thinking about my claim and shrugs. "I guess so. I better get to work then. You ready to come, baby?"

The truth is I was ready the second she stepped out of the damn elevator, but I know how much my Duck loves the foreplay. It's just another one of the million reasons I love her.

I watch in rapt attention as she rides me like I'm some bucking bronco, her body undulating as she takes every inch of me into her and then raises herself up so I'm barely inside her. It's maddening and sensual and about to drive me out of my fucking mind, but it's the best feeling in the whole goddamned world.

Like she thought, she doesn't last long, and before I know it, she's collapsing onto my chest while her entire body quakes from her orgasm. "Jesus, Marius...I needed that."

As always, I know what she needs, and I happily give it to her.

"You didn't come," she whispers, and I can practically hear the pout in her voice.

"Not yet. Time for part two. On your knees," I command as I ease her off me.

She does just as I say, and I position myself behind her. Grabbing hold of her hips once again, I lean forward and plant kisses up the length of her spine until I reach the back of her head. I tighten my fist around her hair and hear her moan. Jesus, I love that sound.

"Marius, you're being a tease," she whines.

In her ear, I say, "Does my Duck want something? All you have to do is tell me."

Pushing back against me, she says in a soft voice, "You know what I want."

I do, so I lean back and thrust my hips forward, filling her completely. Duck grabs the sheets and holds onto them tightly as I begin to fuck her. With each time I drive my cock into her perfect cunt, she moans and whimpers, making my need to come even greater.

As much as I want this to last all night, I can't keep myself from coming before long. With one last plunge inside her, I still as my cock pulses and I come hard.

The two of us finally collapse onto the bed in a sweaty mess of afterglow. As I try to regain my ability to think straight, she flips her hair back so I can see her face and smiles.

"I'm thinking we should order in tonight. You in?" Duck asks.

I wrap my arm around her waist and pull her to me before softly kissing the tip of her nose. "Whatever you want. I'd be fine with bringing up some crackers and something to drink and staying in bed all night."

She rests her head on my chest, and with every breath, I feel warmth dance across my skin. "Good."

We lie there in silence, and all I can think is I don't want to imagine a time when she isn't mine. In the eyes of the rest of the world, I'm a manwhore who couldn't care less about love. The reality is very different, though.

I'd be lost without this woman. Someday, everyone will know about us and how crazy I am about her. Until then, though, it's just the two of us.

Which is fine by me.

CHAPTER THREE

den

AFTER MAKING A BAG OF MICROWAVE POPCORN, I settle in to watch one of my favorite series. I've cleared the entire day for this marathon. After a hard week at work, I deserve to relax.

Naturally, not halfway through the first episode, my phone rings. I glance down and see it's Ava. If it were nearly anyone else on the planet, I'd let it go to voicemail, but not for my best friend.

"What are you doing?" Ava asks when I answer the call, and I mute the TV.

"I'm watching something. Nothing big."

There's silence on her end of the phone, and then finally Ava asks, "Are you watching Air Disasters again?"

The judgment in her tone comes through loud and clear.

"Yes. Is that a crime?" I wish I didn't sound so defensive.

She chuckles and says, "No, but I don't think it's normal, especially for someone who's afraid to fly."

"I'm not afraid to fly," I say defiantly, knowing the truth is I loathe flying. "Anyway, I don't watch this show to look at what's flying or what's not flying for that matter."

Ava chuckles again and says, "I know why you watch this show, and I'm not going to lie. I think it's strange. Is this an episode with him in it?"

"Of course." Not that I don't watch episodes he's not in but not usually.

"Well, should I let you get back to it?"

"Don't worry. The DVR is taking care of it."

"Do you DVR every single episode of Air Disasters?"

She asks that like it would be bizarre if I did. "No, just the ones with him in it."

"You don't even know his name, Eden. What's the point of this?"

The frustration in my friend's voice is palpable. I don't understand why this bothers her, though. So I like to watch a show about airplane crashes? Who is that hurting?

"Why does there have to be a point to it? I like looking at him, so I watch the show. It's not a big deal. And I certainly don't need to know his name."

"I think it might be a big deal. It's sort of weird."

"It's not weird. You just think it is because you have your dream man, and he's always right next to you, and he's crazy about you, and he does everything you want, and he thinks you're the best person he's ever met. Well, I don't have that in my life. Let me have fantasizing about the guy from Air Disasters, okay?"

I don't usually resort to the you-have-everything-so-just-let-me-be defense for anything Ava thinks is strange, but I'll use it for this occasion. It's not a lie. She does have the perfect life with Matthias and those two little boys.

Ava falls silent for a few moments before she quietly says, "I know. I… I… I didn't mean to say that it was weird. I'm sorry. I want you to have everything I have. I want you to have the man of your dreams. I want it all for you. Is it possible this guy is the man of your dreams?"

I throw my head back and laugh as I catch a glimpse of him on my TV. "I don't think so, Ava. He's more fantasy material."

"Okay, well, I'm sure he's hot, right?"

For a few moments, I study the man on the screen. "In an official, civil servant wearing a government uniform way, I guess. I'm not sure. All I know is he works for me. That's it."

"All right. Well, I guess if he works for you, that's great. I'm not going to give up trying to set you up with guys, though, because I want you to not have to watch shows about planes crashing to see a hot man."

"Aww, that's nice and I appreciate that, but it's okay. I'm happy with my life."

That's another little white lie. So what? I know Ava, and if I told her the truth, she'd want to have a whole discussion about it filled with sadness and pity for me. Those are the last things I need.

No, it's better for Ava to think I'm the friend she's always known. Single and perpetually- looking Eden.

"Okay, then I guess I'll get down to why I called. We're having a little get-together next weekend. You'll come, right?"

When I don't immediately answer, she tries to sweeten the offer. "You know, Marius will be there. He told me the other day he's sticking around for a while. I think he wants to keep an eye on Ronan. Whatever his reason is, it's nice to have him around. He's always such a good time when he comes to stay."

"Is he staying at the estate?"

"He is."

Always curious about that King brother, I ask, "Why doesn't he get his own place instead of constantly crashing with you guys? He has the money, so it isn't like he can't afford it."

"Oh, I don't know. I've never asked. Maybe he likes coming back to the house where he grew up? I'm not sure, but I love having him around to spend time with his nephews, and I know Matthias likes having him around."

I catch a glimpse of the man I like on this show and watch him for a few seconds before saying, "Well, I guess if nobody minds, it's not like you don't have room."

"You know…"

Ava stops talking for a moment or two, but I can almost hear the wheels turning in her head. Ever since I mentioned being interested in Marius King almost seven years ago, she's tried to get us together.

"What if we make the party like a sleepover? I know

we're all too old for that, but you could stay here at the house after the party. That way you can drink whatever you want and not have to worry about driving."

I love my best friend. I really do. She's one of the kindest, sweetest people in the world. I don't think Ava could hurt a fly, even if she tried.

But this suggestion of hers screams desperation.

"So what are you saying? That maybe I'll get drunk and he'll get drunk, and we'll end up together?"

She doesn't answer my very pointed question and instead makes that noise that sounds like a hum that she always does when she doesn't know what to say. Finally, though, she quietly answers, "It wouldn't be the worst thing in the world, would it? I just think you two would be perfect together, Eden."

"Why is that?"

"Well, I thought you liked him. Also, we're best friends, and he and Matthias are brothers. It sounds perfect to me."

Of course, it does. Ava would love nothing more than for the two of us to be sisters-in-law. I love her for that.

"I'll tell you what. I'll be at the party, and if by chance Marius and I have a good time talking and getting to know one another, then I'll call the night a success."

"How much more do you have to know about him? You two have talked a bunch of times. Every time you're here you talk."

The guy I'm watching this show for appears, so I check him out for a few seconds before saying, "And all I've found out about him through those conversations is he's a bust ass who's also a manwhore. You seem to think there's more to him than that, but I don't get to see that guy at your parties."

Ava sounds utterly crestfallen when she says, "I just thought it would be nice. I hope you'll still come to the party. You don't have to stay the night. It can just be like a regular party we have."

"Not to worry. I'll be there with bells on, honey."

And just like that, she's back to being happy. "Oh, great! Don't worry. It's going to be so much fun! I've got that new woman helping, so the boys will be safe and taken care of while we're having a good time."

Her mention of the new nanny makes me cringe. I had a feeling my cousin wouldn't be a good fit, but Ava was so desperate and Sabrina jumped at the chance since she said she loved kids. I really did hope it would work.

"I'm sorry about what happened with my cousin, Ava. I didn't think she was that flighty to leave after only a couple weeks."

"It's okay. I liked Sabrina, but Lynn is good too. She's working out great. You don't have to worry. I don't hold anything against you for how things turned out. Sabrina found something else that worked better for her. It's all good."

"Are you sure? I don't want you or Matthias to be mad at me."

"I'm positive. Seriously, don't worry. I was really thankful for the help she gave me, and to be honest, I think she may have helped Ronan even more, so that's a good thing."

Ava may be my best friend, but she's also terribly naïve. I know my cousin left the job as the kids' nanny because Ronan got back together with his high school girlfriend. I never told Ava, but I had a feeling she might try to snag one of the brothers. Since Ronan and Marius were the only free ones available, it wasn't a surprise she chose the youngest King.

Marius King is simply a handful to deal with. For my cousin, that would mean far too much work.

"I'm glad he's doing better. Ronan has always been such a nice guy."

"Oh, he's doing great! To be honest, I really think we have Sabrina to thank for getting the ball rolling with him. Sure, Kate is the one who made him see there's a whole world out there waiting for him, but it was Sabrina who helped him out in the beginning when she got here. So you don't have to worry. I hold no grudge against her."

I chuckle at the thought of Ava holding a grudge against anyone. It's not in her DNA. Anyway, since she got the man of her dreams, she's had a hard time being angry at anyone for very long.

A perfect life with a sexy man who gives you everything your heart desires has a way of making everything else in life seem much less important.

"Thanks. I told my aunt you would probably be cool with what happened, but she was worried. Let's just say she wasn't surprised Sabrina flaked. I guess parents know their own kids."

Ava doesn't respond to my comment, so I turn my attention back to the TV. It's a new episode now, and from what I can see, my favorite guy isn't in this one.

"Hey, it's time for the boys to eat breakfast. Will I see you before the party next weekend?"

"Assuming work doesn't grind me into dust, I could

probably do something one night this week or next. Any chance you can be free? We can grab a drink or go for coffee."

"Oh, I'd like that! Now that I have Lynn, I'm sure I can. Just let me know when. I think I hear Matty crying, so I better fly. Text me when you're free."

She rushes off before I can say goodbye, but that's okay. Now I can get back to enjoying my weekend binge of my favorite show.

CHAPTER FOUR

M arius

THE NOISES OF THE HOUSE WAKE ME UP, AND WHEN I
open my eyes, I'm treated to the sun streaming through
the window. Throwing my arm over my head, I try to
block it out, but it's too late. My nephews and the sun
have conspired against my sleeping in this morning.

I reluctantly roll over toward the blinding light and
grab my cell phone off the nightstand. 8:30.

"Fuck," I groan as I turn onto my back to read any
messages that may have come in since I fell asleep five
hours ago.

I scroll through the texts from friends and my
assistant Sam, not caring about any of them until I get to
the one from Duck. "What time are you coming today? I
have to go out for a few hours, but I don't want to miss
you."

With a smile, I notice her insistence on being grammatically correct in her texts. She's the only person I've ever met who uses commas in her messages. I mentioned it once, and she thought I was making fun of her.

I wasn't. In fact, I never make fun of her. She's the only person on Earth who gets to say that. Well, her, Eleanor, and Ava, but they're different. Everyone else is fair game.

Even without being fully awake, I text her back, knowing she's probably not out of bed yet since she doesn't have work on Sundays. "I'll be home by late afternoon. See you then. Love M"

And to think there are those even in my own family who believe I hate love.

Scrubbing the last of the far too few hours of sleep I got from my face, I swing my legs out of bed and begin walking toward my bedroom door. I stop a few feet before I reach it and look down my body.

Morning wood and no fucking clothes on. I wouldn't have to ever again stop myself from busting ass with Eleanor or Ava if I showed up downstairs in the kitchen like this. They'd probably both drop dead from shock.

I turn around and head over to my dresser to grab a pair of black shorts and an old navy blue and red Penn t-shirt from back when I was dating that girl who went to school there. Might as well stop in the bathroom too before I go downstairs.

As I head toward the door again, I grab my phone and catch a glimpse of myself in the mirror, quickly adjusting my hard-on. The last thing any of the women in this house need to see is my hard dick before nine o'clock on a Sunday morning.

I walk down the stairs as I listen to two babies who sound particularly loud this morning laugh and scream gibberish. Theo has finally started to say a few words, but Matty is a long way off from talking since he's only a couple months old. That doesn't mean he doesn't enjoy joining his older brother in making as much noise as they can on days like today. Hopefully, Ava and that new nanny take them out to the pool to burn off some of their energy.

By the time I reach the first floor, they and Ava are singing that bus song I'm going to be hating by this time next week if they keep belting it out day in and day out. Since it's her house and not mine anymore, I plaster a friendly expression onto my face just before I walk into the kitchen so nobody can see how much I never want to hear that song again.

"Good morning, Marius!" she says in that sweet yet so awake way of hers.

I look at the table and see Ava, Theo, Matty, and my brother, and when I look across the room, I see Eleanor poke her head out from behind the refrigerator door. No Ronan, though. I wonder if he didn't come home last night.

Seems the reunion tour with Kate is still in full swing.

"Morning all," I say in what sounds like more of a grunt. "Is there coffee? Please tell me you've got some because if not, I'm going to die."

Matthias laughs and points at the counter where the coffee pot holds the nectar of the gods. "You look like you didn't get much sleep. Why are you awake so early?"

As I pour myself a cup, I answer, "I had to know what happened to the wheels on that bus. I hear they go round and round, but I'm wondering if they ever just drive the bus off toward the horizon or maybe they come off altogether."

The room falls silent, and when I look over at my brother and sister-in-law, they're giving me strange looks. I sit down next to little Theo and take a sip of black coffee before shrugging.

"What? Don't keep me in suspense. What happens to the bus?"

"We didn't mean to wake you up," Ava says sheepishly.

She shouldn't do that. This is her house now. I'm just being a pain in the ass relative who's likely overstayed his welcome.

I shake my head and sigh. "No, that was wrong of me. I'm sorry. Too little sleep made me forget I don't get to call the shots here. But no kidding, I do want to know how that song ends. Does the bus come back? Drive off a cliff?"

Neither Matthias nor Ava answers, so I turn to my nephew and grab one of his Cheerios off his high chair table. "What about you, buddy? Can you hook me up with some info on that bus I keep hearing about?"

He stares at me like he thinks I'm insane, his dark brown eyes like his father's and mine searching for the answer to some child's question he can't ask yet. No, I'm not insane, Theo. Just tired and a smartass. You'll understand when you get older.

"So, next Saturday night, we're having a party. Nothing big. Just us, Ronan and Kate, Kellen and

Salem, and a few other people. You'll be there, won't you?" Ava asks.

I nod, happy to join in the fun like always. "With bells on. Should I assume I'll be the only single person there as usual?"

"No. Eden will be there, and since she broke up with that guy she was with in the spring, she'll be single too. Nice coincidence, don't you think?"

Smiling, I bite my tongue, but the words come out anyway. "Not really a coincidence since you've been telling me she likes me for over five years."

My sister-in-law shakes her head but smiles. "She hasn't been single that whole time, Marius, but now she is. So what do you say?"

I take another sip of coffee and turn my head to look at my brother. "Is she asking me if this is going to be the party where I make a move on Eden?"

He doesn't answer and simply stands up from the table to leave, kissing Theo before he begins walking toward the hallway. "I think I have a meeting scheduled."

Eleanor laughs over near the sink, and Ava rolls her eyes. "That's not what I was asking, Marius. Now look what you've done. You've chased your brother away to his office, and on a Sunday, no less."

Matty makes a gurgling noise while Theo throws some Cheerios at me, almost as if he understands I'm the bad guy at this table right now. Matthias stops behind Ava's chair and leans down to kiss her before kissing Matty on top of his head.

"What do you say to taking Theo into your office this morning, honey? He can hang out in his baby walker."

Matthias shrugs and walks back to pick up Theo

from the high chair. "Seems your mother thinks you should be put to work, little man. Time to go make a living with your father."

I can't help but smile at how easygoing my older brother is now that he has Ava and kids. It's like all those years of being miserable disappeared when they came into his life. That's good for him, though. He's got enough problems to deal with at King Industries. I'm happy he has a family he loves to come home to.

He walks out with Theo in his arms, leaving Ava holding Matty, Eleanor cleaning up something over on the countertop, and me. I can tell by Ava's expression that she isn't finished with the conversation about the party and Eden. I'm just not sure I'm awake enough for it.

"So you'll come?" she asks.

"As always. Maybe I should bring a date. That way I'll fit in more," I say, joking.

Her blue eyes get big, and she seems frustrated when she says, "The first time Eden's single and you want to bring a date? Just tell me you don't like her. That would be simpler."

I want to joke that bringing a woman to her party would actually be much simpler than telling her I might not be interested in her friend, but I don't. The truth is I'm not disinterested in Eden. I just don't like my family being in my personal business, especially my romantic business.

"Just trying to fit in. Okay, single Marius will be there with bells on."

Like a gift from the heavens, Ronan walks in through the kitchen door, thankfully taking the attention off me. "Hey, everyone! I thought I'd come by to visit."

Ava stands up with Matty still in her arms and gives Ronan a hug. "It's so good to see you! Come, sit down, and tell us what you're doing up so early on a Sunday."

He sits next to me, so I say, "Seriously, dude. You're with the woman of your dreams, and you're not in bed with her on a weekend morning?"

Ronan twists his expression into a grimace for me but then smiles at Ava. "I couldn't sleep, to be honest. Kate's father and I were talking about a prosthetic hand last night, and I swear I didn't get any shut eye all night. All I could think about was the possibility that I might get my hand back."

"Oh, that's wonderful!" Ava coos. "I'm so happy for you, Ronan."

I nudge him with my elbow and smile. "Sounds like a reason to celebrate."

"Ooh, it does! That's perfect. We're having a party here next Saturday, and we really want you and Kate to come. Can you?"

My youngest brother nods. "Sure! I'll have to ask Kate if she has anything planned, but I don't think she does. It's the weekend before Labor Day, so she'll be working all that week."

"Then she's going to need a party to blow off some steam," I say, practically shuddering at the thought of teaching a room full of third graders.

"Right?" he says, laughing. "She found out she has twenty students. Twenty eight-year-olds, five days a week. She's going to be great at it, but damn, I don't know how anyone does that."

When Ronan gets up to ask Eleanor if there's any breakfast left over, I lean in toward Ava and jokingly ask, "Why does my little brother get a hug when he walks in, but I get nothing?"

"I said good morning. Doesn't that count?" she answers with a smile.

"Hmmm…I see how it goes now."

Covering Matty's ears, she levels her gaze on my face and lowers her voice. "If you must know, I find hugging men who have raging hard-ons a little awkward when they aren't my husband."

Sometimes Ava surprises me. Now's one of those times.

Ronan hears what she says and laughs loudly as he sits down with a plate of scrambled eggs. "Don't ask questions if you don't want the answers, dude."

I guess so.

"In my defense, if I stayed away from people every time I had a hard-on, I'd be a hermit living in the wilderness somewhere."

Ava glares at me from across the table and points at the baby on her lap. "Marius! Little ears!"

I could tell her he's going to have hard-ons all his life, but I don't. Instead, I apologize, like the good brother-in-law and uncle that I am.

"Sorry." Looking at Matty, who at the moment seems very interested in his own toes, I say, "Sorry, little man. You'll know what I meant in a few years, but it's cool. Just come to your Uncle Marius if you have any questions."

Next to me, Ronan nearly spits out his eggs. "Come to you? For what? All you're going to tell him is—"

Before he can get the rest of his sentence out, Ava quickly stands up with Matty. "Okay, no more talk about my son's winkie. This is the stuff of parents' nightmares."

She hurries out of the room, followed by Eleanor, leaving just Ronan and me at the table. When I know they're all far enough away that they can't hear me, I look over at him and say one word.

"Winkie?"

The two of us burst into laughter. "Give her a break, Marius. I bet hearing about your kid's penis is jarring, at the very least."

"Sure, but winkie? Anyway, I should be thanking you. Ava was telling me about this party they're having and was more than happy to let me know that her friend is single again."

He doesn't say anything for a long moment as he stuffs a forkful of eggs into his mouth, but after he finishes chewing, he stands up and heads over to the refrigerator to get a glass of orange juice. When he returns to the table, he shakes his head like I said something wrong.

"What?"

"Just get it over with already. Sleep with the woman so she can hate you with the heat of a thousand suns like every other girlfriend you've ever had. Then Ava will never mention it again."

"What makes you think every woman I've ever slept with hates me?"

I'm tempted to tell him I've been with someone for two years and she definitely doesn't hate me, but that would mean I'd have to deal with the million or so questions all my family members would have. Since I'm never in the mood to answer them, I keep my mouth shut.

Ronan finishes his eggs and sits back against his chair. "You're always single. I never hear you say anything about any of your exes, which means they all hate you and you hate them."

I open my mouth to defend myself but stop before I say a word. If the choice is either letting my family think I'm a complete tool when it comes to women or having them know about my relationship, then tool it is.

"Well, you never know, Ronan. Maybe now that you're heading for the altar, maybe it's my turn."

He stands up, taking his plate, fork, and juice glass to the sink and not saying a single word about the idea that I could possibly find love and be happy. I wait for him to come back to the table, but he walks out of the kitchen, leaving me sitting alone.

Looks like I've been very convincing with my claims of not being interested in love all these years.

I feel like finding him and telling him that just because a woman doesn't hold my balls in her purse doesn't mean I'm against love. I just don't want the kind of love he thinks is great. I need something a bit more.

On my way up to my room, I overhear Matthias and Ava talking in his office. When she mentions me, my ears perk up.

"Matthias, I'm thinking since Marius doesn't want anything to do with Eden that maybe you could invite someone from work to join us at the party? You have to know someone nice at King Industries who may like Eden, don't you?"

My brother doesn't answer for a few seconds but

then says, "There's Rob. He's the head of our IT department. Nice guy. Good department head. I've had some productive meetings with him, and at the Christmas party we shared some laughs. Remember him? Light brown hair, just under six foot, thin. Any chance she might like a nerdy IT guy?"

An IT guy? Is my brother kidding? He probably wears a pocket protector and is always pushing his thick, black, birth control glasses up the bridge of his nose.

I wait for Ava to nix that idea since she has to know Eden won't like a geeky IT guy, but to my shock, she thinks it's a fabulous suggestion. "Okay, yeah! I remember him. He was quiet but nice. Not exactly her type, but maybe it's time for her to expand her horizons. Now I just need to decide if I'm going to mention it to her or just have him come to the party and maybe they'll organically get together."

Ronan walks up behind me as I spy on Matthias and Ava and taps me on the shoulder. "Hearing anything good?"

I nearly jump out of my skin and push him back away from me. "What the fuck? You scared me half to death."

Of course, that gets my other brother's attention and Ava's, so they walk out to join us in the hallway. "What are you two doing out here?" Matthias asks, likely already knowing the answer to that question.

Ronan answers, leaving me standing there wishing I was anywhere but here right now. "I was upstairs, and I saw Marius lurking outside your office door when I came down to leave."

All three turn to look at me like they're expecting me

to explain myself. Sorry, but they're going to be disappointed. I have no plans to do anything like that.

When I don't say a word, Ava says, "Since you probably heard me ask Matthias if he'd invite someone from work for Eden, I can ask you a similar question. Would you like me to ask another of my single friends to come so you aren't the only single person at the party? I don't want you to feel left out."

Ronan elbows me hard in the side and laughs. "You better have her do it. You don't have her friend Eden to adore you anymore now that Ava's trying to set her up with someone from King Industries."

God, I really need to spend more time at my own place.

"I'm as I've always been. A very happy bachelor," I say proudly.

Before any of them can comment, my phone vibrates in my shorts, so I fish it out and look at it with a smile as the first words of a message appear. "Now if you'll excuse me, I have a dirty text to read."

I escape to my room to read the rest of Duck's message, happy to know my private life is still very much a secret.

CHAPTER FIVE

den

As Ava digs through the diaper bag to find what she needs to change her very smelly younger son, I hold Matty in my outstretched arms trying to avoid the stink. It doesn't work. I don't know what speed the smell of baby shit travels, but it has no problem conquering the just over two foot length of my arms.

"Jesus, Ava, what are you guys feeding this kid?" I ask as customers at the mall walk by and stare, their expressions pure revulsion.

She triumphantly pulls out the baby wipes that must have sneaked their way to the bottom of the diaper bag and waves me toward where we know there's a bathroom in one of the stores. "It's going to be okay. Don't worry. A little baby poop never hurt anyone. We'll just pop into that place over there and use the ladies' room."

As I follow her while she pushes the stroller, Matty squeals with delight and I continue to breathe through my mouth and try to avoid the nasty glares of fellow shoppers who clearly don't agree with Ava's belief that everything is okay and a little baby shit never hurt anyone. I love my friend and her kids, but at this very moment, I'm wondering if I side with the disgusted people more than her.

Ten minutes, half a dozen baby wipes, and one little boy who pees when he's cleaned because like most males he can't control himself later, the smell is gone and we're finally able to return to what we came to the mall for in the first place. Ava said she wanted to go shopping to find a gift for Eleanor's birthday, but I have a sneaking suspicion we're here for another reason.

One that has more to do with me.

Ava touches the sweaters on the cardigan rack and sighs. "I spend every day with this woman, but I swear I don't know what she'd like for her birthday. What should I do?"

I glance at a forest green sweater with fake wood buttons down the front and cringe. "Not buy that. What does Eleanor like to do in her spare time?"

That question stops Ava in her tracks, and she stares at me like I just asked her to explain the meaning of life. Matty makes a cooing sound I hope to God doesn't mean he's going to the bathroom again. Seriously, what are they feeding this child?

"I don't know," Ava answers looking completely dejected. "How can that be? The woman lives in my house. I've known her all my life. I see her every day, and we talk. Like real conversations, not just what the weather's like and what's for dinner. What is wrong with me, Eden?"

She looks like she's about to break down into tears, so I quickly wrap my arm around her and give her a sympathetic squeeze. "Nothing is wrong with you. You just don't know what gift to get someone. As for your kid, well, there may be something up with his digestive system. Did he just shit again?"

Ava glares at me for my language, so I quickly apologize. "Sorry. I forgot we aren't all adults here. I think he's stinky again, though."

Bending down, she takes a big sniff of the stroller and then stands up, shaking her head. "No. It's just residual stink. Now help me find something Eleanor would like. Please?"

I don't bother to ask what residual stink is, and we continue to look through the department store, the two of us vetoing every idea each of us comes up with. Finally, I stop her and ask, "She's like your mother, right? Well, what would you get your mother if it were her birthday?"

She thinks about that for a minute and says, "Either a pair of slippers or something for cooking."

Not exactly what I would want for my birthday, but I'm not Eleanor.

"Okay. What about a new appliance she might like? Something that would make her job easier?"

That sounds horrible to me. It's like buying a woman a vacuum cleaner for a present. Who the hell wants something like that for her birthday? Women want wining and dining and great sex to cap off a wonderful night. Or jewelry. Anything but appliances.

Then again, Eleanor has to be close to sixty, and I've never heard Ava say anything about a man in her life, so perhaps she'd enjoy something utilitarian for her birthday. It still seems like a lame gift.

Ava pushes the stroller through the store like a woman on a mission now. I follow along, happy we have some direction and that Matty's butt isn't giving off stink anymore. She stops in the kitchenware section, and even though I think this is the last place to search for a gift for a woman you love, she points to a set of pots and pans.

"What do you think?"

I struggle to find the right words. "It's nice?"

She sees through my poor attempt to hide how little I think of this gift. "It's terrible, isn't it? Who wants to get a set of pots and pans for a birthday present? God, what is wrong with me? I want to get her something that shows how much I love having her in our lives, and I'm blowing it."

"Aww, Ava, you're putting too much pressure on yourself. Let's just look around and see if anything jumps out at you. I bet we can find her something really nice that she'll love."

As we set off again walking through the store, she says, "By the way, Matthias is inviting someone from work to the party. I thought maybe you might like to meet him."

There it is. The real reason she wanted me to come along on this shopping trip.

We pass the mixers and blenders, and I say, "Okay, but I'm not really interested in a relationship right now."

That completely normal statement gets me a look of disbelief. "Do I need to remind you that you haven't had a boyfriend for more than a few minutes in nearly two years since you and Justin broke up on your trip to Vegas?"

"Maybe I want to be single."

She laughs at that perfectly acceptable statement. "You sound like Marius. I guess that's why you two have never succumbed to my matchmaking efforts."

I smile at how adorable my friend is when it comes to being Cupid. "Blame that on him. I've always been more than happy to take a ride on Marius King."

"Are you still talking about what that old girlfriend of his said?"

Maia did like to brag that after being with Marius she always walked funny. She wasn't wrong, although I thought she walked funny all the time. Then again, she may have been telling the truth.

My friend has never said anything about Matthias, but she did seem to be walking oddly one day. Ava has always been somewhat secretive about her relationship with the oldest King, though, and I've never come right out and asked.

Today seems like a good day to remedy that.

"All I'm saying is I hear the King boys have been blessed, and I don't mean by all those billions of dollars," I say with a grin.

When she doesn't take the bait, I come right out and ask. "Well, you're married to one. What's the verdict?"

Ava stops dead, practically running into the stroller, and turns around to look at me with eyes as wide as saucers. "Eden! We're in the middle of a store at the mall!"

"So?"

Flustered, she answers, "So, I don't want to talk about that here."

"Just nod if he's well-endowed or shake your head and put on a sad face if he's needledick the bug fucker. That's all I'm saying."

She points at the baby and scowls at my language before quickly scanning the area around us to see if anyone heard me. There's not a soul close enough to have heard my comment, so she doesn't have anything to worry about.

"Well?" I ask as her cheeks get bright red. "Good to go or itty bitty winkie?"

My best friend has never been one to kiss and tell, so I'm not surprised in all the time she's been with Matthias that she's never shared if he's got the goods or not. I have to think he does. The man is six foot four and built like a god. If he has a tiny peen, then what hope is there for the rest of the men in this world?

"I can't believe you're asking me this," Ava says as she starts to push the stroller again.

Oh, well. So much for dishing on the size of the King brothers.

And then, just when I think there's no chance to find out the answer to my question about Matthias, she turns to look at me and nods with a big smile. I knew it!

"You lucky girl!" I say, practically squealing with delight. "No wonder you couldn't say no to him. I mean, the money is definitely nice, and Matthias is seriously easy on the eyes, but a man who has the goods and can lay some pipe is worth his weight in gold."

Now Ava's face is beet red. "You know my son is

right here. You're talking about his father's you-know-what right in front of Matty."

I lean down and smile at the baby lying in the stroller. "Hey, Matty. Can you understand your mom and I are talking about your father's junk? No? Didn't think so."

After tickling his belly, I stand up and smile at Ava. "He doesn't understand a thing."

She rolls her eyes and sighs before we start walking again. "Please tell me you'll consider this guy Matthias is inviting to the party. He's the head of the IT division at King Industries."

A geek. That's who she's setting me up with. Nice.

"Great. So you get a big hanging man with billions and gorgeous looks, and I get Mr. Wizard. Or worse, that weird guy from The Big Bang Theory."

Now it's Ava's turn to make a joke. "Which one? They're all weird."

"If he looks like he's got a tiny dick, I'm not going to be anything but civil. I just want that out there now."

Once again, she throws me a dirty look. "Language, please. Little ears."

"That don't understand anything."

"I swear you and Marius are so bad. I had to reprimand him about his language too this morning, and I swear the two of you have winkies on the mind."

Cringing at the sound of that word, I shake my head. "You can trust me. I do not have winkies on the mind."

Big hanging men? Sure. Winkies? That word is the surest way of making me dry. I don't bother to explain that to Ava, though.

We stop in the jewelry department and look at necklaces, even though I don't think I've ever seen

Eleanor wearing a necklace in all the times I've been to the King estate. When Ava doesn't find anything she likes, we continue to the case with pins.

Ava points at one that looks like a peacock. "What about this? She might like it and wear it on her coat. I know she has other pins. I've seen them on her winter coats before."

A worker comes over to offer help, so while he and Ava talk about what the stones are made of in the peacock's feathers, I crouch down to check on Matty. I swear I still smell something when I'm close to him, but it's not as bad now. Maybe it is residual stink like Ava claimed.

He is an adorable little guy. Smiling at me, he kicks his legs excitedly. I tickle his belly and then play with his chubby little feet.

"You're not too bad, little man. I could have one of you. That might be nice, right? Your mommy and I could raise you guys like cousins, best friends like us. What do you think?"

That makes him grab at my hair, so I quickly stand up to avoid that. Ava's finally decided on a gift for Eleanor with that peacock pin, so now all we have to do is wait for the salesperson to box it up.

"I bet she'll like that," I say, sensing my friend is still upset with me from my comment a few minutes ago.

When she doesn't respond, I give in and promise her what she wants. "Okay, if Bill Nye the Science Guy isn't awful, I'll talk to him. No promises after that, though."

That makes her smile, and she turns to face me, looking very excited. "Great! He's obviously smart. I mean, he's the head of the IT department. Matthias says he's a nice guy. I met him at the King Industries Christmas party, and he seemed very sweet."

Great. Just what I need. A sweet and nice geek.

Maybe he'll be hiding something good in his pants. A girl can hope, right?

Gift in hand, Ava begins pushing the stroller through the store again as she talks about what she's planning to serve everyone at the party. I'm more concerned about what my potential date looks like than the food since I can always count on whatever Eleanor makes to be top shelf.

Ava's phone rings, so I take over pushing Matty out of the store. Still kicking his little legs, he's pleased as punch to be in this thing. My youngest brother was like that. He loved his playpen so much that my parents kept him in it all the time. My father used to joke they'd be lucky if he didn't become a criminal after getting used to being confined all the time.

"What happened?" Ava asks the person who called, so I stop and listen to what's going on.

"Oh, no. Is she okay? Where is she now? Okay. We'll be right home."

Ava stuffs her phone into her purse and grabs a hold of the stroller. "We have to go now. Something's happened to Eleanor. That was Ronan. He sounded like he was going to cry. It must be bad. Oh, God! I don't know what I'll do if she isn't okay, Eden. Eleanor is like a mother to me. Hurry! We have to go!"

Tears fill her eyes as she rushes through the mall to get to the car. After losing her own mother, all Ava's had for a mother figure in her life is Eleanor. The same can be said for Matthias and his brothers.

God, I hope she's going to be okay.

CHAPTER SIX

*M*arius

THE KITCHEN DOOR OPENS, AND IN BUST AVA, EDEN, and Matty in his stroller. Looking around, Ava asks, "Where is she? Where is Eleanor?"

She looks like she's about to cry, so I quickly explain, "She's resting in her room. Ronan's sitting with her. Matthias is in his office making some calls to see what can be done. And I'm here."

That last part seems unnecessarily obvious, but after finding Eleanor collapsed on the kitchen floor, I'm a little frazzled. It's not every day the only woman you've been able to rely on for most of your life scares the hell out of you.

Ava lifts the baby out of the stroller and hands him to Eden. "I need to go see her and make sure she's comfortable. I'll be right back. If he gives you any trouble, just give me a holler."

A second later, she rushes out of the kitchen, leaving the three of us alone. Not that I've never been alone with Eden or Matty before. It's just that at this moment, things feel odd.

"What happened, Marius?" Eden asks as she sits down with Matty at the table.

I sigh, blowing the air out of my lungs. "I came in here for something to drink and found her on the floor. I was just about to start CPR when she opened her eyes and said she didn't remember anything. One minute she was standing at the counter, and the next she was blacked out on the floor."

That sounds far more relaxed than what it actually felt like. I wanted to collapse myself when I saw Eleanor on the floor looking like she was dead. She's the only mother we've had around this house since our own died. To lose her would be devastating.

Eden reaches out and touches my hand. "Are you okay? You don't look right."

"I'm fine. Thanks, though."

We sit without saying a word for a few minutes while Matty plays with his feet, which seem to be his newest favorite things lately. I wish I knew what to say, but right now, I'm a little freaked out.

Eden breaks the silence and says, "I'm sure she'll be fine. She's a tough lady."

That makes me smile as I remember all the crazy things my brothers and I have made her deal with in her time here with us. "She'd have to be to handle the five of us."

I don't know why, but just thinking about how long she's been in our lives makes me choke up with emotion. Eleanor has been in my life since my parents brought me home from the hospital. She helped my mother when we needed cuts cleaned and bandages put on our many childhood wounds. Then when my mother died, she took over worrying about us, truly taking care of all five of us when my father wasn't able to. If it wasn't for Eleanor, I don't know what we would have done in those months when my father was too lost in his grief to even pay attention to us.

"Marius, are you sure you're okay?" Eden asks, tearing me from my memories.

"I'll be fine. Little..." A noise in the hallway makes me cut my sentence short, and a second later, Matthias walks into the kitchen. Tickling Matty's feet, I smile up at him. "Little guy here is growing like a weed."

Both he and Eden look at me like they think I'm crazy, but after a few seconds, Matthias says, "I spoke to her doctor, and he thinks she may need some time off. When she gets back to work, he believes a nurse would be helpful for the first few weeks. He's been treating her for high blood pressure, but she hasn't been willing to take any medicine. She told him she wanted to treat it with a better diet and no salt. I don't think that's been working. Once she feels up to it, we're going to take her to the hospital. He's ordered tests to find out what's going on."

I nod like I know what he's talking about, but I have no idea about any of this. All I want is for Eleanor to feel better and to see her smiling face whenever I'm here at the estate. We don't need any more upheavals in this family right now. I'd like just a few months without a baby being born, someone proposing, or someone getting in trouble.

"My mother has high blood pressure," Eden says as Matty lets out a high-pitched squeal. "It can definitely be handled with medication. My mother wanted to do it the natural way too, so she cut out all the salt in her diet. Didn't work. She still had to go on the pills. Once she did, though, she was fine. I'm sure Eleanor will be too."

Matthias smiles like he's relieved by what she's said. "Thanks, Eden. Here, let me take the baby from you. Let you relax for a while."

He and Matty walk out, leaving Eden and me alone. I'm not in the mood to make small talk right now, so I quickly excuse myself.

Talking about the weather or what she and Ava did while they were out shopping is not high on my list of things I want to do. What I really want to do is leave because just thinking about the possibility of Eleanor not being okay is making me feel more emotional than I like at this moment.

By the time I reach my room, my stomach is in knots. I'm not good with this kind of thing. Happy times are what I excel at. Jokes, laughing, and generally being a smart ass are my strengths. This emotional stuff is not.

I lie back on my bed and try to get a handle on my feelings, but they're all over the place. I need to get my shit together. Ronan's a mess because Eleanor has been the only mother he's had since he's ten years old. Matthias isn't much better.

Then I realize something we all overlooked.

Nobody told Kellen.

For a few seconds, I consider mentioning it to Matthias or Ronan, but that's not going to work. Kellen doesn't need either of them unraveling when they call to let him know. That means it falls to me.

Assuming I can keep it together.

I reluctantly pull out my phone from my pocket and do what has to be done. Kellen answers immediately, catching me off guard.

"Marius, what the hell is up?" he asks in his usual good-time style. "Sick of just lounging around day after day so you call me?"

"Yeah, pretty much."

"Well, what's new? Are you still in town? You should come over to see Salem and me. We always like having you over. What do you say? I've got a ton of work to do today, but another night this week would be great. I can tell Salem to invite her sister Ever to join us. You liked her that one time she stopped over when you were here. Remember? I think she's single now since Salem mentioned something about her breaking up with her boyfriend."

"Yeah, sure. Um, Kellen, I'm calling for a reason. Something happened."

I don't get any more out before he turns deadly serious. "Something happened? To who? Is it Ronan? What happened?"

So much for being the one who's calm and cool to tell him the news so he doesn't get upset.

"No, it's not Ronan. He's fine. He's here, in fact, out at the house. No need to worry."

Kellen lets out a heavy sigh. "Then if it isn't Ronan, what happened? Clearly, you're fine. It isn't one of the kids, is it? Ronan told me little Theo got out of his crib and they couldn't find him a few weeks ago."

"No, it isn't Theo or Matty. That was something else entirely." I swallow hard and continue. "It's Eleanor, Kellen. I found her passed out on the kitchen floor a little while ago. She's awake now, but the doctor wants to run some tests."

I swear I can hear my younger brother's sadness come right through the phone, even though he's not saying a word. Kellen has always been Eleanor's favorite. His charm never fails to work its magic on her. Losing her would be like losing our mother all over again for him too.

"Thank God she's okay. Is she talking? What did she say happened?" he asks, his voice full of emotion.

"She didn't know. One minute she was doing something at the sink, and the next she was blacked out and waking up on the floor. Matthias spoke to her doctor. He thinks it has something to do with her blood pressure, but they won't know until they run tests."

His words come out shaky when he says, "I'm going to come out to the house right now. I'll see you in a few, Marius."

Before I get the chance to say anything more, the phone goes dead. I don't know if it was the right thing to do by telling him, but if any of us should know about how Eleanor is doing, it's him.

This has been one hell of a day. And here I thought I'd get to relax since one of the kids was out of the house with the other one spending time with the nanny.

. . .

I MUST HAVE BEEN TIRED SINCE I DON'T EVEN remember falling asleep. I look outside and see it's still daytime, so I couldn't have slept for long.

Stretching my limbs, I feel like someone's been beating on me repeatedly for hours. Unsure why, I sit up as I try to figure out if I was restless when I slept. I'm not the type to have nightmares—never was even as a kid—but as I try to piece together what could be making my body hurt like this, a vague memory of something I must have dreamed comes to me. I was in Ronan's apartment. At least I think I was in the dream. It's all very hazy, but I think I was looking for the light. He kept asking me to find the light switch and turn on the lights, but I couldn't find it.

Weird. I rarely remember my dreams, but I never remember nightmares. Not that being unable to find a light switch is the stuff of horror, but knowing Ronan was in the dream and he wanted me to help him makes me think it might have been a nightmare.

Rolling off my bed, I make sure I'm dressed since I usually don't sleep with clothes on and then head downstairs. All the emotional upheaval of the day must have worn me out.

Since I hear noises coming from the kitchen, I make my way there to find Ronan, Kellen, and Matthias sitting around the table eating something that looks like apple pie. They all look up when I walk in but don't say anything.

"Jesus, is Eleanor feeling that much better that she made an apple pie? By the way, I hope you left me some. I'm starving."

I sit down next to Matthias while my younger

brothers shake their heads. "She's still in bed, asshole," Kellen says, clearly still upset.

Holding up my hands, I say, "Sorry. I was just trying to make a joke. You know, lighten the mood?"

"Well, it wasn't funny."

I shrug and walk over to get a fork out of the drawer. "Not every one can be a winner, you know."

"Kellen's just worried," Matthias says. "You know how close he is with Eleanor."

As I sit down again, I throw Kellen a smile. "Don't worry. She's going to be fine. Eleanor is a tough lady, and I'm sure Matthias here has the best doctors in the world to take care of her. You watch. In no time, she'll be back up on her feet and making you those butterscotch cookies you love so much."

That puts a smile on his face, and he chuckles. "She does make me some great snacks."

Ronan laughs and says, "Do you remember the time she found Theo in the game room with that girl? She came running down here, and Kellen and I were sitting right where we are now. We were too young to know what was wrong, but I swear when she walked back upstairs with the can of Pledge and that dust cloth, we heard someone scream. The girl came running past us right out the door with him following. Then when Eleanor came down, all she said to the two of us was, 'The game room is clean, in case you boys want to go up there.' And that was it."

"That was a few months after Mom died," Kellen says. "I asked her about it one time, and she said she felt it was her responsibility to keep Theo's reputation intact.

I didn't have the heart to tell her he'd probably ruined it by that time."

The four of us throw our heads back and laugh at the very thought of Theo ever having a respectable reputation. Out of all of us, he made sure to leave a past full of deeds Eleanor would have blanched at.

"Poor Eleanor," Matthias says as he stops laughing. "She had no idea about who Theo really was."

"Or maybe she did," I say, sure Eleanor wasn't as naïve as it seemed.

"She was probably trying to help the girl out more than him," Ronan says. "Something tells me Eleanor knew exactly who our brother was."

"If she didn't, the rest of the world did," I say under my breath.

My three brothers turn and look at me, and Matthias says, "Theo liked to have a good time. Everyone knew that. You and I were part of the fun with him more times than I can count."

And, of course, Kellen jumps in to defend Theo. "Yeah. Theo was always a good time."

While I'm not normally in the mood for revelations, something about what happened with Eleanor makes me feel like I want to make an exception today. "Yeah. A good time and a backstabbing dick. So a little bit of everything."

Now the three of them glare at me. I've broken the unspoken King family rule of never speaking ill of anyone once they're gone. Well, I'm not into that today, especially about that brother. He's had far too long being a saint, in my opinion.

That ends right now.

"Theo was not a backstabbing dick, Marius. What the hell makes you say that?" Kellen asks.

I stand up to get a drink from the refrigerator. "Because he was. You wouldn't know about that because he never screwed you over, but Matthias and I know full well what Theo was capable of, especially when it came to women."

Matthias gives me an odd look, and for the first time, I wonder if he truly doesn't know what Theo did to keep him and Ava apart all that time after they got together those snowy couple of days that December. He can't honestly not know, can he?

"What are you talking about?" he asks, and I stand behind the refrigerator door stunned this is going to be the day he finds out what actually happened.

I grab a soda and walk back to the table as I try to think of the right words to explain everything to him. Kellen scowls at me, and while I'm not in the mood to get into a fight with him, if he's going to try to defend Theo, he's not getting a free pass from me today.

After taking a sip of my drink, I look at Matthias and tell him the truth. "Theo knew you were crazy about Ava. He always knew. He knew what happened when you two were alone on those snowy days when we were stranded in the city and you guys were out here. He knew and made sure he didn't give you the message she gave him before she went to her aunt's in New Hampshire."

My older brother stares at me in shock as I spell it all out. "She trusted him because she thought he was her best friend so, of course, he'd give you her message that she had to go. Every time he busted your chops about needing to get laid or needing to get a girlfriend while you were home on break, he knew you two had been together and that he had made sure you never heard that she wanted you to know she had to leave because of her father, who by the way, also knew you two had gotten together while we were all gone. It wasn't Joe who kept you two apart, though. It was Theo. Then when he felt like he wanted to settle down, he came back, and since you were being a dick to Ava because you felt like she ran away, he took advantage of the situation."

"That can't be right. Theo wouldn't do that to me," Matthias says unconvincingly, his voice barely above a whisper.

To show him he's not the only one of us who Theo screwed over, I say, "And by the way, want to know who Maia was with after me? None other than Theo. He knew I was fucking crushed when we broke up, and what did he do? He slept with the woman I was still in love with. Maybe I should thank him. It showed me I was wasting my time thinking about her."

Now my brothers look confused, like when we all found out Santa Claus wasn't real. Sorry, guys. Good old Theo, who everyone loved, had no problem screwing over his very own brothers.

"Did you ever confront him about what he did to you?" Ronan asks me.

I nod, remembering exactly the moment I realized Theo King wasn't the person everyone always thought he was. "Yeah. He said it was no big deal. It wasn't like he slept with her while I was still dating her. To him, it wasn't a problem. Son of a bitch was having a hell of a month. First, he dicks over Matthias and Ava, and then he fucks around with my ex, who he knew I was still crazy about. Hell of a guy."

The four of us sit in silence after I finish. I expect Kellen to try to come to Theo's defense since that's been his favorite pastime since he died, but he doesn't say a word. Maybe now he can understand that King brother wasn't a great person or a great brother.

He and Ronan quietly get up from the table and walk outside, leaving only Matthias sitting with me. His expression is pure sadness, but I don't know if that's because of what I just told him or what's happened to Eleanor today.

When he finally speaks again, I understand it's probably a mixture of the two affecting him. Looking down at his plate, he quietly says, "You know, I felt like the worst person in the world when I ruined things between Theo and Ava and he left here. I never got the chance to tell him I was sorry. I never got the chance to say goodbye. I've beaten myself up about those things all these years."

He stops and lifts his head to look at me. "I had no idea what you said happened. I don't think Ava knows either. I would have never dreamed in a million years that he'd do something like that to me or to her. And what he did to you isn't any better. He was my best friend in the world. I would have trusted him with anything, and now I find out he did everything he could to keep me from Ava."

I hate seeing Matthias like this, so I say, "Theo was selfish. He felt like the world was his oyster, and whatever he wanted, he took. It didn't matter if what he wanted was someone else's. He didn't care. Don't beat yourself up over him anymore. Yeah, what you said that broke him and Ava up wasn't great, but she would have never been with him if he hadn't gotten between you two."

Like the good person he's always been, Matthias leans over toward me and whispers, "Don't tell Ava anything about this. I don't want her thinking he was a bad guy. We can't change anything that happened now anyway, so there's no point in her finding out the truth, okay?"

Happy to do what he wants, I nod my agreement. "My lips are sealed. I'll take it to the grave, Matthias."

He thanks me and leaves me alone in the kitchen. Maybe I should have taken that secret to the grave for him too.

CHAPTER SEVEN

*M*arius

For two weeks, Ronan and I stay at the house to make sure Eleanor is okay. Kellen comes by every afternoon, and I swear that's the happiest she is all day. He's a clown, but he's a lovable clown when it comes to her.

All the tests came back telling her doctor her blood pressure was dangerously high and she may have had a stroke that afternoon she collapsed in the kitchen, so Ava and Matthias have ordered her to take it easy and do nothing around the house. She, of course, fought against that, but as of this afternoon, we've all worked to make sure she hasn't done anything but relax.

Sitting in the kitchen with Ava and little Theo as she feeds him something dark green in a jar, I think about what she'd have to say if she ever found out her firstborn son was named after a bastard who only thought of himself. Let's just hope this Theo doesn't grow up to be like that uncle.

"Thanks for staying around, Marius. I know Eleanor's been thrilled to see everyone rally around her."

I wave off the idea that what I did was anything incredible. "You know me. I love to hang out here with you guys."

She slips a tiny spoonful of that dark green stuff into Theo's mouth before turning to look at me. Hesitating, she says, "Not that I don't love having you here, because I do, but I'm wondering why you've never gotten your own place. Is it just a nomad thing?"

It's questions like that one that make me feel like a shit for lying to my family, but if I told them the truth about my life, then they'd be in my business all the time. God knows I can't deal with that.

I shrug and flash her a smile. "I guess I'm just a wandering soul."

"Well, I'm glad that when you decide to rest your head somewhere it's here. I think it's good for Matthias to have you around. Without Theo, I have the sense that he was feeling a bit disconnected, like he was so much older than the rest of you guys. Having you hang out bridges that gap for him."

Once again, I shrug and smile. Ava's always been too naïve when it comes to her years as Theo's best friend. That kindness and thoughtfulness he never cared a damn about is good for Matthias, and unlike the second born King, the oldest one of us has never not known exactly how lucky he is to have Ava.

I watch her tenderly clean her older son's face before

she refills his bottle. When she sits down again, she lets out a heavy sigh.

"Seriously, tell me how your mother had five kids and so close together. Two are wiping me out."

"You're doing a great job, Ava. Never doubt that. Even more, never doubt how much Matthias and the boys are lucky to have you around."

My compliments surprise her, and she stares at me oddly for a moment or two before smiling. "Thank you, Marius. Are you okay? You seem very...I can't think of the right word, but you seem different today."

"Maybe a little more introspective than usual. Don't worry. I'll be back to my usual joker ways soon," I say with a chuckle.

"I like your joker ways. I always have. I like them even more because they lighten my husband's mood. You have a good effect on Matthias, you know that?"

Waving away that idea, I stand up and tussle the baby's hair before putting my dirty glass in the dishwasher. "Speaking of the man himself, where is he today? I don't think I've seen him all day."

"He drove into work today to handle a few things. I think he might be stopping by Kellen and Salem's place to say hi. Salem's been so busy with that client of hers lately. I talked to her last week, and she sounded like she was going to pull her hair out."

For a moment, I try to remember if I know who Salem's new client is. Oh, yeah. The university president accused of embezzling millions of dollars and running off with a student.

"Is that guy still refusing to behave?" I ask as the memory of something I heard about him flying off to some island instead of sitting down for a scheduled interview floats through my brain.

Ava nods. "From what she was telling me, this guy makes Kellen look like a choir boy."

I laugh out loud at that idea. "That's saying something. No one has ever accused that brother of being good."

"Kellen just has middle child syndrome. He wanted to be noticed, but I bet it was hard being one of five. Strangely, you don't have that. I think Theo did, though."

Even though I want to say Theo was just an asshole, I bite my tongue. "I think those two operated on the principle that any attention is good attention. I prefer the exact opposite. No attention at all. I make sure to live my life below the radar."

"Is that why you never wanted to try anything with Eden? Because then we'd all be in your business?"

Her question catches me off guard, and I'm not sure how to answer. Lie? I can't tell her the truth, so I guess lying is the only option.

"Yeah, I guess."

The new nanny walks into the kitchen with Matty and walks over to the refrigerator. "Someone's hungry now that he woke up from his nap."

Ava jumps into action, hurrying to get the bottle warm enough for the baby to eat while checking that his older brother doesn't need anything. I consider offering to take Theo for a little while to give everyone a break, but before I can, Lynn lifts him out of the high chair and announces she's going to give him a bath.

"I'll leave you guys to this. I have some stuff to do today."

"Oh, please don't leave on our account. It's just that we're trying out a new schedule with the boys to see if we can get them to sleep through the night together," Ava says as she sits down with Matty in her arms.

I smile and shake my head. "I don't know how you do it. I'm getting tired just watching you with these kids. I think I have a new appreciation for my mother."

Ava sighs and gives me a smile. "Tell me about it. Well, have a good day. I think once we're done eating and Theo is done with getting cleaned up, we're all going outside for some fresh air and pool time, so if you want to get in on some of that, we should be hanging out for the rest of the afternoon."

"Hopefully, my business in the city works out the way I want it to so I can get back to take a dip with my nephews. See you later!"

I leave as Ava juggles Matty and his bottle. I really do love hanging out with everyone here, but I've got something even more important to deal with today.

THE ELEVATOR DOORS OPEN, AND I STEP OUT, noticing how quiet the apartment is. Then again, it's two floors and way too minimalist for my taste. We seriously need to get some real furniture in here. The last owners of this place must have been the type of people who think the word sparse is something positive.

"Hey, Lucy! I'm home!" I call out in my best Ricky Ricardo imitation.

I get no response, but she may not have heard me. I'll just walk around and see where she's hiding herself.

By the time I finish searching the first floor and haven't found her, I'm starting to wonder if she's even here. She texted and said she was waiting for me. Maybe she meant in the bedroom.

Excited by that idea, I start to undress as I walk upstairs. I've got my shirt off and I'm ready to strip off my pants when I see her pacing back and forth across the master bedroom floor.

I come up behind her and wrap my arms around her body. She feels warm against me, and I close my eyes to enjoy it. "Didn't you hear me when I yelled?" I whisper in her ear.

She turns out of my hold, a sure signal she's not happy about something. Standing with her arms across her chest and giving off some serious pissed off vibes, she levels her gaze on my face.

"What's up?" I ask as I toss my shirt on the back of that weird minimalist chair that's basically a hunk of wood and a single piece of what looks like gray pipe holding things together.

"We need to talk, Marius."

Never in the history of all mankind has a woman said those words and then the conversation turned out to be pleasant. Seriously. Do they teach females this that day they take them all out of the classroom in grade school when they claim to tell them about their periods? Is it something like they show them the ins and outs of menstruation and then spend the rest of the time instructing them on how to make sure males understand they're unhappy?

I reach for my shirt since I get the feeling this isn't going to be one of the great naked times we have together. "Oh?"

Although she probably wants me to say something more, I've found that saying as little as possible when a woman is upset is the best plan of action. Say too much and they have a ton of ammunition for whatever fight they want to have.

No, the best course for a man is to say the least amount possible. Oh, and be affectionate. That confuses them, which gives the man a chance to avoid the worst of it.

Her green eyes practically stare bullet holes through me. Did I happen to mention that these tactics work on most but not all women? Unfortunately, I'm in love with one of the women they don't always work on.

Like right now, for example.

She looks gorgeous today. Not that she isn't always beautiful, but something about her long black hair against the royal blue tank top she's wearing makes me want to sweep her up in my arms and haul her off to bed, which is conveniently just a few feet away.

Too bad the frown on her face says we won't be having any good times in the bed anytime soon.

"Marius, I can't keep doing this. I know you want me to, but I can't. Not anymore."

We've had this conversation before. At least I know how it goes, not that I enjoy it any more because I'm familiar with it.

"Why?"

Her dark eyebrows come in toward her nose like

angry black slashes. Smiling, I lean in and kiss her, hoping to make that expression disappear.

"Did I ever tell you how beautiful you are when you're furious with me? It's confusing yet arousing all at the same time."

She puts her hands on my naked chest and pushes me away from her. "I'm serious. I can't do this anymore."

So we're really going to do this right now. Fabulous.

"Can we at least move this conversation down to the kitchen? I'm starving. Since Eleanor isn't up on her feet yet, we've all been cooking, and let me tell you it's been eye-opening how bad most of us are at that. Ava's pretty good, and surprisingly, Ronan makes a mean fajita dinner, but the rest of us better not quit our day jobs."

A pout mars her beautiful face. "You aren't taking this seriously. I can't keep lying to everyone anymore. It's too much."

I slide my arm around her waist and pull her to me. God, she feels so fucking good pressed against my body. Do we really need to have the same conversation we've had dozens of times before when we could be having a much better time between the sheets?

Since I made the mistake of asking that very question the first time we had this discussion and found out just how stupid that was, I don't give voice to my idea. When she's this serious, it's best to just confront the issue head on.

"It won't be forever. I promise."

When she gives me a look that screams she doesn't believe me, I add, "Have I ever lied to you?"

She sits down on the edge of the bed and sighs. "No,

but we've been lying to everyone for ages. I don't want to do it anymore."

I push her hair back off her face and bend down to kiss her. "What's this all about?"

She hesitates for a few seconds and then says, "You have no idea how much I wanted to be there for you when Eleanor got sick. I was in the same room as you, and I couldn't show any support or affection for what you were going through."

Oh, so that's what the problem is. I can deal with this.

Smiling, I say, "It's okay. I knew you were sympathetic. It was practically coming off you in waves the whole time you were there with me. I knew, so it's not like you couldn't show me affection. I felt it. I really did."

Surprisingly, that doesn't make her feel better.

She stands up and pushes me away before storming off, so I follow her down the stairs, the whole way trying to explain that I know how she's feeling. When we reach the first floor, she spins around and folds her arms across her chest again.

Never a good sign.

"You think you know how I feel? Tell me, Marius, how does it feel to lie to your best friend? Or even more, how do you think it feels to be alone more nights than I'm with you? We've been together for two years. I agreed to hiding our relationship because I understood you wanted to keep things just between us. That's not working anymore, though."

I don't say anything to that because she's right. Every

word is the truth. I was the one who asked her to keep things hidden all this time.

"In my defense, I'd say I've been lying to my best friend since I've been lying to Matthias."

She screws her face into a look of complete disgust and walks away, so once again, I follow her. If I had known this conversation would involve so much moving from one place to another, I wouldn't have worked out this morning.

I catch up to her in the kitchen, and I'm secretly thrilled because I'm starving. As I head for the refrigerator, she groans behind me.

"I'm listening. I swear I am. It's just that I'm hungry."

"Not to worry. Thank God I make sure that refrigerator is always full. You know what I am? It just dawned on me. I'm your Eleanor. I'm the person who makes sure you're happy, just like she did when you all were growing up. If I washed your clothes, I'd really be like your own personal housekeeper."

I grab some ham and cheese before closing the refrigerator door and heading for the island, sort of creeped out about her referring to herself as my personal Eleanor. "You're not that at all."

As I search for the bread, she turns serious. "Marius, I've loved you for so long I can't imagine my life without you. I can't do this anymore, though. I want the world to know about us."

Her words stop me dead, and I turn around to look at her to see if she really meant what I think she said. "What are you saying?"

She's calm when she answers, "I'm saying I can't do

this anymore. If we can't tell the people we love that we're together..."

I watch as she stops herself, unable to finish that sentence. This is usually the part of the argument where I tell her it won't be much longer, but I doubt that's going to work today.

Maybe it's time for the truth.

Walking over to where she's standing on the other side of the island, I slide my arms around her and pull her to me. I'd be lost if I didn't have this woman in my life. She has to understand that.

"I've never had anything all to myself like this relationship. Growing up, I was the middle of five sons. Our relationship is special because you're all mine. I don't want to share you with anyone. I don't want to have my family in our business. Why can't it just be the two of us like it's always been?"

"Because I'm tired of lying. I love you. I'm starting to wonder if it's something you don't want to tell me. Are you ashamed of me? Is that it?"

That she can even ask that tells me she's far more serious than usual about this issue.

"I love you, Duck. I promise someday it won't be like this."

Unlike before, she doesn't spin out of my hold. That's a good sign. I might be winning this argument.

"When, Marius? I want children. I watch Ava with the boys, and all I can think is I want to have kids of my own. Not someday in the distant future. Soon. How does that happen when I can't tell anyone who the father is?"

So much for winning.

"I don't know. I promise it will happen, though. In

the meantime, I give you anything you want. We travel. We stay in the most incredible places. I buy you every piece of jewelry you point out to me. You hated us sleeping in hotels, so I bought you this penthouse. Whatever you want, I make sure it's yours. That has to show you how crazy in love with you I am, doesn't it?"

She kisses me and then steps out of my hold. Looking around, she says, "I know you think spending money on me is what I want or that it makes up for having to lie about us, but neither of those things is true. I don't love you because you have money or because you bought me a penthouse. I don't even get to tell anyone I own a goddamned penthouse, Marius! I'd love to invite my parents here to show them this place. And what about Ava? She's my best friend. You don't think I'd love to bring her here and tell her the man I love bought me a damn penthouse?"

"I promise, Eden. Soon," I say, reaching out for her.

"When?" she asks, like the tenacious creature she always is.

To be honest, I usually love that dogged way she has of never giving up. Right now, though, it's making me wonder how long I'm going to be able to keep us a secret. I don't want to share her or us with anyone. Why can't she understand that?

"Just a little longer. Please? Let us be just us for a little while longer."

Eden relaxes against me and rests her head on my chest. "Don't make me leave, Marius. It would break my heart."

She has no idea what it would do to me if I lost her.

CHAPTER EIGHT

den

As I join with Ava to slather the boys in sunscreen, I can't help but wish I could tell her the truth. Marius has no idea how hard it is to keep this lie up. There are so many times I've wanted to share something sweet he did for me, and I've gotten to share exactly none of it with exactly zero people.

That says nothing of how much I love him. I've never been this crazy about a man in my entire life, and ordinarily when something that incredible happens, a woman gets to share it with her best friend. Me? I get to pretend I'm some happy single girl who gave up on love a long time ago.

"You seem quiet today. Anything wrong?" Ava asks when we finish the slathering.

I force a smile and shake my head. "All good here.

Maybe I should put some sunscreen on too. All these years of tanning are going to make me look like an old leather car seat at some point."

Ava laughs at my attempt to distract her from my mood. "You've always been so lucky. You never burn. I don't know what's wrong with me. We're both brunettes, but I burn every time."

"It's the blue eyes."

She nods like that news disappoints her. "I guess. It would be nice to have some color sometimes. I wonder if the boys will get their father's complexion."

The two of us look at Theo on her lap and Matty still in the stroller with their brown hair and brown eyes just like Matthias has and then at each other. Laughing, I say, "My guess is you're going to be the only one in the family who never tans. Sorry."

When we're talking about lighthearted things like this, I can tell myself it's not a big deal that my entire life is currently a lie. It's when we're serious that I have terrible bouts of guilt. I so want to tell her how happy Marius and I are. I want to tell her how we got together since that's such a great story. I want to share with her how he bought me that diamond necklace she always says she loves. When she asked me about it, I had to lie and tell her my boss bought it for me for a job well done on some project. For months, she was sure I was sleeping with him.

It's not like I'd even have to tell her everything. I just want to share the great stuff with my best friend.

"By the way, Matthias told me that guy from work said he'd be happy to come to the party. I hope you like him. I have a really good feeling about this one."

Ava has set me up with no less than five guys since I got together with Marius two years ago. Each time, they were perfectly nice people I had to pretend to give a chance and then let down gently because I don't want anyone else.

My best friend would know that if I didn't have to keep lying to her.

"I'm sure he'll be fine," I say, confident I don't sound as enthusiastic as she would like me to be.

Thankfully, Ava is preoccupied with Theo, who at the present moment has decided that his fingers belong in his mouth. All ten of them. At the same time.

"Can you hand me one of those baby wipes? He's got my entire arm covered in spit."

I laugh and hand her the container of wipes, positive she's going to need more than one. I don't know what that kid's fascination is with his mouth, but he's constantly shoving something in it. It would be one thing if he swallowed everything, but what he seems to do more often than not is put things in his mouth and then remove them covered in saliva, which he then gets on everyone.

As she attempts to clean herself up, someone walks out from the house. Assuming it's Matthias, I don't turn around, but then I see Marius walk over to join us instead. Like always, I have to pretend I'm not happy to see him, so I grab my phone off the table and begin to scroll through my emails.

"Ladies, are we swimming on this beautifully sunny day?" he asks and then crouches down to talk to Theo. "You're definitely swimming, little man. You're like a fish."

"In his own spit, maybe," Ava says. "I need to get him cleaned up first. You can take Matty in, though."

Marius looks over at the stroller and stands up. "Okay, then he and I will do some uncle-nephew bonding. Ready, buddy?"

Even as I pretend to read some email, I sneak a peek as he strips out of his t-shirt to reveal his muscular arms and chest, to say nothing of the washboard abs. How this man expects me to pretend that we aren't together when he insists on doing stuff like this is beyond me.

He lifts Matty out of the stroller and pats his bottom. "You sure these things you put on them don't make the pool a mess?"

I look up and see Ava shaking her head. "Don't worry. They do the job. You won't be swimming in baby poop or pee."

Turning to face me, Marius smiles, and it's real work not to show how he makes my stomach do a flip when he's so sexy. "That sounds delightful. Sure you don't want to come in with me and the little guy?"

With a shrug, I answer, "Not today. Thanks."

He winks at me and then walks away with Matty to get into the pool. I swear he does that on purpose because he knows I have a hard time pretending we aren't together. It would serve him right if I came out and told Ava the truth while we're sitting out here today.

"Come on, Eden. Don't be a stick in the mud," Marius calls out from the pool as he lifts Matty in the air like some Lion King redux.

Looking around, I don't see Ava or Matthias, so the coast might be clear for a few seconds, at least. I walk over to the edge of the pool and look down at Marius.

"What's the end game here, dear? Do you want me to spill the beans? If not, then I'm not sure why you're acting like this."

If it's possible, he looks even better wet. How can someone always look so good? It's impossible, yet Marius King somehow achieves that.

He glances over toward the door of the house to see if anyone's around and then up at me. "No, Duck, I don't want you to spill the beans. Just get in the pool. We can have a good time, and no one will be the wiser."

I shake my head in disbelief. "Are you kidding? If his mother sees you and me having a good time together, she's going to try ten times as hard to get us together. It's tough enough pretending now."

As Marius considers what I said, Matty splashes his little hands in front of them. I'm fine with coming clean and telling Ava everything. In fact, I'd be happier if we did tell the truth. It's Marius who wants to keep us under wraps.

"At least sit down on the edge?" he says in a way that makes me feel like I'm being the bad guy here. "I promise Matty and I won't splash you."

Even though I don't believe him, I sit down on the edge of the pool and let my bare feet dangle in the water. "Now there's a lie if I've ever heard one."

He positions Matty in front of him, hiding behind his little body while he says, "Aunt Eden, how could you think someone as innocent as I am would do anything like splash you on purpose?"

"It's not the kid who I think is going to do that. It's you. Just remember I'm not wearing a bathing suit, okay?"

Marius pokes his head out from behind Matty and pouts. "You're no fun at all, Aunt Eden. No fun at all."

Ava and Theo join us not ten seconds later, and it's like his entire demeanor changes. Gone is the playful, flirty man I adore, and in his place, a man who acts like he doesn't even know I exist appears.

"All the stickiness is gone, thankfully," she announces as she walks over to the pool. "Marius, how is Matty liking the water? He cried yesterday when Matthias took him in, so I wasn't sure how he'd deal with it today."

"He's fine," Marius says as he bounces up and down with Matty in his arms. "He was just saying to Eden that she's a flat tire for not coming in with us. I told him that wasn't nice, but he refused to apologize. I have to admit he may be onto something."

Ava throws me an uncomfortable look that says she's sorry her brother-in-law is being a jackass and laughs it off. "If Eden wants to just dip her toes in the water, that's fine with me. I'm sure it's fine with Matty too."

With that, she walks into the pool with Theo in her arms and proceeds to let him splash around, soaking her. "Eden, if you decide to change your mind, I've got a bunch of swimsuits. Just say the word."

"Yeah, say the word, Eden," Marius says, mocking me.

Thankfully, Matty chooses this very moment to suddenly burst into tears. Marius looks completely confused, like he isn't sure what to do, so he walks across the pool to stand in front of where I'm still relaxing on the edge.

"Here, he doesn't seem to want to swim any more. I

think he's missing the stroller," he says before handing Matty up to me.

I reluctantly take him, although when I set him on my legs, he gets me drenched. "Thanks for the advance warning. Now it's like I went swimming too."

As I stand up to walk the baby over to where the towels and his stroller wait for us near the table, Marius lifts himself out of the pool and follows us. I get Matty dried off and check to see if he's dirty. Since he's not, I do as his mother instructs me to and set him down in the stroller. Not a minute later, he's fast asleep.

"Ava, he's out cold. Do you want me to take him upstairs to his crib?"

She thinks about it but shakes her head. "No, he loves the stroller, so he's fine there. Just make sure the brake is on so he doesn't start rolling away. Then come over and hang out with me. I can't get out yet because Theo's still having a good time."

Since Marius is drying off and can watch Matty, I head back toward where Ava and Theo are enjoying themselves in the pool, but just as I'm about to reach where I was sitting, I feel hands grab me around the waist. A second later, I'm soaring through the air.

I hit the water with a thud and sink to the bottom. Son of a bitch! I'm soaked from head to toe. What was he thinking?

Furious, I come up from under the water and glare at Marius. "What the hell is wrong with you? I'm fully dressed here, you idiot!"

Other, far more adult words come into my mind, but I remember little ears are listening, as Ava always says.

What I really want to scream at Marius is, "What the fuck did you do that for?"

He stands on the pool deck grinning like some fool, and I swear when I turn to face Ava she looks like she's so stunned she doesn't know what to say. Furious, I climb out of the pool and storm toward the house, unsure what I'm going to do since I don't have any dry clothes here.

Thankfully, Ava calls to me, "You can get a pair of shorts and a t-shirt from my closet."

I don't turn around to thank her because if I see Marius, I think I'm going to smack him. Matthias walks into the living room just as I'm marching through, and I point toward the stairs.

"Don't come up to your bedroom. I have to get some of your wife's clothes because your brother is an asshole."

Matthias nods and gives me a shrug. "Okay. Marius, I'm assuming?"

Without looking back, I answer, "You'd assume right."

Goddamn him! He makes it so I have to lie to my oldest and dearest friend, and then he does shit like this.

As I stomp up the stairs, I try to remember why I love that man. At the moment, nothing is coming to me, but I have a list as long as my arm why I hate him right now.

Ten minutes later, at least I have dry clothes on. My underwear and bra are still drenched, so let's hope my friend and her husband don't have a problem with me going commando. I don't give a damn what Marius thinks.

On my way back out to the pool, a bedroom door opens and he pulls he into his room before slamming it shut. As usual, he's wearing a smile, like he's happy he pissed me off.

"Don't bother telling me you're angry because I know you're not. You're just pretending for Ava and my brother."

Jesus, he can be utterly clueless sometimes!

I push against his chest, catching him off guard and sending him back a few feet into the wall. "I am angry, Marius! I told you I didn't want to go swimming. Did I have to say I didn't want to get wet too?"

Now that he has a real sense of how furious I am, he stops smiling and walks over toward me. "Oh, don't be mad. I was just having a little fun."

I narrow my eyes and glare at him. "I'm going now. Don't try to talk to me for the rest of the time I'm here. That's how angry I am at you."

Of course, that doesn't stop him from sliding his arms around my waist and pulling me into him. Looking down at me, he studies what I imagine must be a truly enraged expression on my face and leans in to kiss me. I shouldn't let him, but I can't deny I do love the man's mouth.

"Don't be angry, Duck. If it was just the two of us, we'd be having sex in the pool right now. Admit it."

I stare up into his dark eyes and shake my head. "Admit what? That I like having sex with you? Okay, fine. I do. Why can't you see I'm angry with you right now?"

He steps closer and presses his bare body against mine. "Because I don't want to see that. Come on. Give me a smile. You know how much I love when you smile. It makes my heart happy."

Wriggling against him, I twist out of his hold. "Well, your heart is going to have to be unhappy this afternoon. Maybe next time go with your heart's idea instead of wherever you got the idea to throw me in the pool."

Marius frowns like I'm the one who caused this problem. "It's not bad enough I have to hear the woman I love is being set up with some guy from King Industries? Now you won't even smile for me?"

This man is going to drive me insane.

"So you don't like that Ava keeps trying to set me up with potential boyfriends? Then let's tell the truth so everyone can know we're together."

He shakes his head to that idea. "So what are you going to do with this guy?"

Seems the man I love is choosing denial today. So be it.

"Well, I thought after dinner I'd tell him to drive to the nearest dark spot and we can fuck like animals. Then maybe I'll ask to go for ice cream since I've been really wanting some mint chocolate chip lately. Nothing big. Just your usual blind date."

Even though he has to know none of that is what I actually plan on doing with Ava's newest potential Mr. Right, Marius looks utterly miserable as he listens to me. When I finish, he grunts like he's disgusted.

"I don't want you to go."

"Then let's come clean and tell the world we're together."

Of course, his answer to that suggestion is the same it's been for two years. Shaking his head again, he says,

"Not yet. That doesn't mean you have to go out with this guy, though."

He pulls me to him and kisses me hard, his hand gently encircling my throat in that way he does when we're alone that never fails to make me weak in the knees. "You're mine, Eden. Not his. Mine."

Barely able to speak I'm so aroused, I croak out, "If I don't go out with this guy, Ava will be suspicious."

I see the jealousy in his eyes when he says, "And if you do go, I'll be miserable."

Against his lips, I whisper, "Then you know what you have to do. It's your call, baby. The ball's totally in your court."

I spin out of his hold again and hurry toward the door. I don't look back because if I do, I'm going to want to stay, and I can't.

He's going to have to accept the fact that as long as he insists we keep our relationship secret, I'll have to keep going on blind dates with the men Ava finds for me. It's completely in his control.

CHAPTER NINE

arius

FURIOUS ABOUT AVA INSISTING ON SETTING UP EDEN, I head down to my brother's office to find out more about this guy from King Industries she's picked out this time. I love my sister-in-law, but this shit needs to stop right now.

I find Matthias sitting on the black leather couch just inside the door. He looks stressed out and utterly exhausted. Too bad. This conversation can't wait.

"Hey, what's going on? Planning on taking a quick nap?" I ask as I walk in.

"Maybe," he answers sheepishly. "You look like you have something on your mind."

Unsure how to phrase this so it doesn't seem suspicious, I try to be as casual as possible when I say,

"Just wondering about this guy Ava says she's setting Eden up with."

Matthias screws his face into a look of pure confusion. "Why do you care?"

"I'm bored. I have nothing else to do."

My brother seems to accept that answer, although that may be because he looks like he hasn't had enough sleep in a year. He stands up from the couch and walks around his desk to sit down in his chair. A few seconds later, he spins his laptop around toward me.

"That's him. Robert Jennings. Everyone calls him Rob. Nice guy. Thirty, I think. He's got an MBA like Kellen. In fact, Kellen suggested him for Eden even before Ava asked if I knew anyone at work for her. Seems like an upstanding guy."

I study the picture of Rob Jennings on the King Industries website and hate him instantly. Like hate that burns hotter than a hundred suns. The kind of hate that makes you want to kill people. I hate his light brown hair. I hate his face, which I'm guessing more than one woman has thought was decent. I hate his smile especially. He looks like he's spent his entire life in a dentist's chair. Eden's going to hate this guy too. I know it. He's an IT guy, for Christ's sake.

Still staring bullet holes through my brother's laptop screen, I ask, "What makes you think Eden wants a guy like this? From what I've seen of her, she's pretty wild. I'm not sure this guy with his buttoned up, white dress shirt and no tie look is going to be able to handle the likes of her."

"Well, I'm not sure he's going to like her since she can be a lot, but Ava asked me for my help setting her up, so

I figured Rob would be a good choice. Anyway, it's just a date. Nobody is saying they're going to get married."

His mention of that word makes me tear my attention away from Mr. Rob Jennings of the land of IT. "Married? Seems like you're jumping the gun, aren't you?"

Thankfully, my brother is too sleepy or distracted by fatherhood to pick up on the seething jealousy that's currently seeping into every syllable I utter. As he spins his laptop back in front of him, he says, "Well, Ava wants Eden to be happy, and she thinks this guy can do that. She promises if they don't hit it off that she'll be fine with it. I think they're going to go out to dinner first, and then they'll be at the party in a few weeks."

Jesus Christ! Two dates? What. The. Fuck?

"Don't you think having a party with Eleanor still feeling under the weather is in bad taste? I mean, I'm not one to stand on formality or manners, but she is still recuperating. Maybe you should push it back again."

Even as I say those words, I know they're bullshit. Eleanor's going to be fine. She's been up and around yesterday and today, and this morning I saw her making breakfast. That doesn't mean I'm above using her recent health scare to make sure this party doesn't happen and Eden doesn't have to spend any time with Rob from IT.

A knock on the office door interrupts us, and Ronan walks in beaming a smile. "Hey, was there a family meeting I didn't know about, or are you guys talking about me?"

"What's new, little brother?" I ask, pleased to see the youngest King so happy.

He plops down on the leather sofa and puts his feet

up on the coffee table in front of it. "I came out to see how Eleanor is doing. Since I know she's okay, I want talk to Matthias about something, but now that you're here, I think I want to talk to you about it too. Either of you have time?"

I turn to look at Matthias and say, "This guy is busy running a dating service, but I have time. What's up?"

Of course, that makes Ronan curious. "Really? What made you decide to buy one of those?"

Laughing, I shake my head at how naïve my youngest brother can be as Matthias explains he didn't buy a dating app. "Marius is busting balls, as usual. Ava and I are setting her friend Eden up with a guy who works at the company. I have some time before I have to take a call from London. What's up?"

"I wanted to talk about a charity I want to set up. It will be for people like me. I wanted to run it by you since you have attorneys on retainer." Ronan stops and then says, "Marius, I was hoping you'd be part of it since you're the only reason I'm still here."

Hearing him say that and seeing him smile as he does makes me happier than I thought I could be today, especially after finding out about Rob the IT guy who's going on a date with the woman I love. "I'm in! Anything for a good cause."

"Cool! Matthias, can you direct me to someone we can trust to set this whole thing up?"

"Sure. I don't think Mattson is the guy you want, but I think someone at his firm would work. I'll look for their number."

Ronan swings his long legs off the coffee table and

stands up. "Great! I think I'm going to go say hi to my favorite sister-in-law and my nephews."

He begins to walk toward the door but then turns around and looks at me. "Hey, explain something to me. Why haven't you ever tried to get together with Eden? She's been into you for years."

"What makes you say that?" I ask, fishing for compliments when I should be keeping my damn mouth shut.

Both my brothers look at one another and then at me. "Seriously? Ava mentioned it before Theo died. I know you were there when she said it."

I don't recall that conversation, not that it matters. Trying hard to seem as disinterested as possible about Eden being crazy about me, I answer, "It just never felt like the thing to do."

"Dude, you're nuts. She's beautiful, and she likes you. What else do you want?"

Waving away his idea, I begin walking toward the door. "She's just not my type, okay?"

I leave Ronan and Matthias to talk about whatever this charity idea of his is because if I hung around in that office for another minute, neither one of them would ever believe I don't give a damn about Eden. When the time comes to reveal the truth about the two of us, they'll know. Until then, I'll keep my business the way I like it.

Private.

On my way up to my room, I think about possibly telling everyone about Eden and me. It might be nice to share that kind of thing with my family. They all seem to like her, and I know they'd be happy for me.

And it's not like I have to worry about any of my

brothers hooking up with her like with Theo and Maia. Maybe coming clean with everyone could work.

I lie down on my bed and stare up at the ceiling as I try to convince myself that having everyone know Eden and I are together won't ruin everything. It would make things easier, and I wouldn't have to lie to my brothers and Ava anymore.

Not that I have an issue with lying. Not in this kind of case.

See, I don't find lying as egregious as so many people do, especially when it comes to someone's private life. Who the hell needs an entire family's opinions on your love life? No, thanks.

Anyway, I love having Eden all to myself. It's like a secret only the two of us share.

Even as jealousy bubbles inside me, I have to believe we're going to be fine if she goes on that date with Rob, the IT guy. Staring up at the ceiling, I silently tell myself I'm getting upset over nothing.

"She won't like him. He's not her type. She's as crazy about me as I am about her. It'll just be one date. She probably won't even want to have him at the party after going out to dinner with him."

I bet right now you're thinking I should just tell the world about us. Then Eden won't go on a date with him, so I won't have to worry.

But you see, that's the thing. I never worry when she goes on these dates Ava sets up for her. I trust Eden more than I've ever trusted anyone before. She's proven time and again by her willingness to keep our relationship on the down low that she can be trusted.

So why am I jealous? Well, that's the kind of man I

am. When I love a woman—really love her—she's mine and I'm hers. I mean, you don't see me going out with anyone else because I'm with her.

Yes, I know this could all be avoided if we just made things public. Then all these stupid blind dates Ava insists on arranging could stop. She'd probably be thrilled her best friend and I are together.

The problem is then everyone would know, and we wouldn't just be the two of us anymore. All my life, I've been one of five brothers. Nothing in my life was allowed to be just mine. I figured women would be since going after one of your brothers' girlfriends or exes breaks a cardinal rule in the bro code.

Theo showed me how wrong I was with that.

So no, for now, Eden and I will remain in hiding. I'll just have to accept the fact that her going on dates with other men is the price I have to pay to keep us a secret.

I'm not worried. This will all be fine.

CHAPTER TEN

den

THIS DATE IS OFF TO A FLYING START. SO FAR, ROB HAS talked about nothing but work since he picked me up at my parents' house, which is where he thinks I live. He's boring, and I'm lying.

Great combination.

"So I told Matthias that I could definitely get things up and running, but it would take longer than the last head of the division thought it would because he was cutting corners left and right."

While he continues to explain whatever he did in his department, I look around the restaurant at the tables with their pristine white tablecloths and the gold sconces on the wall as I wonder what this man could have said to Ava at any point that made her think he was perfect for me. I smile at an older woman sitting with what looks to be her granddaughter. I bet they're having a good time. My grandmother isn't the type of person I'd want to go to dinner with, but right now, I'd even take having her sitting here with me talking about how she thinks my hair needs to be cut and asking me why I wear such dark eyeshadow all the time over having to listen to Rob drone on about himself.

"So what about you? Tell me about you. I feel like I've been the one talking this whole time," he says before stabbing his fork into a mozzarella stick.

I watch him cut that fried piece of cheese into four precisely the same size pieces and force a smile. "I don't think I've ever seen anyone use a knife for mozzarella sticks."

"Oh, yeah," he says as he pops one of the teeny-tiny pieces into his mouth. "I'm very careful about choking. Do you know that's one of the biggest hazards in life? You definitely want to be cautious about eating and choking."

Nodding, all I can think of now is this man has never had a blowjob in his life. No way. Not with that worry about choking.

Then again, he might just be a selfish prick who has no problem with a woman choking on his dick. Not that I think he's got much going on there. This guy screams tiny penis.

To think that I have an incredibly sexy man with more than enough to satisfy me but because he insists on us keeping our relationship hidden, I have to go out with guys like this. I know Ava means well, so I don't blame her.

I blame Marius.

And just as I think that, the man himself walks in the door of the restaurant. Oh, this date just got a hundred times worse. If I'm lucky, he won't notice the mozzarella sticks cut up into baby-size portions. Even better, if I'm really lucky, he won't see us here at all.

That thought barely crosses my mind when he waves to me and starts heading in our direction. Sweet baby Jesus. What the hell is planning on doing?

God, please no. No, no, no.

"Are you okay?" Rob asks as I feel my stomach drop. "You look really pale all of a sudden."

That says it all since I'm as tan as I've ever been in my entire life sitting here with him. Why do these things happen to me?

"Eden? Funny seeing you here," Marius says when he stops at our table.

I paste a smile on my face as I study him for a second or two. He got dressed up in his dark gray suit for this little scene he's about to make. At least there's that. It would be infinitely worse if he came to this nice restaurant dressed in shorts and a t-shirt. At least when they have to escort him out because he becomes a problem, they'll think he's a well-dressed professional who may have had a few too many and got out of hand and not some guy who looks like a frat boy fresh off a bender.

"Marius," I say through gritted teeth.

The two of us stare at one another for what feels like forever before Rob quietly asks, "So you two know each other?"

Of course, Marius beats me to the answer. Turning to

look at my date, he smirks. "Marius King, the brother of your boss. Nice to meet you."

I notice he doesn't offer to shake his hand. Nice touch.

"Really? Now that you mention it, I can see the strong resemblance. Nice to meet you."

Rob does offer his hand, so as the two of them do the gentlemanly handshake thing, I say, "I've known Marius and his family for years. We all went to the same prep school as kids."

Why I say all of that I have no idea. What I really want to do at this very moment is stand up and walk out of this restaurant, never looking back at either of these men.

Grinning like a damn Cheshire cat, Marius returns to staring at me as he says, "Oh, yeah. I've known Eden forever. It's like she's a part of my family I've known her for so long."

His voice sounds unnecessarily sexy, which makes me wonder what the hell is going to come out of his mouth next. If only he had just agreed to tell the world about us, none of this would have to happen.

"Do you also work at King Industries?" Rob asks. "I'm the head of the IT department, and I don't think I've seen you at any of the company functions."

The very idea of Marius appearing at the King Industries company Christmas party makes me want to burst out laughing, but I can't do that so I press my lips together and hope I can keep my composure. Another comment like that from Rob and I'm going to lose it.

"No, I leave the workaday life to my brothers

Matthias and Kellen. I'm one of the Kings who prefers a more carefree life."

Rob nods, and I can hear his disdain for Marius come through loud and clear when all he answers is, "Oh."

Marius hears it too, but his reaction isn't to get angry. Instead, he laughs. Fabulous. Oh, God, I feel like I'm on a train that's lost its brakes and is careening down the tracks while on fire and heading for a cliff.

Thankfully, he takes Rob's lackluster response as his cue to say goodbye. "Well, I better get going. I'm just here to pick up dinner before I have to meet with my assistant Sam. Have a wonderful evening, you kids!"

And with that, he breezes away like everything that just happened was perfectly normal.

I watch him walk out to the entrance where I swear he flirts with the very attractive redhead hosting. He looks back at me and smiles before leaving, and I turn my attention back to Rob who works in IT.

"Interesting guy. He seems nothing like his brothers, particularly Kellen."

If I keep fake smiling like I know I must, my face is going to hurt all day tomorrow. I don't have a choice, though. Ava really wants me to give this guy a chance, and even though there's no possibility we could ever be a couple, I don't want to hurt his feelings.

"True. He and Kellen are very different. To be honest, I feel like Marius is sort of a mixture of the youngest King, Ronan, and the second oldest, Theo. He died in a car accident a few years ago, but you know what I mean."

Terrific. Now I'm rambling. Maybe we should call this date what it actually is. A disaster.

Rob nods, and I push the lettuce around on my plate. Definitely not my best date. Not by a long shot.

I don't think I've ever been so happy to see a server less than a minute later when he brings us our entrées. That joy immediately disappears when he sets down Rob's plate of salmon with the dill sauce he explicitly asked it to not have.

"Excuse me, this wasn't supposed to have the sauce on top. I specifically said no sauce. Weren't you listening when I gave you my order? It's not rocket science. I say what I want, and you write it on your little pad and tell the kitchen. You're going to have to take this back, and I want a brand new entrée prepared, not just someone scraping off the sauce."

The server looks mortified, although I'm not sure if he's bothered by the mistake with Rob's food or the pretentious way he sounds when he explains the mistake. Personally, I find him rude and would have no issue with walking out of this restaurant right now.

If I didn't promise Ava I'd work really hard with this guy to give him a chance.

That there's no possibility we could ever be a couple doesn't negate the fact that I said I'd keep an open mind about him. It's just that he was such a pompous ass talking to the server like that. Marius is a billionaire, and never once has he ever spoken to anyone waiting on us so rudely.

"Can you believe that?" Rob asks, likely assuming I think he's in the right.

He finds out very quickly he's mistaken. "You didn't have to speak to that man like that. Someone made a mistake. They'll fix it. This is a very good restaurant."

"That's not the point. The point is I specifically asked for no sauce on top of the salmon. It's not rocket science. Just don't drown the damn fish in sauce."

Since I don't plan on ever seeing this guy again, I could tell him I think he's a jackass and walk out, but I can't because of what I swore to Ava I'd do. So instead, I force myself to keep smiling as I slice off a piece of steak from my New York strip.

My phone vibrates in my purse, so I lean down to fish it out to see who's messaging me. Marius. This can't be good.

"Nice stick in the mud. I know you're pretending to like him but don't you think that's cruel? Meet me at our place in an hour. I love you."

Only Marius King could irritate and charm a person all in one text message.

The kitchen fixes Rob's salmon, so after waiting for only a couple minutes, the two of us can finally enjoy our meals. I'm thrilled when he stops talking as he eats, giving me a reprieve from his boring conversation and rude complaints about the server.

I wait for the right moment just before he's finished to let out a tiny groan that gets his attention. Looking concerned, he asks, "Are you okay, Eden?"

Grimacing like I'm in agony, I lean forward and croak out, "I'm not sure. I don't feel well."

Rob from IT is a clueless boob, but he can see I'm not doing well by the fake look of pain on my face. "Oh, I bet it's something that requires sodium bicarbonate. I have some at my apartment, if you'd like me to give you a dose."

The last thing I want is this guy to give me a dose of

anything, so I shake my head and gently groan again. "I think I just need to go home. I'm so sorry, Rob, but I'll have to cut our date short. I hope you understand."

His eyes get big as he nods. "Oh, I definitely understand. If we had time, I could tell you about the week I spent with an upset stomach. I almost landed in the hospital because of that. Choking and upset stomach are definitely my bugaboos. I'll get the server to give us our check right now."

It's hard not to burst out laughing as he's talking, but I need to keep this sick act up for just a little while longer. Then I'll be free.

Although Rob is a terrible bore and possibly the least sexy man I've ever had dinner with, on top of being rude to service people, he surprises me by getting and paying the check in a matter of minutes so we can go. I keep up my sick routine all the way to my parents' house, and when he puts the car in park, I get the feeling even being ill isn't going to let me escape a good night kiss.

"I had a lovely time. I hope you did too, although I know being sick can make you feel like you don't want to think of this as a lovely time."

I try to smile, but I'm worried if I make it too good, he'll think I'm okay, so I nod and reach for the door. "I'm so sorry, Rob, but I think things are worse now. I hope you can forgive me."

He thankfully doesn't try to kiss me when I quickly open the car door. "Can I see you again?"

Clearly, I need to step up my acting skills. Bending over like I'm in real pain, I look into the car at him and groan. "Oh, you have my number. I wish I could talk more, but I have to go. Good night."

I hurry into the house and slam the door behind me, relieved this night with Rob is over. Now the second half of my night begins.

CHAPTER ELEVEN

$\mathcal{E}$den

"MARIUS KING! YOU COME OUT HERE RIGHT NOW," I bark when I step out of the elevator into our penthouse apartment.

He walks out of the kitchen wearing nothing but a pair of black basketball shorts. "Was your date awful, dear?" he asks with a chuckle.

I glare at him for a few seconds before walking past him on my way to our bedroom. "Well, my date was rude to the waiter, and you thought it was a good idea to crash the whole show. Awful doesn't cover it."

Behind me, Marius laughs. "Rude to the waiter? Seriously? Where does Ava find these guys? I think I'll have to tell my brother to fire that son of a bitch. Being rude to wait staff is so fucking…well, rude."

Spinning around, I stop and shake my head as I look

at the man I love with utter astonishment. "And you showing up wasn't rude?"

That gets me one of his trademark smiles that never fail to remind me of a pirate. "That wasn't rude, and if it was, it was only rude to you. He was rude to a perfect stranger just trying to do his job. Big difference. I ordered in food. You hungry?"

"It's been a hell of a night, Marius. I lied through my teeth to Rob from IT because I can't tell my best friend I don't need to be set up with any more guys because I already have one I'm normally perfectly happy with, although at this moment I'm not sure about that. I had to fake being sick so I could end the date early, which I guess is more lying. You know what? I'm tired of lying. I don't want to do it anymore."

He walks over and wraps his arms around me in a hug I had no idea I needed so much. "Aww, let Marius take care of everything."

I look up at him and sigh. "You're part of the problem, you know."

"I know, but you love me."

This man is going to drive me nuts. "And somehow that makes it okay? I thought I was going to throw up when you were standing at the table with us. I had no idea what you might say from one word to the next."

He throws his head back and laughs. "At least I brought a little excitement to what sounds like a pretty terrible time."

I sigh and hang my head. "What am I going to do with you?"

Marius slides his finger under my chin and lifts it so I

can't avoid looking up at him. "For starters, you can eat some of the dinner I had delivered."

"I'm not hungry," I say defiantly, setting my jaw. "I'm not going to be seduced by food, Marius."

He tilts his hips forward so his hard cock presses against my abdomen. "Oh, don't worry about that. The real seduction is what happens after we eat. As you can tell, I'm all ready to go."

I look into his dark eyes and say, "What if I don't want that?"

That question assumes I could say no to him when it comes to sex, which has never happened in the entire time we've been together. Sometimes I think I should hold out and not sleep with him so he'll agree we should tell everyone about us, but I'd be hurting myself if I did that.

When you're crazy about someone like I am about Marius, sex is something you want to share with them. When they're as good at it as he is, it's ridiculous to even think of denying yourself such an incredible time.

He knows all of this, so the fake look of hurt and shock on his face right now is all for show.

"You don't want to go upstairs and have mind blowing sex for the rest of the night? Where did my Duck go, and how can I get her back?"

"Your Duck is right here, Marius. She's just sick of being a rotten liar."

With a grin, he says, "So you do want to have mind blowing sex all night. You just don't want to lie about it? Is that what I'm understanding?"

Frustrated, I place my hands on his naked chest and push him away. Turning on my heel, I head for the stairs.

"You're intentionally being obtuse, Marius. You know what I mean."

Behind me, he sighs. "I do, Eden. I was just trying to be playful."

I turn around to see him looking sad as I set my foot on the first stair. Whenever he uses my given name, I know he's being serious. "I know, and I love that about you. I'm just unhappy about lying to everyone."

"What if I promise to make you forget about everything tonight? Will that put a smile on your face?"

I could respond that what would put a smile on my face is telling the people we love the truth about us, but I don't feel like talking about that anymore. I don't know if it was the terrible date with Rob or feeling like I had no control over anything at dinner tonight, but I don't want to think about anything until tomorrow.

Marius walks over to where I'm standing on the first stair and kisses me. "I love you more than I can say, Eden. I know you want to go public, but can't we have just have a little while longer when it's only us?"

Nodding, I smile because this isn't an issue that's going to be solved tonight. "I love you too. Let's table this discussion because I don't feel like talking about it anymore."

His eyes hopeful, he asks, "Then you'll come into the kitchen for dinner first and then a night of great sex?"

Marius King is many things, but easily discouraged is not one of them.

I kiss him and whisper against his lips, "I'll tell you what. Forget dinner and meet me upstairs in five minutes. Be ready to rock my world because after that date tonight, I need to be reminded that sexy men who know how to take care of a woman still exist."

That gets me a huge smile. "Dinner is forgotten, my lady. As for my taking care of you, well, not to toot my own horn, but I've never disappointed you, have I?"

I bite my lip as he leans against me, pressing his hard cock into my thigh. "Never once."

Looking into those gorgeous dark eyes staring at me, I try to claw back some control. "You know, I should be furious with you."

He knows I'm not really upset with him, so he simply smiles at my statement. "I just needed to see that guy. That's all. You can't blame me for being jealous."

"I don't believe for a second you were jealous, Marius. You're everything he isn't. You know that."

Marius pulls me to him and groans as my body melts into his. "He was out with the woman I love. The woman who makes my world go round. Of course, I was jealous. I wanted to tear his head off, and that little crack when he heard I don't slave away at a desk nine-to-five every fucking day like he does with his bullshit job pissed me off. He's lucky I didn't put my fist through his smug fucking face."

Okay, maybe I was wrong. Maybe he was jealous.

I want to mention the one thing that would have made that dinner date an impossibility, but I'm beginning to sound like a broken record with that. Even more, I don't want to think about anything but how much I love this man tonight.

Cradling his face in my hands, I kiss him on the lips. "You're the only man I want, baby. You know that."

"I do, but that doesn't change the fact that I had to

see you with another man tonight. And before you say it, I know. It's all my fault that it happened in the first place. I know. I just don't want to share you with the world yet."

He really is just the sweetest man sometimes. "You don't have to share me. Not tonight, at least. Tonight, it's just you and me."

That brings a smile to his face. "Just me and my Duck."

For the first time, I understand what he means when he says he wants it to just be us for a little while longer. When we're together like this, only the two of us, we both get to be who we truly are. I don't have to be Eden controlling the million things I have to do at my job or the version of me who makes sure to do the right thing so my parents think I'm a good daughter or what Ava thinks I should do so I'm a good friend in her eyes.

And for him, he doesn't have to be the protective big brother or the King everyone thinks only wants to have fun in this life. Although I know those are both his nature, when he's alone with me he doesn't have to be that man. He can just be happy, and that's all I want for the man I love.

"I love you, Marius. Never forget that."

He sighs like the weight of the world has been lifted off his shoulders. "I never do, Eden. I hope you never doubt how much I love you."

I shake my head and smile. "Give me a couple minutes to grab a shower. I need to wash this night off me before we're together."

The truth is I don't know if I smell like the restaurant

or even like Rob's cologne. I just don't want to be with Marius with any hint of tonight or that date on me.

"Take all the time you need, Duck."

By the time I get into the shower and adjust the temperature of the water, I've almost completely forgotten how awful my time with Rob was. Ava means well, but what if I actually was single? Is that the best there is out there now?

I don't want to think about that, so I squeeze some shampoo into my palm and wash my hair. Next, I grab the conditioner because if I don't use it, I'll have hair that looks like a long, black haystack, and no one wants to see that.

Lost in thought about whether I should shave or not, I don't hear the door to the shower open. Suddenly, I feel hands on my back, and I spin around to see Marius standing in front of me as water streams down over his head.

"I got tired of waiting, so I figured I'd join you," he says playfully. "Aww, I missed the shampooing. I love that part."

He can be so silly sometimes. "Sorry to tell you I've already moved on to the conditioner portion of the show."

Marius slides his hands through my hair and smiles. "Did I ever tell you how much I love your hair?"

Since he's mentioned it many times, I simply shrug. "Maybe once or twice."

He pushes my hair completely off my face and kisses me long and deep. "It's one of my favorite things on you. Your eyes too."

I know what he's doing. This is his way of apologizing. I don't want that, though.

"You don't have to make up for anything tonight, baby. I know why you showed up."

Without saying another word, he lifts me up so I'm at the perfect height for him to slide into me. I wrap my legs around his waist, and a second later, he fills me like his cock was made only for me. I close my eyes and bury my face in his neck as he fucks me like no other man ever has.

Expertly. Passionately. Perfectly.

My fingers scratch across the top of his shoulders, making him groan, but I don't stop. When we're like this—utterly lost to how much we need one another—it's like I forget everything but the sensual way he envelops me. It's like he's everywhere around me, inside my head, deep inside my body taking possession of my very soul.

He feels so damn good pumping into me that I can't control myself. I sink my teeth into his earlobe and moan in his ear, "Oh, God, don't stop...God, don't stop."

Marius doesn't say a word and keeps fucking me like a man on a mission to come and get me off too. I cling to his neck, hanging on with all I have. We're wild and raw, and I wouldn't want it any other way right now.

"I hated seeing you with him, Eden," he says as he slows his pace so our fucking becomes much more measured for the moment.

"We were two people at a table in a restaurant. That's all."

He looks into my eyes but says nothing. Marius knows this can all end if he agrees to us going public. I know seeing me having dinner with another man hurts him, but only he can put an end to Ava's matchmaking.

"I still hated it," he grunts out before driving his cock deep into my body and touching a spot no one has ever reached before.

We return to not speaking, and it doesn't take me long before I'm on the verge of coming. It never takes me long for the first orgasm with Marius. The man knows how to make a woman happy. There's no denying that.

He senses I'm close too and begins to pump into me harder, stabbing into my pussy with abandon. My release unravels inside me until I feel like I'm going to explode, and a second later, it's all I can do to hold on to him as my body kicks into overdrive. I buck against him, desperate to make this feeling last as long as it can.

I don't know how long my orgasm lasts, but I finally collapse against him, my head on his shoulder as the hot water from the shower beats down on my back. I'm utterly satisfied and secretly hungry now, but I don't say anything about that since he hasn't come yet.

Marius begins to fuck me again, but I stop him with a shake of my head. He looks confused but eases out of me and sets me down on the tile floor.

"Is something wrong?" he asks, and I sense a hint of hurt in his voice.

"No. I just thought I'd like to do something else. Can you let me around you to get to the soap?" I ask with a smile.

Still unsure what I'm talking about, he steps aside. I push down on the dispenser to get a palmful of the coconut soap that smells heavenly and turn back to face him.

Without telling him what I'm doing, I wrap my fingers around his cock and give it a few strokes. Then I say, "Time to rinse off."

He does as I suggest, but I can tell he doesn't understand where I'm going with this. "Okay. Is this some new thing you read in one of your magazines? Because if it is, I have to say I'm fine with it but it doesn't go far enough, in my opinion. But I'm game for anything."

God, I do love this man. I stand on my tiptoes and kiss him on the lips before whispering against them, "Now relax and let me take care of you."

As I slowly lower myself to the shower floor, Marius finally realizes where I'm going with all of this and grins like he just won the lottery. Since kneeling is out of the question on these tiles, I crouch like a catcher and take his long, thick, and now coconut scented cock in my hand. Stroking him, I watch as he closes his eyes and lets out a heavy moan.

He really is the most sensual creature I've ever met. Of all the things about Marius King I adore, this part of him is the one I love most.

I take my time playing with him, but finally he opens his eyes and looks down at me with pure need in them. "Duck, you're killing me here. You aren't trying to torture me because of what I did tonight, are you?"

Clearly, that's enough foreplay for now, so I flick the head with my tongue a couple times and slowly take as much as I can of him into my mouth. He's far too big and long for me to take him all the way, but I get most of his cock in. It's enough for him to let out a moan so full of desire I think he might come before I even get down to business.

Staring up at him, I suck his cock and watch as he revels in how incredible it feels. The first time I went down on him, I was amazed at how much he loved getting head. Justin never liked it, so I rarely gave him a blowjob, and when I did, he loved to say that he was different from other guys and just didn't prefer that kind of sex.

Thank God I'm not with him anymore. I much prefer a man who appreciates a woman wanting to please him.

Marius moans loudly again, tearing me out of my thoughts about my ex, and I see a wildness in his eyes now. Sure he's close, I suck hard just like he loves and gently squeeze his balls, and that's enough to send him over the edge. He explodes, filling my mouth with cum, while he holds my head on his cock.

When he finishes, he blows the air out of his lungs and sighs again. "Jesus, Eden. You should have warned me you were going to go down on me. I nearly passed out there when you were doing that thing with your tongue on the underside and cupping my balls."

I stand up and kiss him, unable to not laugh at how serious he is right now. "Why would warning you have made a difference?"

"Well, if you told me, I would have had more to eat. I think I almost blacked out at least a couple times during it."

"Did it make you feel good?" I ask as I maneuver around him to let the water rinse me off.

"Hell yeah!" he says before wrapping his arms

around me and nuzzling my neck. "I definitely think I need to eat something now. Woman, you make me weak in the knees."

I turn in his hold and smile at how cute he is. "Well, you go eat. I'm going to rinse this conditioner out of my hair since it's been in there for nearly twenty minutes. I'm going to have the softest hair in America tonight."

"The softest hair for the most beautiful woman in the world," he says as he slides my hair through his fingers. "Are you going to eat too?"

I shake my head. "No. You go enjoy. I think I'm going to do some upkeep since I deep conditioned."

"If you're sure," Marius says, waiting for me to change my mind.

I kiss him and point toward the shower door. "I'm sure. Now go and eat something. I'll meet you in the bedroom after I'm done."

He starts to move toward the door to leave but looks back at me and says, "Just checking one last time because I got coq au vin, which I know is one of your favorite things."

"Save me a little. I'll have it tomorrow."

With one last sweet kiss, he leaves to go downstairs, so I rinse the conditioner out of my hair and follow him out of the shower to focus on my nails. It's been weeks since I had a mani-pedi, but since I don't foresee me having much time in the near future to remedy that, I'm going to have to take care of things myself.

An hour later, my fingernails and toenails are a matching plum color, and my hair is as soft as silk. Maybe I should keep that conditioner in longer more often.

Or maybe I should just have sex with Marius in the shower more often.

I walk out of the bathroom and see him already fast asleep in bed. I guess he wasn't exaggerating about how much sex sapped him of his energy. I'll have to remember to have him eat before I go down on him the next time.

The moment I slide underneath the covers, he begins tossing and turning. I try to stay as still and quiet as possible so as not to wake him, but it's like he's having a nightmare. I watch as he shakes his head like he's telling someone no to something, but then he reaches his hands out in front of him. A few seconds later, he wakes up, and I see he's drenched in sweat. His eyes are filled with fear, and he doesn't seem to know where he is.

I reach over and gently touch his cheek. He turns to look at me, and slowly, I see the man I know return.

"Are you okay? You were shaking your head and tossing and turning. Did you have a nightmare?"

He thinks about that for a long moment and then shrugs like nothing ever happened. "I don't know. Maybe I was beating up that Rob from IT guy in my dreams."

I roll my eyes and smile, but I know it wasn't that. He wouldn't wake up in a cold sweat if he was dreaming about beating the hell out of Rob.

As I snuggle up against his side and he wraps his arm around me, I wonder if I should mention this isn't the first time he's acted like he was having a nightmare. On the nights we've spent together since Ronan tried to kill himself, Marius has woken up like this more than a few times.

"Are you sure you're okay, baby?" I ask, looking up at him.

"Whenever I'm with you, I'm all good, Duck," he answers before sweetly kissing the top of my head.

I wish I could believe him.

CHAPTER TWELVE

*M*arius

AVA'S PARTIES NEVER FAIL TO SERVE UP SOME GOOD times, but as soon as I walk in and see that Rob guy again, I'm pissed off. Eden told me he was a total jackass. The shithead couldn't even be nice to the damn server. Why is he here for what would be considered their second date?

I pull Eden aside the first chance I get before most of the partygoers start arriving, practically dragging her into the powder room on the first floor. "What the hell is he doing here?"

She looks incredible tonight in a dark green tank top dress that shows off her tan. I wish I had said something about that before I asked about that guy. I love when she wears that color. It looks incredible next to her black hair and green eyes.

Before I can say anything like that, she snaps back, "The same thing he was doing when we went out on a date, Marius. This is all happening because of what you insist on with us, not me. You want to make sure this never happens again? Then let's go out there and tell everyone the truth."

I lean in and nuzzle her neck just under her ear. She smells like that perfume I love and can never remember the name of. I always think of Eden when I smell it.

"Why does it have to be that? I told you I want to keep you all to myself."

She pushes me away and shakes her head. "Then you can't complain when I have to pretend to be with some guy Ava sets me up with. You can't have it both ways, Marius."

Seriously? All I want to do is keep our relationship to only the two of us for a little longer. How can she not understand how important that is to me?

"This isn't fair. How would you feel if I showed up with some girl?"

Anger fills her eyes, and she takes a step toward me so we're pressed against one another. "I'm warning you, Marius. We can't go on like this."

"Are you giving me an ultimatum?"

I love when she gets feisty, but I'm getting the sense she's about a mile past that right now. Eden knows I only want to be with her. For Christ's sake, if I didn't constantly have to put out fucking fires with my brothers and their goddamned problems, I'd tell her I want to move away to wherever she wants to go. I'd buy us a big house, and we could live out our lives together.

That's not the case yet, though. Matthias and Kellen seem to be okay, but Ronan is still dealing with everything from his accident. Sure, he's got Kate by his side, so he's doing better. I just can't walk away from him completely yet, and as long as I have to live around here near my family, I don't want to let them in on the greatest part of my life.

Not yet.

"You call it what you want, Marius," she says in a serious voice that tells me that was, in fact, an ultimatum. "All I'm saying is this can't go on indefinitely."

I reach out to push her hair behind her ear. "Promise me you won't kiss him. I know you won't sleep with him, but even the thought of you kissing him bothers me, so promise."

That gets me a look of confusion mixed with disgust. Never a good combination.

"Are you kidding me? What makes you think you can put all these rules on me but you don't have to follow any?"

Leaning down, I sneak a kiss. "I follow a bunch of rules with you. Remember when you told me you hated that I didn't put my toothbrush in the cup? I've never not put it away since that day. And remember when you said you didn't want to see my socks on the floor near the hamper because that bothered you? Tell me, have you seen any recently? See? Those are only two very good examples of how I follow rules very well when it comes to you."

She stares up at me and then shakes her head. "You're unbelievable."

"I'll take that as a compliment."

Rolling her eyes, she sighs. "I need to go before someone figures out I'm in here with the only single King who, by the way, isn't single, but he doesn't want anyone to know that."

I slip my arms around her waist and pull her to me, loving how good she feels against my body. Staring down into those gorgeous green eyes of hers, I smile as the perfect thought crosses my mind.

"What do you say to us doing it right here? I'm sure there's something purely Freudian about that since this used to be where my mother would bring each of us when we scraped our knees, and she'd kiss our boo-boos, but putting the freaky deaky psychological issues aside, I don't think I've ever wanted you more than I do right now. Can you feel my hard-on? I swear I could cut fucking glass with my cock right now."

I'm more than a little disappointed when she pushes me away and reaches for the doorknob. I grab her and push her up against the door, loving how excited she makes me.

"Marius, do you hear yourself when you say things like that to me?" she asks, the anger rising in her voice with each word.

Shrugging, I answer, "I was only sort of joking about the Freudian business. Forget that. It's not a big deal, and I promise it won't affect me. I'm ready, willing, and able to roll. Come on. What do you say?"

She draws her dark eyebrows in toward her nose to make them like two very angry slashes. "I say I think you're insane. If I didn't love you, I'd want to smack your face. In fact, I think I want to anyway."

I slide my hands down her back and squeeze her perfect ass. "I don't mind if we do things rough. Oh, baby."

She squirms out of my hold and glares at me. "What the fuck is wrong with you? Are you going to be like this all night? I don't think I'm going to be able to handle it if you are."

I choose to ignore her questions since I don't believe there's anything wrong with me, and to be honest, I'm not sure how I plan to handle the rest of the night. "So that's a no to a quickie here in the powder room? It was the Freudian stuff, wasn't it? Mental note to self: Eden does not like any talk about psychology when it comes to sex."

Her mouth hangs open as she looks at me in horror. "Marius, I don't know what's going on with you, but I have to go now. It's only a party, the man is no one to me, but I have to pretend that I like him for Ava's sake. Now unless you want to tell everyone the truth, I have to get back out there."

She leaves without my answering her. It's not that I don't want the world to know I'm in love with her. I just want to keep that between us for a little while longer. I keep telling her that, but she doesn't seem to understand.

Unfortunately, Rob from IT and this being their second date has gotten to me. I thought tonight would be a chance for Eden and me to sneak away to have some fun. Now it seems I'm going to be stuck watching the woman I love pretend to like a man while all the other couples act like it's some kind of fucking reboot of the Love Boat.

Well, I'm not doing it.

A half hour later, Ava begins to gently herd us all into the formal dining room for dinner. I don't immediately join them, so she comes over to where I'm standing near the front door and nudges my arm.

"Hey, dinner is ready. Aren't you joining us?"

"Oh, yeah. I'll be right in. I'm just waiting for someone."

She looks at me like she doesn't understand what I mean. "Waiting for someone? Is someone coming as your date tonight? I didn't set out enough place settings if that's the case."

Always the consummate hostess.

I wave away her concern about dishes and silverware. "Don't worry. She can share my plate. It's all good."

"Oh. Okay. Well, when she gets here, you two make sure to come to the dining room. I'll tell Eleanor we need to hold dinner until then."

"It's okay. No need to stress Eleanor out. Have dinner now, and when my plus one gets here, we'll join you."

I can see by the look in Ava's eyes that she's dying to find out about who's coming to dinner as my date. She doesn't ask, though. That's good because I have no interest in explaining myself. What I'm doing is more to show Eden how it feels to watch the person you love on a date with someone else. Nobody else needs to know what's going on.

Ava smiles and begins to walk toward the dining room. "Okay, Marius."

I head outside and see my assistant Sam pull up a couple minutes later. When she gets out of her car, I have to admit I'm a little impressed. I told her to wear something nice that shows some skin. I didn't expect her to wear a long, red, backless dress with slits up to her hips and a nice bit of cleavage.

She might need to get a raise after this.

"Marius, this place is stunning!" she says as she stares up at the house I grew up in. "Do you live here?"

If you're wondering why Sam doesn't know anything about where I live, it's because she's my assistant for my photography work. I pay her handsomely to essentially be a calendar that sends me texts when I have a shoot.

"Used to. This is where I grew up. Now it's my brother and sister-in-law's house. Their names are Matthias and Ava, by the way. I'll introduce you to everyone. It's basically my family, some guy from my brother's work, and Ava's friend Eden. There might be a couple other people, but I don't know them."

"You look great, Marius," she says with a big smile as her gaze travels down my body and then back up to my face. Reaching out, she runs her hand down my arm. "I never get to see you dressed like this. I love this black dress shirt! It looks so good on you."

"Thanks. You look good too," I say, stepping back from her.

"I had to borrow it from one of my roommates. Are you sure it's okay? I hoped you'd like it."

"Yeah. It looks great. Let's head in."

She continues to stare wide-eyed while we walk inside the house. I guess it's a pretty nice place. I just don't look at it like that since I grew up here. To me, it's just home.

"I'm not overdressed, am I?" Sam asks nervously as I take her hand in mine.

"You look great. Remember what I told you. We want people to think we're together tonight, so no talking about you being my assistant, okay?"

She nods and gives me a big smile. "Got it. What do I say if anyone asks me details about us being together?"

I stop a few feet outside the dining room to think about that question. "Just say you've known me for a while."

That should work if Ava starts interrogating her, which I know she will. My sister-in-law is nothing if not curious.

"Maybe we should come up with a story. We can say we got together while we were in Aruba. That was a great trip, wasn't it? You took some great pictures, and we had dinner at that really great restaurant with those giant lobsters. Remember how big they were? We can tell everyone that was the night we first got together."

Her memory of that trip is much better than mine. All I remember is that damn model complaining about sand in her crevices for half the day I was shooting her. After that, I don't remember a thing, but that isn't surprising since I spent the night alone in my hotel room trying to drown my sorrows after the day I had and because I was missing Eden.

"Better to keep things vague. When you start getting into fine details, that's when things go wrong."

Turning to look at Sam, I give her one final once over. Her long blond hair looks perfect tonight. That red dress is a showstopper. And as always, her pretty face impresses.

Let's see how Eden likes it when the shoe is on the other foot.

Have you ever heard someone say when they walked into a room the entire place fell silent? Like they could hear a pin drop? That usually means everyone in that room is shocked by what they're seeing.

Well, that's what happens when Sam and I walk into the dining room. I notice Ava looks stunned, which seems strange since I told her I'd be bringing someone just a few minutes ago. All three of my brothers are equally as surprised, as evidenced by how their mouths drop open when they see us. (Let's be honest. That reaction is for Sam, not me. They've seen me all their lives.)

The best reaction, however, comes from Eden. Even though Rob from IT is clearly talking to her, she instantly ignores him to stare wide-eyed in our direction as I direct Sam to my seat.

"Not to worry, Ava. Sam and I are fine with sharing. Sorry, we're late, everyone. I sort of sprung us on Ava at the last minute. How is everyone doing tonight? This lovely lady is Sam. Sam, my family."

Nobody says a word. They all just stare like Sam and I are from outer space, and they don't know how to talk to aliens.

"Hi! It's so nice to be here," Sam sweetly says.

The meal doesn't even begin before I see Eden get up from the table and storm out. I have to stop myself from running after her since that's my kneejerk reaction, but that would look odd since supposedly the two of us mean nothing to one another.

Ronan is the brother closest to where I'm sitting, so I

lean over and say with a chuckle, "Maybe Eden and Ava are fighting tonight."

Baffled, he shrugs. "I have no idea. Who is Sam over there? You've never mentioned this person before, but now you think you should bring her to Matthias and Ava's party?"

"Yeah, why not? Everyone else gets to bring a date. Why not me?"

He looks around me at Sam and then returns his attention to me. "Dude, how old is she?"

"I don't know. Twenty? Maybe twenty-one. I'm not sure."

He stares at me, his eyes as wide as saucers. "That's pretty young."

"Age is just a number, dude. What matters is what people have in common."

Leave it to that brother to get all moralistic about Sam's age. She's over eighteen and an adult. What more matters?

Since I don't want to talk to him anymore, now seems like a good time to find out where Eden went since she hasn't returned to the table. Turning to Sam, I whisper, "I'll be right back. By the way, you're twenty-one, right?"

She smiles and shakes her head. "I don't turn twenty-one until next February, Marius."

"Great. Well, if anyone asks, just say you're already twenty-one, okay?"

Sam starts to say something, but I quickly get up and head in the direction of where I last saw Eden run off to. It doesn't take me long to find her in the kitchen standing at the sink.

"You're going to miss dinner if you don't come back."

When she turns around, I see tears in her eyes. I take a few steps toward her because I naturally want to make things better, but she stops me dead by holding her hand up.

"What the fuck do you think you're doing?" she asks sharply.

I know this woman as well as I know myself. She can't hide an emotion once she has it, and at this moment, she's so angry she wants to kill me.

"Well, right now, I'm coming to find you because I saw you storm away in a huff from the table. I'm sure Rob from IT is worried too, but since he's a clueless tool, he's not coming to find you anytime soon, I bet."

"You know what I mean."

Best to come clean, at least on this issue.

"I figured turnabout was fair play. No?"

She wipes under her eyes and sniffles away her tears. "I told you I wanted to let the world know about us and that I want to have a baby soon, and this is how you respond?"

"Doesn't feel so good seeing someone you love with another person, does it?"

Eden takes two steps toward me and stops, but I get the sense if she had anything big and sharp, like a pike, my head would be sitting atop it right now. Rage fills her expression, even as tears continue to fill her eyes.

"I pleaded with you to tell everyone about us. I pleaded, and you said just a little while longer. I could have handled that, Marius, but now you've gone and done this, and I can't do it anymore. I'm done. Whatever you thought you'd accomplish with this little stunt of yours, you did a lot more that I don't even think you realize."

Before I can say anything more, she pushes past me and marches out to the dining room. I follow her, and as I pass where she's sitting on the other end of the table, I hear her tell Rob from IT that she's sick. A minute later, Ava walks the two of them out, leaving me miserable and angry at how things happened.

"I wonder what's wrong with that woman," Sam whispers to me.

"Probably sick. In fact, I might be coming down with something. I think I need to bow out of this party. Maybe another time."

As I stand up from the table, Ava walks back in and gives me an odd look. "Are you going too?"

"I don't feel well. Must be something I ate earlier today," I say as I nudge Sam to get up also.

She looks at me strangely too, but as she stands up, she politely says to Ava, "You have a lovely home. Thank you."

My brothers all stare at Sam and me as I hurry her out to her car. Can't people get sick? It's not like any of them are dependent on us to have a good time tonight.

By the time we reach her car, Sam is asking what's going on, but I'm not in the mood to answer questions. I just want this night to be over and my life to go back to the way it was.

"Marius, is that it?" she asks when I open her car door for her. "I thought we were going to stay for the entire party."

"Yeah, thanks. I promise to give you a nice bonus in your next paycheck for being so cool about things tonight. I guess something I ate for lunch is the problem."

Looking up at me, she smiles and reaches out to rub my stomach. "I hope you feel better. I'd like to do something when you're up to it."

"Maybe. I don't know. It's probably not very professional of me to date people I employ, though."

That's a pretty lame excuse now. Like hello, maybe shut the fucking barn door before you watch all the horses run out.

"I don't mind. I think you're very professional," she says, and I hear almost begging in her voice.

"Drive safely, Sam. I'll talk to you soon."

Before she can try to kiss me since that seems to be where this is going tonight, I walk back into the house and straight up the stairs to my old room. I'd go to the penthouse, but the idea of waiting around for Eden to get home after Rob the IT guy doesn't exactly sound like how I want to spend my night.

I flop down on my bed and close my eyes as I silently recap the night. My assistant now thinks I want to sleep with her, which wouldn't be problematic if she hadn't made it perfectly clear she's into me for the past six months. Okay, you don't have to say it. That was a shitty thing for me to do. Trust me. I know. If I give her a really big bonus like buying her a new car or a paid vacation to some island resort with all the bells and whistles, maybe that will fix things?

And then there's the issue with Eden. All I wanted to do was show her how much it fucking hurt to see her with someone else. Why couldn't she understand that?

I bet you're saying I deserve whatever she's going to

do. Fine, you might be right, but if I know my Duck, it's going to be big and bad and hurt like a motherfucker.

Maybe I'll give her the night to cool down.

As I drift off to sleep, I know things will be okay. She loves me, and I love her. We'll be good after she has some time to think things over.

CHAPTER THIRTEEN

den

My phone vibrates across my desk as I look at the time on my laptop. Just a few minutes after five. Normally, I'd be in a hurry to get out of the office and go home, but what's the point? It's been a week since Ava's party, and all I do is go to work and then go back to the penthouse to climb into bed and hide underneath the covers.

I don't have to look to see who's messaging me. It's the same person it's been all week.

Marius.

He thinks I'm still angry with him, but that's not true. I passed anger the day after. All day Sunday, I wanted to scream and then kill someone. That night, though, a strange calm came over me, and I finally knew what I had to do.

Now I'm just in the stage of a breakup that feels the worst. The one where all you want to do is cry until there are no more tears left inside you.

Marius has texted me over and over every day. It started out with I'm sorry, and then it went from there to I'll do anything to make it up to you. The crazy thing is I think he would, except for the singular thing I need him to do.

I haven't responded to even one text. I half expected him to show up at the penthouse. It wouldn't be out of the question. He did buy it, so it wouldn't be outrageous to think he'd try to find me there.

Part of me wishes he had. Then again, what else is there for us to talk about now? He finally pushed me too far. I had no choice but to do what I did.

My phone vibrates again, but this time it's a call from Ava. I take a deep breath and put on my happy voice before I answer so she doesn't know anything's wrong.

"Hey, mama! What's up?" I ask in an exceedingly cheery way that is very unlike me.

She picks up on that immediately, just like I should have known she would. "Hey, are you okay? You sound off."

"Just a great day at work. Living the dream. It's also Friday, so who doesn't like the idea of two whole days off? What's going on with you and those beautiful babies?"

I say that knowing anytime anyone mentions her children Ava is off to the races talking about them. It's not a great thing to pull on my best friend, but right now, I just don't want to talk about how I'm feeling because I don't know if I can stop myself from telling her everything.

Or completely breaking down into a sobbing mess. It could go either way.

"Oh, Theo actually said ma-ma today, or at least it sounded like he did. Matthias hasn't stopped bragging about how he said da-da first, so it might be wishful thinking. As for Matty, he really is such a good baby. I'm hoping to break him of his love of that stroller, though. I don't think it's healthy to stay in that thing as much as he does, even if he does love it."

And just like that, Ava isn't paying any attention to how I sound.

"You are so lucky. You have a great husband and those two beautiful boys. I hope you know how lucky you are."

For a moment, she doesn't answer. I probably sound pretty pathetic, and she wants to ask what's wrong. Since I can't tell her, I should have kept my mouth shut.

Finally, she says, "I'm sorry Rob didn't work out. He told Matthias he thought you had feelings for someone else. I told my husband he's nuts, but it's okay. There are more fish in the sea."

"If it's okay with you, I'd like to cut bait for a little while when it comes to men and dating. I think I just need to figure out what I'm doing with my life."

The disappointment I expect to hear doesn't happen, thankfully. "Sure! I'm not worried about you. You're going to find a great guy who's crazy about you. I bet he walks into your life when you least expect it."

I had a great guy who came into my life at the very

moment I needed him. I thought we'd be together forever.

So much for the fairy tale romance.

"I want you to come over tomorrow. We're having the last pool party of the year, and everyone will be there. One last summer blast before we have to close the pool."

Everyone? I don't think I can handle seeing Marius yet.

"I don't know. I'm still fighting whatever that was that made me leave the party early."

Ava isn't going to take that lame reason for an answer. I know her far too well. I should have said I have to work this weekend.

"Please? I like hanging out with the guys and their girlfriends, but I like having my best friend around too. Ronan and Kate will be there, as will Kellen and Salem. I haven't seen Marius much this week, so I don't know if he'll be there. He's been downright surly lately, so probably not."

"Maybe his girlfriend is giving him a hard time. Perhaps she lost her binky, and he hasn't bought her a new one."

My snide comments make Ava laugh. "That was so weird, wasn't it? Marius never brings anyone to our parties, and then he shows up with that girl. Ronan said he thinks she's only twenty. Marius is nearly thirty! What is he thinking?"

I don't answer, but in my mind all I can think is I have no idea what that man thought he was doing. Did he actually think him bringing that beautiful girl with the giant boobs and gorgeous, young face was anything close to the same thing as my having to go out with Rob, the man who worries about choking on food so he cuts everything up into tiny pieces like Ava does for her kids?

"Not sure," I answer, not wanting to continue talking about Marius and his date.

"Well, I highly doubt he'll be there, with or without her, so say you'll come over tomorrow. Matthias is going to be manning the grill. He's very excited about it too. He's closing his office door and taking the entire weekend off. We've got hot dogs, hamburgers, steaks, shrimp, the works! You just have to come."

I don't have the heart to disappoint her a second time she has a party, so I reluctantly agree to go. "Need me to bring anything?"

"Just your bathing suit. We're swimming until we get pruney. See you at noon!"

"I'll be there."

Even if I really don't want to.

WHEN I WALK OUT ONTO THE PATIO, I SEE EVERYONE has arrived already. All except Marius. That's probably for the best. I have to admit a small part of me had hoped to see him today, but that's likely just habit. Every time I've come to see Ava in the past two years I've hoped to see Marius here.

"Eden!" Ava squeals as she hurries over to give me a hug. "Did you bring your bathing suit? You have to get in today. It's the last official party of summer!"

I lift up my t-shirt to show her my suit. "I'm here and

ready to swim!" I say far more enthusiastically than I feel.

"Okay, drop your purse off near the table. I'm in with Matty, and Theo is hanging out with his uncles. Matthias can make you anything you want to eat. We have a ton of food!"

Her excitement for this party is nothing more than her usual happiness to have her friends and family around her, but my stomach is already in knots. It started as I was driving up to the house, and now that I'm here, it's much worse.

The last time I was here, I had to pretend to be sick. This time, I might not have to lie about it at all.

And if Marius shows up, it'll be worse. If he shows up with that young girl, I might just throw up all over the patio.

I force myself to smile and make small talk with Matthias, Kellen, and Ronan before saying hi to their girlfriends. It's all one big happy family and me. Well, one big happy family with one member missing.

Knowing I have to put on my usual act, I jump into the pool and play with Matty and his mom for a while as everyone else drinks and laughs and occasionally joins us in the water. After a while, I forget about my worrying and let myself enjoy the party. Ava is my dearest friend in the world, and her family has always been great to me.

I don't know how they're going to feel when they find out the truth. I guess they might not think I'm so great when it all comes out.

Two hours into the party, we've all eaten and swam enough for an entire weekend. The boys fall asleep, Theo in his Uncle Kellen's arms, and Matty in his usual spot in the stroller. The margaritas are flowing, and we're all having a great time. I even forget about my worries that Marius will show up and demand to talk to me.

And then what had been a perfectly wonderful day goes to hell in a matter of minutes.

"Marius! I didn't know if you'd be joining us today," Matthias announces, and my heart skips a beat.

I turn to see the man I still love walk out to join all of us. He looks tired, like he hasn't slept in days. The dark circles under his eyes tell that story. And his beard says he hasn't shaved since the party last week. The way he looks at me when he sees I'm here tells a completely different story, one that I can't hear today.

Leaning over to whisper to Ava who's sitting next to me drinking a margarita, I say, "I'm going to go change out of my bathing suit. Do you want me to bring anything out when I come back?"

She smiles and nods her head. "If you see Eleanor, tell her to come out and join us. Everyone I love is here, and we're living our best life. I don't need anything else."

I nod and hurry inside the house. At least one of us is living the dream. Too bad my life has become a nightmare.

After hiding out in the powder room for ten minutes, I can't avoid returning to the party anymore. I open the door, poke my head out to see if the coast is clear, and happily, there's not a soul to be found.

I don't get two steps out of the bathroom before Marius appears in front of me. He doesn't say a word and pulls me by the arm into the kitchen. Not exactly the room I'd choose for our final showdown, but he's calling the shots for now.

He looks at me, and I see such love in his dark eyes. I've always loved the way he looks at me. It's a mixture of caring and sensuality that never fails to make me fall in love with him all over again.

And if I'm not careful, that's exactly what's going to happen.

Taking my hand, he presses it against his bare chest just over his heart. "We both proved our points, so now we can start fresh. I'm sorry, Eden. Please, say you forgive me."

When I shake my head but don't say anything because I'm on the verge of crying, he continues. "This can't go on. I miss you, and I know you miss me. Have you gotten all my messages? I've been texting every day. I'm sorry. You have to believe me."

"You look like hell, Marius."

He tries to smile, but it never really happens. "I haven't been sleeping very well for the past few nights. I miss you, Duck. I've been miserable without you. You miss me, don't you?"

Tears well in my eyes, making it hard to see as pull my hand away and say, "I wanted to go public about us, and what did you do? You brought that girl to the party."

"You were with that guy. How is what I did any different?" he asks with so much hurt in his voice that I almost want to say I'm sorry.

I can't stand here and talk about this with him right now. I have to go before I fall apart and everyone sees.

"Don't follow me. I have to go say goodbye to everyone, and if you're with me, I'm not going to be able to do it without crying."

He follows me, even though I just told him not to, so it's practically a herculean effort to act normal when I return to the party. I make a beeline for Ava in the hopes that I can bid my farewells and leave as soon as possible before anything more happens.

"Ava, I have to go. Thank you for a great time."

She jumps up off the chaise lounge and gives me a hug. "Thank you for coming over. I'm so glad you were here."

"Me too," I say, barely holding back tears. Turning to everyone sitting at the table, I say, "Thanks for a good time, guys! Matthias, as always, thanks for letting me monopolize your wife's time."

They all say goodbye, but one King says nothing. He simply stands near the door to the house like he intends on intercepting me on my way out. Why can't he just leave things alone? Doesn't he understand I'm not ready to forgive?

As I make my way toward the house, Eleanor appears in the doorway with a man. Dammit. I forgot to tell her to come outside.

Behind me, Matthias asks her, "Is something wrong, Eleanor? Everything okay?"

I swallow hard and try to push past her and the man, but it's no use.

"I'm fine, Matthias. This man is a process server."

When I look back, Ava is wearing a worried expression. "What's this about, honey?"

Matthias walks over to the man and smiles back at his wife. "Nothing to worry about. It's par for the course when you run a company as big as King Industries. They usually serve me at my office in the city, though. This guy must be working overtime."

It's like everything begins to move in slow motion as the process server explains to Matthias he isn't the King he's there for. Confused, the oldest King looks around and asks, "Then who?"

And that's when the entire world stops.

Walking out of the house, the man holds up the envelope containing the papers he's been hired to serve. "I'm looking for Marius King."

Never in my life have I felt like I wanted to burrow into the ground like I want to do right now. I don't regret what I've done. I just assumed this would happen when nobody was around, not in the middle of one of Ava's parties.

Marius looks at me with confusion and then back at the man. "I'm Marius King."

As he hands him the yellow envelope, he says, "This is for you then. Have a good day."

I don't know how it's possible, but I don't faint dead away when Marius opens up the envelope and begins to read the papers. I want to run away from this house as fast as I can, but I'm not able to move my feet. It's like they're encased in concrete.

I'm stuck standing here watching the man I love read the words no man ever wants to see.

When he looks at me again, all I see is pure pain in his dark eyes.

Holding the papers up in front of him, he walks over to me and asks with so much hurt in his voice, "What's this?"

I hang my head, and in a tiny voice, I answer, "Please, Marius. Don't do this."

"I could say the same thing to you. Why Duck?"

As much as I want to avoid meeting his gaze, I lift my head and say, "It's okay. Sometimes things just don't work out, even when you want them to more than anything. Don't make a big deal about this. It's just the way it is."

Marius takes a step toward me, and I know he wants to reach out and touch me. "I don't agree."

"Just sign the papers, Marius. I don't want anything. Sign them, and we'll be done."

He shakes his head. "No. I won't sign them."

I have no choice. He didn't want to make us public, but now his family is going to finally find out everything.

"I've waited for you, Marius. For the first year and a half that we were married, we didn't even live together. Maybe I'm partly to blame for this. I don't know. I went along with everything you wanted because I loved you. I waited and waited, and every time I asked why we couldn't tell everyone we were together, you said because you wanted a little more time. What I want is for someone to choose me. You didn't, so we're done."

I couldn't stop the tears now if I tried. All week, all I've wanted to do was cry my eyes out. I couldn't. Maybe because it wasn't definite.

Now it is.

"Duck…Eden, I won't let us end like this," he says, and the agony in his voice makes me feel like someone's squeezing my heart.

Unable to look at the hurt in his eyes any longer, I run into the house to escape. Ava catches up to me just as

I reach my car parked out front. For a second, she just shakes her head, like she doesn't know what to say.

Then, finally, she steps toward me and wraps her arms around me. That's all it takes for the tears to come full force. I sob like a baby as my best friend hugs me, all the while likely wondering what the hell kind of friend I am to keep something so big hidden from her.

When I calm down, I step back and lean against my car. "So, yeah, I've been your sister-in-law for two years."

Her mouth drops open, and she stares at me in pure shock. "What? How? I don't...I don't understand."

I sniffle and try to think of a logical way to tell her the story of Marius and me. It's quite a tale to tell.

"Do you remember when I went to Las Vegas for the week with Justin two years ago?"

She nods. "Yeah. You broke up with him because he was a jackass the whole time."

I wipe the tears from under my eyes and finally tell her the truth. "I was only with him the day we arrived there. Marius was at the same hotel for a pool tournament. Justin got nasty with me, and Marius saw it."

"What do you mean he got nasty with you?"

"Let's say Justin got a little rough and pulled my hair because I wouldn't do what he wanted."

"He got rough? What the hell was wrong with him?" she asks in horror.

"Yeah. Marius saw, and he decked him, but in the middle of it all, I got punched in the eye. Then he got Justin thrown out of the hotel. I had nowhere to stay, so he invited me to his suite. One thing lead to another, and we slept together."

Ava listens, but I can tell she wants me to cut to the chase. "Okay. That's good, right?"

She's always trying to be positive. I love that about her.

With a smile, I answer, "It was great. Really great. So great that he and I spent the entire week together. That Saturday, I was supposed to leave, but we were having a great time. It's hard to explain, but I was in love within a few days, so when he suggested we get married, I said yes."

"You got married in Vegas? Like an Elvis impersonator officiated?"

My best friend really is the sweetest person in the world. Only she would ask that question.

Shaking my head, I have to laugh. "No, it was a regular person, not some fake Elvis. Since then, we've been husband and wife."

"I don't understand. Why didn't you tell me? Why didn't either of you tell any of us?"

This is the part I didn't want to talk about. It's too embarrassing to say.

Hanging my head, I answer, "He didn't want to tell anyone. Maybe he was ashamed of me. Maybe it's like he's always said that he just wanted to keep us to us. I don't know."

I look up at her as tears begin to come again. "All I know is I can't do that anymore. So I served him with divorce papers, as you just saw. I have to go now, Ava. I want to crawl back under the covers like I've been doing all week, but this time I'm not sure I want to ever come out again."

Ava starts to cry and wraps her arms around me again. "You were my sister-in-law, and I didn't even get to enjoy that. That's not fair, Eden. It's not fair."

"I know, but life isn't fair. Go back inside and enjoy that wonderful husband of yours and those two sweet babies. I need to go before Marius comes out here and wants to talk. I can't talk to him anymore. I've got no more words left."

We stand there at my car in the middle of a beautiful late September afternoon sobbing like babies ourselves. Ava cries for all the things she thinks she missed out on by not knowing I was married to Marius, but I cry for all the things I'm losing.

Even if I know what I'm doing is the right thing for me.

CHAPTER FOURTEEN

*M*arius

MY BROTHERS ALL LOOK AT ME LIKE THEY HAVE A million questions they want to ask but can't figure out how to ask them or which one to ask first. Kate and Salem hurriedly gather up some plates and glasses before taking them inside, clearly not interested in witnessing any more of the shitshow that's become my life.

When it's just the four of us and the two sleeping kids, Matthias walks over to me and asks, "What the fuck is going on? Are you telling me you and my wife's best friend, who she's been trying to set you up with for years, are married?"

Just as I start to say something, Ava walks out the back door and marches right up to me. I've never seen her so upset. She looks like she either wants to bite through a piece of steel or cry harder than she's ever done before.

"How could you do this?"

"You don't understand."

That's all I get out of my mouth before she slaps me hard across the face. I'm stunned for a few seconds, especially since Ava is the least violent person I've ever met in my life. My brothers look like they can't believe this person who's always been so kind to all of us just slapped me.

"You were married to Eden for the past two years? My best friend was my sister-in-law, and you chose to hide that? Why? Were you ashamed of her?" she asks, her voice cracking.

"No. I wasn't ashamed of her. That's not why I wanted to keep things quiet."

Tears stream down her face as she glares at me. "Then why? Was it because she doesn't come from the kind of money you do? Eden is an educated, successful, intelligent woman who makes good money as an investment analyst, and by the way, it's not like she came from the wrong side of the tracks so she's not worthy of you. Her family is wealthier than mine ever was. Do you feel the same way about me?"

Matthias tries to come to my rescue, which is nice, but Ava's not having any of it.

"Honey, I'm sure it's not about money," he says, but his wife spins around and huffs like she's about to breathe fire.

"No, Matthias! I want to hear what this was about from Marius."

When she turns back to face me, I brace for her to

slap me again, but she collapses into one of the patio chairs and simply shakes her head. "Eden thinks you were ashamed of her, so that's why you didn't want to tell everyone you two were together."

Ava buries her face in her hands and sobs like a baby. My heart clenches in my chest, not only for what all of this is doing to her but also for what Eden must be going through. I wish I could go to her, but I know the woman I love well enough to be sure she needs some time.

"I've never been ashamed of anything I've ever done, including marrying Eden. Ava, I swear to you. It had nothing to do with her."

She surprises me when she jumps up from the chair shaking her head. "I need to go find her. She can't be alone right now."

As she hurries off, leaving me with just my brothers, I think about how this day has gone. The woman I love served me with divorce papers. My sister-in-law, who up until today I would have counted as one of my biggest fans, slapped me across the face and likely hates me. My brothers haven't said much, but I get the feeling that's because they're in shock.

And everything about my life has descended into pure shit. Hell of a day.

Kellen is the first to break the silence with a low chuckle before he says, "Well, I guess I am going to be the last one to get hitched."

Matthias, Ronan, and I look at him in disbelief that out of everything that's happened today *that* is his takeaway. Then again, Kellen always does like to play the clown.

"Dude, read the room," Ronan chastises him.

Matthias pulls up a chair and sits down in front of me. He hesitates, opening his mouth and closing it a few times, before he finally asks, "What's this all about, Marius?"

That's a loaded question. It's also one I know the answer to all too well.

I start to explain, but Ava comes rushing out of the house again waving her phone in front of her. "Where is she? I've called her five times, and she's not answering. I called her parents' house, and they say she hasn't been at their house for more than an hour or so in months. Where is she, Marius? I need to go to her."

Grabbing a white napkin off the table, I look at Matthias. "I need a pen. Do you have one?"

He hands me a pen, so I write down the address of our building and hand the napkin to Ava. "She'll be here. I'll contact the lobby staff and tell them to let you up. It's the penthouse."

She stares at me for a long moment and then turns to Matthias. "Honey, I need you to look after the boys. Lynn can handle most of it, but I need you to make sure they're okay. I have to go find Eden."

He kisses her and smiles. "Go. I've got everything under control here."

Ava hugs him and then turns to leave, but not before she throws me a nasty look. "You better hope she's okay, or I'm going to have something to say about it."

Great. Now the one person who I know has always liked me now thinks I'm public enemy number one. This day can't get much worse.

"And just in case you don't know who Eden's father

is, you should know he's not going to be happy when he finds out about this."

She doesn't explain that any further before storming out, and when I look around for someone to tell me what she meant, Matthias says, "I'm guessing you haven't met your father-in-law yet?"

Shaking my head, I shrug. "No. Why?"

Ronan chuckles, and Matthias looks uneasy. "I'm assuming you know Eden's maiden name, right?" Kellen asks.

Nice. Like I'm some asshole who marries a woman without even knowing her full name. "Yeah. Giordano. So?"

Once more, Matthias looks like he's unsure he wants to have this conversation. "Let's put it this way. Family is very important to Mr. Giordano, particularly his only daughter."

"Mr. Giordano? Who is this guy that we have to be so formal?" I ask, still fucking confused about why I should care about who my wife's father is.

Before Matthias can say another word, Kellen exclaims, "Family, dude! He's a fucking mobster! Have you been living under a rock? Everyone under the damn sun around here knows about the Giordano family."

Fucking super. Now I've got the problem that my father-in-law is probably going to put a hit out on me. This day just keeps getting better.

"Somebody needs to start explaining what the hell is going on because I'm lost," Ronan says.

When I don't say anything, Kellen chimes in. "As far as I can tell, Marius is married to Eden, but for some reason he wanted to keep that a secret. Not sure, but I think she didn't like that, which resulted in that process server giving Marius divorce papers. Oh, and Eden's father doesn't know his only daughter and the apple of his eye married this guy, and since he's a mobster, our brother is probably living on borrowed time as of tonight. Did I miss anything, Marius?"

I shake my head since he actually encapsulated this entire mess pretty well. "Nope. That about covers it."

"Yes, you did miss something," Matthias says, sounding particularly confused. "Why the hell did you want to keep this from us? You told Ava you weren't ashamed of being married to Eden, so why not share the good news?"

That's a much harder question to answer.

After blowing the air out of my lungs and trying to find the right words to explain what I was thinking, I say, "I need a drink. I'll be right back."

They don't stop me, so I walk inside and head for the bar since it's definitely a bourbon kind of conversation we're about to have. I pour myself a glass and down it before pouring a second glass. I have to call the doorman at the building so Ava can get up to see Eden, and then I take a deep breath in and brace myself for what's to come.

When I get back outside, I see my brothers are waiting for some answers. Just the fact that I'm expected to explain to them all that's happened with Eden is proof I was right about hiding our relationship.

I sit down and take a big gulp of my drink. There's no escaping the King brothers inquisition.

"So start from the beginning," Matthias says like he's speaking for the family.

Glaring at him, I say, "The fact that I have to explain myself at all is part of the damn problem."

All three of my brothers look at one another and then train their focus on me again. "What does that mean?" Matthias asks.

Clearly, he is in charge of speaking for the family.

I take another drink and answer, "It means I've never had a single goddamned thing to myself. I've always been one of five. The five King brothers. The problem is I've never been anyone special. I'm not the oldest like you, Matthias. I'm not the youngest like you, Ronan. I'm not the one destined to be a businessman and follow in Dad's footsteps like you, Kellen. Even when Theo was still alive I wasn't special like him. I've always been the exact middle King and that's it. All my fucking life I've been known as one of five. But with Eden, it was just me, and I loved that as much as I loved her."

I stop for a moment and correct myself. "Love her."

"You're the photographer in the family, Marius. That's something none of us have," Matthias says.

Shaking my head at his attempt to make me feel better, I smile. "No, because you're the artist in the family."

"So that's why you didn't want us to know you were married?" Ronan asks, and I hear the hurt in his voice.

"I just wanted to have something all to myself. That's what my relationship with Eden was for me."

Nobody says anything for a few minutes. All the better. I can't think of anything but what Eden must be feeling right now anyway.

"So it's a real love thing between you two?" Kellen asks in an uncharacteristically serious way.

I nod as I can't help but smile. "Yeah. I'm crazy about her. That penthouse Ava's going to? It's Eden's. I bought it for her."

Matthias stares at me wide-eyed after hearing that. "You bought a million dollar penthouse for a wife you were keeping hidden?"

I chuckle at that ridiculous price for a penthouse on the Upper East Side. "Try fifteen million."

The youngest King steps forward and says, "You bought her a fifteen million dollar penthouse? I don't understand this, Marius. I mean, I get that you didn't want to tell us, although I really don't understand why, but you clearly care about this woman. What did you think would happen when you insisted on the two of you keeping your marriage a secret?"

I shrug because I'm not sure what they want me to say. "I didn't think of anything but wanting to keep her all to myself. It was so nice to just be one person with another person. I didn't have to be anyone but the man who married her. You have no idea how great that felt."

None of my brothers respond, not surprisingly. They've never felt like they got lost in the shuffle of being one of five. Each one of the men around me has always been able to live with the niche they were assigned by birth. They have no idea how envious I've always been of that ability of theirs.

Matthias may have always hated the expectations put on him, but he's handled them well and even enjoys being in charge of the family business now. Ronan may have wanted to be anyone but the youngest son growing up, but he knows he's enjoyed the benefits of that spot in the birth order. And Kellen may not love the fact that

Matthias didn't have to do a thing to get to be the head of King Industries, but he's been able to be the person he's always known he wanted to be even with Matthias being above him.

And me? All I've ever been is Marius King, the younger brother of Matthias and Theo and the older brother of Kellen and Ronan. That's how teachers referred to me every year of school. That's still how people refer to me. No matter what I've tried to be in life, it was never more important than being one of the five King brothers.

"I had no idea you felt this way, Marius. I'm sorry if I've done anything to make you feel like you weren't special in your own right," Matthias says.

"It's not anything any of you have done. It's just the way it is. Don't get me wrong. I'm not blind to all the benefits I've gotten being one of Max and Elizabeth King's children. I've got enough money to last my lifetime and more. I can do whatever I want in this world. There are billions of people on this planet who would probably wish they could be me. I know that."

For a second, I stop and then let out a heavy sigh. "But I also know I liked it when it was just Eden and me."

Leave it to Ronan to ask the one question I don't want to answer.

"I know what you're saying, but how do you think that made Eden feel?"

For a long moment, I don't say a word because I don't want to admit the truth. I know how she felt. She's been telling me for the past two years that she wanted the world to know about us. She's said it in every way possible, and still, I told her I needed more time.

Today's little visit from that guy with divorce papers shows how that went.

"I knew how she felt. In hindsight, I guess she was more unhappy about it than I understood."

Normally about now, I'd be uttering the words in my defense, but this time, there's no use. I have no defense. I know that.

"The girl? Sam? The one you brought to the party last week? What was that all about if you and Eden were married?" Ronan asks.

God, the questions keep getting harder. What a fucking mess I've made.

I blow the air out of my lungs and shrug. "Just more of me being stupid. Ava kept setting her up with guys because she didn't know we were together. I told Eden I didn't want her to even pretend to be with him, but she said Ava would know something's up if she didn't. She was doing what I wanted by keeping us a secret, but I hated it because I was so jealous. So I called Sam and told her to come over. I thought I was showing Eden how if felt to see someone you love with another person. I think you know how that went over."

My brothers simply stare at me like I'm some complete moron. Maybe I am. I have an incredible woman who loves me as my wife, and I spent the last two years keeping her hidden away.

"So are you going to sign the papers?" Matthias asks as he gets up to check on Matty in the stroller who's starting to make noises like he's hungry.

I shake my head at that ridiculous idea. "Hell no! I'm

not getting divorced. Eden and I will be able to work this out."

"How's that?" Kellen asks with a chuckle.

Shrugging, I answer in the only way I can. "She's still in love with me, just like I'm still in love with her. All I have to do is make her see that."

Kellen stands up and looks at me like I'm out of my mind. "Dude, she went to a divorce lawyer already. She served you with divorce papers. This isn't going to be something like just convincing her the way you always put the toilet seat down is proof you're a wonderful husband." He stops and looks over at Ronan. "Damn, I'm never going to be able to get used to that word being used to describe this guy. I thought he'd be single forever."

As the two of them talk about me like I'm not there, Matthias sits down in front of me holding his younger son. "I need to feed this little guy, but here's my two cents, for what it's worth. Don't listen to Kellen and Ronan. I can attest to the fact that even when it looks like you've done something that you can never come back from, if she truly loves you, then there's always a chance."

I can't help but smile at how big a romantic my older brother has become since falling for Ava. "Look at you. It's like looking at a walking Valentine's Day advertisement. I'm not worried. She'll take me back. I know she will."

"Good. Any chance you want to explain why? She looked pretty upset when she left here today," he says as Matty makes louder noises that say he's already hangry and if Matthias waits any longer, we're all going to be treated to his piercing vocal talents.

"She loves me, and like you said, if she loves me, there's still a chance. I'll just win her back."

Matty loses his patience and begins to cry loudly, so Matthias hurries him inside to eat, leaving me to figure out exactly how I will win Eden back. It's not impossible. I know that. I just have to do it right.

CHAPTER FIFTEEN

den

I HEAR A NOISE DOWNSTAIRS IN THE KITCHEN, AND instantly, my stomach twists into a tight knot. I can't see Marius right now. We'll just end up in a big fight, and that's the last thing I want to do with him.

"Eden! Where are you?"

Throwing the covers off, I jump out of bed and hurry down the stairs to see Ava looking around the penthouse like she's in awe. "Not too shabby, huh? The man is an ass, but he does know how to buy a girl a gift."

She looks at me and her mouth drops open. "This doesn't belong to both of you? He bought you this place?"

I nod, knowing how incredible that makes Marius sound. "Yeah. I told him I wanted a place of our own instead of us spending all our time in hotels, so the next week, he bought this penthouse. Doesn't mean he's a good man or anything. Just that he has money."

Why I say that I don't know. Marius King is a good man. He's never lied to me, and he's always been the man he said he would be when we got together.

But I'm not in the mood to sing his praises right now.

Ava doesn't respond to my attack on Marius and instead just opens her arms to invite me in for a hug. That's all it takes to make the waterworks start all over again. I stumble over to her and practically collapse against her as she wraps her arms around me.

Sobbing, I say, "I hated not telling you. You have no idea how much I wanted to tell you we were sisters-in-law."

She rubs my back and starts to cry too. "I know. It's not your fault. It's his. I want you to know I was so mad at him that I slapped him right across the face."

I lean back and sniffle as my tears continue to come. "You did?"

Ava nods and tries to smile. "I did! He was so surprised. Then I told him if you weren't okay when you found you, that he was going to have to answer to me. And then I said your father was going to be furious when he finds out, and I know Matthias has explained to him by now what that means since he didn't look like he knew what I was talking about."

"Oh, you're the best friend a girl could ever have, Ava. I love you."

"I love you too, Eden. So this has been your home for the past two years?" she asks as she looks around at the penthouse.

Sheepishly, I admit the truth. "Not exactly. I've only been here for a couple months."

My best friend shakes her head in confusion. "Wait, I don't understand. You and Marius have been married for that long, so where were you living before here?"

I lower my gaze to the floor. "I was living at my parents' house. Marius was living at your house or in hotels when he was on shoots."

When she doesn't say anything to that bizarre revelation, I lift my head and see her expression full of questions. "I know. It's strange."

"It's not strange. I just don't understand. You got married and then didn't live together? Why? Because you were keeping everything secret?"

God, I wish the answer was that simple.

I look around at my beautiful home and sigh. "It's hard to explain. I don't know, honestly. We got back after getting married, and then he had a job he had to go to and I had to go back to work. So he left, and when he returned from wherever he was on whatever shoot he went on, we spent time together, but then he'd leave again for work. Then last spring when everything with Ronan happened, he wanted to keep an eye on him, so he started hanging out a lot more at your house."

Even I know that explanation isn't great. It's not that Marius and I ever came right out and said we didn't want to live together. Things just conspired to make it not happen.

"I wish I knew, Eden. I would have told him he should be home spending time with his wife."

"He felt he had to watch over Ronan, and I understand that. To his credit, the first time I said I didn't want to sleep in hotels anymore, no matter how nice they were, Marius bought me this place."

She smiles and asks, "Want to give me a tour of your gorgeous home?"

"No. Maybe later. Right now, I just want to crawl into bed and pretend this day never happened."

"Then we'll both do that."

We walk upstairs to the bedroom Marius and I share, and Ava stops dead as soon as she sees the enormous master suite. "Oh my God! This bedroom is bigger than the house I grew up in."

I wave away her comment. "Don't be ridiculous. It's big. Yeah. But it's not bigger than the entire house you lived in, Ava."

She looks over toward the king size bed in front of a bank of huge windows. "Your bed looks almost lost in here, and it's huge too!" Then she turns to look at the fifty inch TV across from the bed. "And look at that TV!"

I know what she's trying to do, but listing all the great things about this place isn't distracting me like she thinks it is. I climb into bed and unpause the TV so my episode of Air Disasters starts again.

When your life comes down around you, at least your favorite show is there for you.

Ava kicks off her shoes and climbs under the covers with me. "Do you remember that time I slept over your house in eleventh grade when you broke up with that boy you were dating? We gorged ourselves on rocky road ice cream that night and stayed up until dawn. Want to do that again?"

I love my best friend, but none of this is working. I

just want to feel bad. It's sounds wrong, but right now, all I want to do is wallow is my misery.

"Not really. I think I'd just like to watch my show and feel terrible."

She snuggles up against me so her head is resting on my shoulder. "Got it. No ice cream. Just hanging out. Let me guess. This is an episode with that guy in it, right?"

"Right."

"So I'll get to see him finally?"

I turn to my left to look at her and force a smile. "Yes, and I don't think I need to remind you that I'm in a very delicate state right now, so if you think he's ugly or anything even remotely negative, please keep it to yourself, okay?"

She smiles so sweetly that I know I don't have to worry. "As long as you like him, who am I to say otherwise? Now show me this man who makes you so happy."

We watch TV for another five minutes before he appears, and I point at the screen. "That's him."

My lovely crush.

"Oh, he reminds me of my father," Ava says. "He's got kind eyes."

I study his eyes until he disappears from the screen. They are kind. I like that.

"Kind is good."

Beside me, Ava says in a quiet voice. "Marius has nice eyes too. They're that shade of brown all the Kings have. You know, that warm chocolate shade."

"You're sweet, but that's your husband who has the

warm chocolate eyes. Mine has more like dark chocolate."

Ava smiles as I say that. "Your husband. I'm still trying to get used to that."

"Well, don't take too long. I hear he got served with divorce papers."

Even as I try to make a joke, my heart aches when I say those words. I hated that I didn't have a choice but to do that.

My best friend hugs me tightly to her and says, "I saw a picture of my father when he and my mother first started dating, and he looked a lot like this guy on Air Disasters. My mother used to say my father fell in love first, but she was secretly crazy about him even before they started going out because he was so handsome."

I look at the TV and can see a hint of similarity in how this guy looks with her father. "That's nice. Your father is a great guy. Sweet and thoughtful and honest. I like that."

Just listing all those wonderful qualities makes me break down again, and I begin to sob like a baby. "Your mother was so lucky. She had such a great guy."

Ava pulls me close and hugs me tightly to her. "Oh, honey. I didn't mean to make you sad again. Marius is a great guy too. He just made a mistake."

That has the opposite effect of what I think she's trying to accomplish here, and I cry even harder. "He is a great guy, but he never wanted anyone to know we were together, so really, how great is he?" I ask all muffled into her shoulder.

"Aww, Eden. Let it out. You'll feel better."

"I wanted things to work out so much. He kept

saying just a little longer, but when I saw him with that girl at your party, that's when I knew he wasn't understanding how much I hated hiding our relationship. Why did he have to do that?"

"Honey, I don't know, but I can tell you as soon as you left that night, he sent her home and went to his room. I don't think they were really together."

Leaning back, I wipe under my eyes. "I know they weren't, but why couldn't he understand that because he wanted to keep everything under wraps, I didn't have a choice but to keep going out with guys you wanted to set me up with? I would have never been at that party with Rob or anyone else if we weren't hiding that we were together."

God, how did my life become so messed up?

"Let it out," she says sweetly. "Get all your crying done so you can start to feel better."

I don't want to tell Ava that isn't going to work this time. I'm never going to feel better. I love Marius. I've never been happier with anyone else in my life, and now it's over. How the hell can I ever feel anything close to okay again?

Even as I think that, I secretly wish something would happen to make me not want to divorce him. But what could that possibly be?

As I watch Air Disasters through teary eyes, Ava asks, "Will you tell me the story of how you guys got together? I'd love to hear it."

Normally, whenever I meet a new guy, I tell my best friend everything about it. She didn't get to enjoy the Eden and Marius story when it first happened, though.

I sniffle and sit up against the pillows. Drying my eyes, I smile as that night comes rushing back to me.

"Well, believe it or not, I finally have my story of a white knight coming to my rescue. Didn't think I was going to say that, now did you?"

Ava smiles and shifts her position so she's facing me sitting cross-legged. "Tell me everything! I need to know chapter and verse and the whole book!"

Since she asked, I guess I have to give her all the details. At least it's a great story.

"Well, it all started the first night of the trip to Las Vegas with Justin."

"Hurry up, Eden! I want to see if we can get into watch that pool tournament," Justin says in a whiny voice I'm close to hating right now.

"I'm coming! Why do you care about some pool game?" I ask as I hurry out of the hotel bathroom in my new black strapless mini-dress I bought especially for this vacation. "So, how do I look?"

Twirling around, I wait for him to compliment me on my new dress. Since he's never seen it, I expect a few ooohs and ahhhs, at least.

"You can't wear that to this. Go back in and change, but hurry because we're missing everything."

I stand there in shock staring at him. "Why? It's a gorgeous dress."

He winces and leans back on his hands on the bed. "It's too slutty. There are going to be a ton of guys at this tournament. Go change, and hurry because I'm not going to wait around."

"I'm not changing, Justin. I bought this dress specifically for this trip. It's not slutty, and even if it is, who cares? We're in Vegas. Have you seen the people here? Just coming up in the

elevator we saw two women I'm sure were hookers. I thought you'd like this dress."

That last comment is an afterthought, especially since by the time I say that, he's watching TV and ignoring me. This trip was supposed to be a way for us to put the spice back in our relationship since after a few months together, we've gotten a little stale. Every date is the same. Same topics to talk about. Same places to eat.

The same sex time after time.

I thought a short trip to Las Vegas would liven things up between us. Since he has no interest in my new, sexy dress, that plan seems to have failed miserably.

When I don't make a move to go back into the bathroom to change, he turns to look at me like he can't understand what's going on. "Why are you still wearing that? We're missing everything, Eden. Come on. Let's go!"

"No, I'm not changing. Either I go like this, or you can go alone."

Rarely do I like to issue ultimatums, but this is a hill I die on. I just hope Justin doesn't let that happen.

I wait, holding my breath and silently praying to God he's going to realize he's making a mountain out of a molehill. Why can't he just be proud to have me on his arm in this dress? I look great in it. Why can't he see that?

Justin stands from the bed and glares at me. "Fine. Then I'll go alone because you aren't leaving this room in that dress. Over my dead body."

With that, he walks out, leaving me standing in our hotel room stunned and hurt. What has happened to the man I met four months ago who loved showing me off when we went out? He never even said a nice word about how I look in this dress.

As tears burn at the back of my eyes, I steel my emotions

because there's no way in hell I'm going to break down and cry. I'm in Las Vegas looking great. He can go to that stupid tournament. I'll just go down to the casino and gamble.

Screw him!

I take a final look at myself in the bathroom mirror and force myself to smile. It's going to be okay. I don't need to be attached to Justin's hip to have a good time.

"You look great," I tell my reflection. "Now go have fun!"

Ten minutes later after a ride down to the main floor with a woman who couldn't gush enough about how gorgeous I look in my dress, I emerge from the elevator with my confidence renewed. Justin doesn't want to be seen with me? Fine. Then I'll make my own good time.

Just as I reach the enormous double doors to the casino, Justin calls out, "Eden! You came down anyway?"

For a moment, I debate whether or not I should even bother to respond to him. It's not in my nature to ignore people, though, so I turn my head and look down the hallway to see him rushing toward me.

"I'm going to gamble, Justin. Go to your tournament."

He grabs me by the arm just as I take a step toward the doors. "It was over by the time I got there. Maybe if you didn't take forever to get dressed, although I can't imagine why it took you so long since there's barely anything to this getup."

Stunned, I stare at him, but he practically drags me toward the front doors of the hotel. At first, I don't fight him because I can't believe he's acting like this. When my brain finally catches up with my body, I yank my arm from his hold.

"Where are we going? If you didn't want me to be seen wearing this at your all-too-important tournament, I can't imagine you want everyone on the strip to see me walking down the street in this, what did you call it? Oh, yeah. A getup."

He glares at me and grabs hold of my arm again. "I'm not having this discussion with you here, Eden. I think we need to leave."

"Leave? We just got here. We're scheduled to stay here for three nights. I'm not going anywhere."

What the hell is he thinking? Leave? To go where? Does he actually think we should leave because of this dress?

Justin gets in my face, something he's never done before, and I swear I see pure rage in his eyes when he says through gritted teeth, "I will not have my girlfriend seen looking like a fucking whore. Get upstairs to that room and change, or I swear to God, Eden, you're going to be walking the streets to find another hotel room."

Something inside me snaps, and I yank my arm away. "Go fuck yourself, Justin! I will not be talked to like that. I don't know what the hell has gotten into you, but if you think you can speak to me like that, you can have the damn hotel room. I'll just get another one. For now, though, I'm going to gamble. Have a nice night."

For a long moment, we stare at each other, and I suspect he's as reluctant to take the next step as I am. I don't know what's causing him to behave this way, but this isn't Justin.

From behind me, I hear a man's voice say my name, and I spin around to see Marius King. As he walks toward me, Justin says in a low voice, "You better go back upstairs and change right now. I'm warning you."

I ignore him and say hi to Marius when he stops in front of me, but a second later, Justin grabs me by the hair and pulls my head backwards. Tears well in my eyes it hurts so much, and now on top of everything else, I'm embarrassed because Ava's brother-in-law is seeing this whole thing happen right in front of him.

"Whoa, buddy. Leave the lady alone. She clearly isn't

interested in whatever you're offering. Go get a drink and blow some money at the tables. Don't do anything stupid," Marius says.

Justin releases his hold on my hair and pushes me aside, now furious with another man instead of me. "Whoa, buddy yourself, dickbag. Who the fuck are you to tell me how to handle my girlfriend? Go back to whatever table you were losing your own money at and leave us alone."

Humiliated Marius is seeing me like this, I lower my gaze and look down at the floor. How did this trip go so horribly wrong?

"Listen, man. I don't want to cause you trouble, but I'm not going to let you treat Eden like this. I've known her since high school, so I guess you could say we're friends, and friends don't let friends hang with shitheads who are so clearly fucking below them. So shove off before this gets ugly."

I don't know what Justin's face looks like as Marius says that, but a second later, he pushes me hard toward the wall. I look up just in time to see him lunge at Marius. Fists fly, and when I don't get out of the way quickly enough, Justin punches me in the eye. I scream, and the two men go careening into the wall nearby. The security guards who were standing in front of the casino doors come running over, further adding to my humiliation.

They pull Marius off Justin, who continues to shit talk, and one asks me if I'm okay. I quickly assure him I'm fine because it's bad enough I've been punched in a public place by my now ex-boyfriend. Strangers feeling bad for me would be too much to bear.

"Mr. King, do you need any assistance?" one of the security guards asks Marius.

He shakes his head and brushes a piece of lint off his black dress shirt. "I'm fine. That man physically attacked this woman." All three men look at me, and Marius asks, "Do you want to press charges?"

All I want to do right now is crawl into a hole and hide. Pressing charges against the man I came here with sounds so awful I don't even know how to answer.

When I shake my head, Marius and the security guards step aside to talk for a few moments. After they're done, one of the men gives me a sympathetic smile before he and his fellow guard walk over to Justin and Marius comes to stand by my side.

"Sir, you're going to have to leave. Now."

"I'm a guest at this hotel, dammit! I won't be treated like this," Justin barks, attracting even more attention to us.

"Not anymore. Let's go."

As they escort him out of the hotel and he loudly complains the whole time, I bury my face in my hands, unable to endure all the stares from strangers passing by. Beside me, Marius slips his arm around my shoulders and pulls me against him in a hug I didn't realize I needed so damn badly.

"Come on. Forget that guy."

I drop my hands and look up at him with tears filling my eyes. "I came here with him. He reserved the room and everything. What am I going to do if they don't have any more rooms?"

"You'll come with me. They comp me a suite here whenever I'm in a tournament, so I have more than enough space. We'll stop at your old room, grab your stuff, and take it all up to my suite. Easy peasy."

Confused by his kindness since his claim about us being friends was a bit of a lie, I ask, "Why are you doing this? You barely know me."

He smiles, and I swear it's like all the bad that's happened in the past hour disappears into thin air. "Not true. I know you and Ava are as thick as thieves, and if Ava is crazy about you, then I have to figure you're all right. Now come on. We'll get your stuff and get you settled in up at my suite."

I nod, wishing I knew how to show him how thankful I am. We begin walking toward the elevator, and it's only us when we get in and he presses the button for his floor.

We don't say anything the whole ride up, but just as the doors open and we step out, he looks at me and winces. "I think we better get you some ice and fast. That eye looks rough."

Could this day get worse?

I hurry back into the elevator and study myself in the gold, reflective walls. I look like some battered housewife. Jesus Christ, how did my life turn into this? Justin was never Mr. Right, but he wasn't Mr. Beat The Hell Out of Me either.

All I want to do is cry. I look awful.

Marius pokes his head back into the elevator and takes my hand. "Let's go, bruiser. You've had a tough fight today, but you came out pretty good."

My head begins to throb as I let him lead me down the hallway. "You're not funny. I look terrible. I feel even worse."

He smiles and points toward his room. "We only have to walk a few more feet. You relax, and I'll get some ice. If you're hungry, I can order room service. I know I could use a drink, and I'm thinking maybe you can too."

I don't say anything because I'm overwhelmed by how wonderful he's being right now. I have to finally ask why he's really doing any of this for me. My being friends with Ava seems like a pretty weak excuse.

"Why are you being so nice to someone who's practically a stranger?" I ask when we reach the door to his hotel room.

Marius shrugs as he opens the door and gently escorts me inside to the biggest hotel room I've ever seen in my life. Even with *only being able to see out of one eye I can tell this suite is enormous.*

I turn to face him and see him smiling at me. "Maybe I'm just a nice guy."

Marius King a nice guy? No way.

Taking a deep breath, I let it out in a rush after telling Ava the beginning of our story. She sits listening like her life hangs on every word, and when I stop for a break, she shakes her head.

"I never liked Justin, but why did you lie to me when you came back? You said you had a great time in Vegas. I believed you because you extended your stay to a week. Why didn't you tell me the truth about what happened with him?"

Like that day in the lobby of the hotel in Las Vegas, I hang my head in shame. "I was too embarrassed. I let him do that to me. I don't know what was wrong with me. I'd never let anyone treat me like that."

"I'm just glad Marius showed up and got him kicked out and gave you a place to stay. It's definitely an exciting beginning to you two."

She has no idea. If she thinks that was exciting, just wait until she hears how we spent the week and then got married after seven days.

CHAPTER SIXTEEN

den

A half hour in the biggest soaker tub I've ever seen gives my anger a chance to rise to the surface, replacing the humiliation I felt before. And to think I bought that dress believing Justin would go crazy for it.

Jackass.

I finally get out of the tub when my fingertips get pruney, and I see a white cotton bathrobe hanging on the back of the door. Did Marius put that there? I don't remember seeing that when I walked in.

Then again, I do only have one working eye, so maybe I missed it. No matter. Whoever hung it there, thank you.

I slip it on, and oh my God, it feels heavenly against my skin! This is no ordinary cotton robe. It feels like the softest cotton known to man. I guess there are perks to staying in a suite here.

When I walk out into the hotel room, Marius is sitting on an enormous black sofa watching something on a large screen TV. He smiles when he sees me, patting the cushion next to him.

"Come sit down and rest. Did you have a nice bath? I ordered room service. Since I didn't know what you liked, I got a bit of everything."

After I do as he suggests, I suddenly feel awkward when I remember my eye probably looks awful. I lower my head and focus my attention on the white hotel robe.

"You okay?" he asks, but I don't look at him.

"Yeah. The bath was nice."

He falls silent, so I assume he's returned to watching TV. All the better. I really don't know what to say right anyway. I don't understand why he's being so nice to me either. Maybe it's because Ava is my best friend and she's with Matthias. It certainly isn't because we're good friends since I don't think Marius King and I have spoken twenty words to one another before today. Yes, we attended the same high school, but he was a year ahead of me. The closest I ever got to him was knowing his ex-girlfriend.

All of this fills my head so I don't pay much attention to him until he taps me on the knee. I look at my leg and notice the robe has fallen open. Great. First, I get punched in the face by my lovely ex-boyfriend, and now I'm flashing the guy who's trying to help.

What a day.

"Eden, are you sure you're okay?"

I nod but still refuse to look at him.

He leans over and slides his finger under my chin. Gently lifting it, he forces me to look at him. "What's wrong?"

"My eye hurts. I don't even want to look at it. I bet it's horrible."

Marius smiles and shakes his head. "Nah. You look great, like always. I think you just need to learn to duck."

His eyes light up, and he says, "That's going to be your nickname from now on. Duck."

Terrific. Other women get called kitten or baby or honey. I get duck.

I don't try to hide my frown at his nickname for me. I've always hated my name and wished for a cool nickname. Duck is definitely not that.

"That pout tells me you're unhappy. Don't like the nickname? What if I make it Little Duck? That's definitely cuter."

Twisting my expression into a grimace, I shake my head. "I bet you've always loved your name, but I hate mine. Always have. And I always wanted a great nickname. I just don't think Duck or Little Duck is great."

He tilts his head left and right like he's unsure what to say to that. "I like my name. It's unique. I've never met another Marius. For that matter, I've never met another Eden. I like your name."

I can't help but smile. I remember Maia saying a lot of terrible things about Marius, but one thing she mentioned over and over was how charming he could be when she was feeling down. As I sit here feeling like I've been beaten down by life, literally, I understand what she meant.

"Thanks. You wouldn't like it if every teenage boy you ever met insisted on saying something about your garden of Eden."

Marius lets out a belly laugh at what was supposed to be a serious point. He realizes I wasn't kidding a second later and forces himself to stop laughing.

"Sorry. I want to say those guys were just assholes, but I'm pretty sure I would have said that to you as a teenage boy."

A knock on the door interrupts our conversation, and he jumps up from the couch to answer it. "Time to eat! I hope you're hungry."

I'm just thankful for a break in the discussion of my name and my new nickname. I watch him walk through the suite and can't help but notice how good he looks in his gray dress pants and black dress shirt. Like all the King boys, he's good looking with an incredible body, but for my money, Marius King is the best looking of all five brothers.

I chastise myself for thinking that since I look like some kind of beat up pathetic thing. It's doubtful he's seeing me as anything other than a damsel in distress, which is never a good look. I prefer to be a woman with confidence, and usually I am, but after what happened with Justin today, I'm struggling to remember who Eden really is.

He leads two men dressed in black waiters' uniforms past me to a big round table on the other side of the room near the giant floor to ceiling windows that offer a gorgeous view of Las Vegas. I watch as they make two trips and then a third and then a final trip in with dishes filled with food.

Marius hands them both hundred dollar bills and walks them to the door. "Thank you, gentlemen. Have a great night!"

"If you need anything else, Mr. King, please call. We'll be happy to help," one of the men says on his way out.

When Marius returns, he points to the table so jammed with plates and food that there's no room for us to sit at it and eat. "I may have gone overboard, but I wanted to make sure you had whatever you wanted to eat. Dig in. There's soda, champagne, and whiskey. Oh, and water, but who the hell wants that?"

I stare at the table, stunned he went to so much trouble for me. "That's a lot of food."

He nods and shrugs like it's nothing to have ordered over a thousand dollars' worth of room service. "You know what they say. Go big or go home. Come on, eat. What do you want to drink? For me, it's definitely a whiskey day."

Standing, I walk over to the table and study all the food I can choose from. French toast, eggs, salmon and steak dinners, four burritos, a hamburger with fries, two ice cream sundaes, pancakes, what looks like some kind of club sandwich, and a charcuterie board, and that's not including covered dishes hiding more food I can't see.

"Um, I guess champagne."

I might as well be drunk if I have to look like I went twelve rounds.

He smiles and pours me a glass. "A woman after my own heart. I might have been disappointed if you said water or soda."

As I reach for the plate with the club sandwich, I say, "Normally, I would, but I'm not feeling myself today. It could be that I had some jackass punch me in the eye. Maybe my brains were scrambled. I don't know. All I know is I feel like champagne."

"Then champagne it is," he says, handing me my drink.

I settle in on the sofa and start eating, famished from all that's happened today. Marius sits down next to me and drags the coffee table toward us so I have somewhere to set my champagne flute. We don't speak as we eat, and when I finish my sandwich, I sit back and let out a heavy sigh.

"Getting beat up gives you an appetite, I guess."

He doesn't respond to my attempt at being self-effacing, so I wait a few minutes before I say, "Marius, I owe you big. Thank you for jumping in with Justin and giving me a soft place to land. I don't think I'll ever be able to repay you for all you've done."

All he does is shake his head while he continues to eat his steak. When he finishes, he sets the plate on the coffee table and downs the rest of the whiskey in his glass.

"You don't owe me a thing. As for your boyfriend—"

I immediately correct him. "Ex. Ex-boyfriend."

Smiling, he says. "As for your ex-boyfriend, if those security guards weren't so close, I would have schooled him on how to treat a woman."

That makes me laugh since I know Justin isn't a fighter. He was never much of a lover either, but he did have his moments when he was kind. Why all of that vanished today I honestly don't know.

"So are you going to put that gorgeous dress back on so we can go have a good time?"

Confused, I point at my eye, which I know is rapidly turning black and blue. "How can I go anywhere looking like this?"

"This is Vegas. Nobody knows you here. You could have been one of the women fighting in last night's bout down the street. If anyone asks, I'll warn them that you're a female MMA fighter, and if they know what's good for them, they'll shut the hell up."

"You won't mind being seen with me looking like this?"

"No."

"People are going to think you're with a woman who's sporting a black eye."

Marius walks over to the bar and pours himself another drink. "I don't care what people think. I never have. Now go get ready and make sure you put that dress back on. We'll go gamble for a while."

Thrilled someone other than me loves that dress, I smile and start walking toward the bedroom where all my clothes wait for me to put them away. I knew that dress looked great on me. Screw Justin and his puritanical nonsense.

From behind me, Marius says, "Duck, don't worry. You're beautiful, even with the black eye."

I thought I'd hate that nickname. Maybe it's not so bad, after all.

WE GET BACK TO THE HOTEL ROOM RIGHT BEFORE MIDNIGHT *after hours of gambling in the casino. I lost all the money I had put aside within the first two hours, but that didn't seem to faze him in the least. He just said we deserved to have a good time and proceeded to pay for both of us for the next four hours.*

Never in my life have I had so much fun with a man. There were no worries about what I was wearing or how much we were spending. We just had the best time.

After hours of drinking and laughing, I don't know if I'm drunk or simply feeling better than I've ever felt in my life. Strangely, Marius doesn't seem affected at all by how much whiskey he drank the whole time we gambled.

"How is it you don't get drunk?" I ask as I kick my shoes off, sending them flying through the living room of the suite.

He shrugs while he walks over to the bar to pour himself another drink. "Hollow leg? I'm not sure. I ate a lot before we left and then when we took that break from blackjack. That's probably it. Want more champagne?"

I beg off, sure if I have any more alcohol I'll fall fast asleep, and that's the last thing I want to do right now. "No, I'm good. Thanks."

We last ate nearly five hours ago. I can't imagine how this man is doing it.

Marius sits down on the sofa and looks over at me still standing in my bare feet halfway across the room. "Planning on leaving?"

"No."

"Then come over and hang out. I don't bite." He flashes a wicked smile. *"Not hard, unless I'm asked to."*

Maybe it's the fact that I'm a little buzzed, but everything about this man excites me, especially when he smiles and makes comments like that. I remember what Maia told me about being with Marius. Now I have to decide if I want to find out for my own.

My legs shake as I walk over to the sofa, and when I sit down, I'm still trembling. I don't know why I'm so nervous. It's not like I'm a virgin.

"So now that you're finally over here, do you want me to put something else on the TV?" he asks.

Up until this very moment, I didn't even realize the TV was on. I turn to see what he's watching. Basketball. Ugh. I hate basketball.

"Anything but that," I say with a chuckle. *"My apologies if you're a huge basketball fan."*

He hands me the remote and laughs. "Not really. I'm not really interested in watching anything, so feel free to find what you want."

I move through the channels, but there's nothing good on. So much for Saturday night television programming. They must put the good shows on when they think people are actually home and watching TV.

Frustrated, I toss the remote onto the sofa next to me. "Nothing good."

"Then I think that's a sign that we should forget watching TV and move to what we're both thinking about," he says, and all I can think about is how sexy he sounds right now.

Never one to make it too easy for a man, I stare at him for a long moment before asking, "And just how do you know what I'm thinking about?"

"Trust me, Duck. I know."

"So a King who reads minds. That would make you a very powerful man."

"Mmmm…so back to what you've been thinking about," he says as he pulls me onto his lap and my dress hikes up to my hips. "That's better."

God, he's hard as a rock and pressing against the front of my panties, which I'm sure are practically drenched. Even more, he's staring up at me with those dark eyes of his that I swear I could get lost in.

Then I remember that I have a nice shiner and probably look like something the cat dragged in.

Lowering my head, I mumble, "I don't look my best."

He tilts my chin up with his finger and shakes his head. "You look as beautiful as you always do. In fact, I think I might have some strange fetish about black eyes."

"You're just saying that."

Marius lifts his hips off the sofa so his cock pushes against my clit. The feeling is nothing less than exquisite.

"No way. See? I'm hard. I think it's the black eye."

I know what he's doing, and while I'm thankful he's trying to be sweet, I'm sure I've looked better. "Not the dress?" I tease, enjoying how playful he is.

Other women likely see Marius and fall for his gorgeous face and muscular body. Still others probably like his money. Me? I thought I wanted him because of what's between his legs, but I found out today he's also genuinely a good time even without sleeping with him.

His gaze travels up and down my body before it comes to rest on my face. "The dress is definitely working for me too. Same with the shoes. I suspect, though, that you could be wearing a garbage bag and still look incredible."

Before I can say a word to that, he leans forward and slides his hand behind my head to pull me down on him. When his lips touch mine and his tongue darts into my mouth, I swear it's like my body wants to explode.

Then only a few seconds later, he sits back and smiles up at me. "You taste as delicious as you look."

Suddenly, doubt fills my mind. I know I shouldn't mention it and ruin the mood, but I have to. "Marius, this morning when I got here, I was with another man. I don't know if we should do this."

He shakes his head and slides his hands along my sides as he says, "He didn't deserve you. I, for one, believe it's good he's out of the picture. Think of tonight this way. I want you, and you want me. There's no need to complicate the situation."

"You have an answer for everything, don't you?" I say with a smile.

"Pretty much. I know what you want, Eden. Admit it, and we'll have a night you won't forget."

"You're pretty cocky. What about you?"

He pulls me up his legs so his rock hard cock is fully pressing against the front of my panties. "What about me? I know what I want."

Oh, God. I've fantasized about this very moment more times than I want to admit. No is the farthest thing from my mind.

And he knows it.

"You know, your ex-girlfriend used to say after being with you, she walked funny."

Marius leans forward and nuzzles my neck. "I promise to do my best to make sure you can say that too."

The feel of his mouth on me makes my eyes roll back in my head, and his cock nudging between my legs backs up that promise of his. I'd have to be crazy not to live out my fantasy with Marius King.

And trust me. I'm not crazy.

I stop before telling Ava any of the sexy details, and she stares at me like I've just deprived her of something she needs to live. "And? You two had sex that first night? Was Maia right?"

"Should you really be asking that about your brother-in-law?" I ask, teasing her.

"Yes! Why not? Marius has always been such a sexual person. Now I'm supposed to pretend he's not? So was she?"

I nod but stay mum on the specific details for the moment.

Ava squeals and falls back on the pillows. "I knew it! I could've guessed the answer since I know what Matthias is like. Still, I love that for you. Marius is gorgeous, has the equipment a man needs to satisfy a woman, and he's loaded. He's the perfect man I've always wanted for you!"

"Yeah, except he wanted to keep us a secret. Not exactly perfect anymore, is he?"

All the happiness drains from her face. She sighs and answers, "Well, maybe things can be fixed. Do you love him? Like love him enough to work things out?"

Again, I nod. I do love Marius.

"Then everything will be fine."

Typical Ava. She never fails to believe good things are going to happen to those she loves.

"It's up to him now," I say, unsure if he's going to do what he has to so we can be together again.

And that's the terrifying part.

CHAPTER SEVENTEEN

M arius

SO NOW YOU KNOW WHAT A FUCKING MESS I'VE MADE of things. In case you're having a hard time keeping up, I have a woman I adore who loves me, and I completely fucked up. Now she wants to divorce me, and I'm sitting outside my brother's house smoking a cigar and trying to figure out how the hell I'm going to save my marriage.

I told you I didn't hate love. I never lied. Not to you and not to Eden.

Still, I'm bright enough to know that's not going to help me now with her. No, I'm going to have to figure out how to win her back.

I think it can work. She loves me. I know that. I've never doubted how much Eden loves me. That she's doubted me hurts, but I know we can come back from that.

So, I just have to decide how.

Matthias and Ronan disturb my peace out here with the tiki torches when they return to the patio. The two of them sit down at the table but don't say a word at first.

After a couple minutes of the three of us looking around like we're strangers waiting for a bus, I figure I should speak. "Nice end-of-summer party, Matthias. Where's Kellen?"

"He and Salem had to go back to the city. She's got some athlete who can't stop fucking up," he explains.

"I'm sure Kellen is happy he's not the guy in need of a reputation rehab this time," I say with a laugh.

We fall into another strange silence again until Ronan says, "So what are you going to do?"

It all comes down to that, now doesn't it? What am I going to do?

The answer is simple. How I'll actually do it is an entirely different story, of course.

I stand up and face my brothers. "Win her back. Show her that she doesn't want to divorce me."

My two brothers look surprised to hear me say that. Or maybe it's the casual way I said it, as if it's a fait accompli, which if I'm being honest is the opposite of what making Eden want to stay with me is. Still, I figure it's good to come out of the gate with a winning attitude.

"Right now, though, I need to clear my head. That calls for a game of pool," I announce before heading into the house without waiting for them to say a word.

By the time I've racked the balls and chalked up my cue, Matthias and Ronan have joined me in the game room upstairs. Whenever I need to think about some problem, I shoot pool. It helps me put things in perspective.

And if ever I needed to get my thoughts straight on something, it's tonight.

The two of them sit down on the leather sofa. Matthias looks particularly confused about what I'm doing and asks, "How is this helping?"

"Are you going to play?" I ask, ignoring his question for the moment.

He shrugs and stands up to grab a pool cue hanging on the wall. "Sure. Are we planning on talking about what happened, or is this part of your living in denial routine you seem to have started?"

I focus on the cue ball and line up my shot. "No denial. Just looking for some clarity. That's all." I send two balls sailing into two different pockets and silently congratulate myself on that trick shot.

"Okay, Matthias. I'm low balls. Since I don't want to run the table, I'll let you take your best shot."

My older brother groans and shakes his head before attempting to sink at least one ball. He fails miserably, and the cue ball just sort of roams around the pool table like it's lost before coming to rest down near me.

"Dude, you suck at this now. What happened to you? You used to be a decent player."

He twists his face into an angry expression before answering, "It's called having kids and a job, Marius. I don't get to play much anymore. Can we focus on what's going on?"

I shrug and line up my shot to send the two ball into the right side pocket. "I told you. I'm going to win her back. It'll work. Don't worry."

"And how do you plan on doing that?" Matthias asks.

With a smile, I look down the table at him and say, "Ah, there's the rub."

My older brother waits for me to continue, and when I don't, he says, "Clever. Who are you? Hamlet? Marius, you need a real plan, and here you are shooting pool and waxing poetic."

"Yeah, if you want Eden back, you're going to have to do something big," Ronan adds. "Like huge. The woman served you with divorce papers. That tells me she's serious."

Why do they keep fixating on those damn divorce papers? "It's not like they're definitive. I think they're more the embodiment of her feelings at the moment, which I can change. I know it."

Already tired of talking about this, I sink the four and seven balls before screwing up a shot on the six ball. I should have just come up here alone. My brothers are making it impossible to get any thinking done.

Ronan and Matthias glance at one another before looking at me. "You sound pretty sure of yourself there," Matthias says. "What makes you think you can change her mind?"

That's an easy one to answer. "I know I can change Eden's mind because I know her. We've been crazy about one another since that first day together. She doesn't want a divorce any more than I do. She was just unhappy about having to keep us a secret, but now that everything's out in the open, all I have to do is find a way to show her she wants to stay married to me."

Nobody says a word for a long moment while

Matthias attempts to put the thirteen ball in the left side pocket. Once again, he doesn't even get close.

Ronan twists his face into an expression that looks like he just tasted a lemon. "Okay, but if that was the only problem, why aren't the two of you together right now? Your relationship isn't a secret anymore."

I wave away that idea since I don't want to deal with that issue right now and set up my shot to put the three ball in the right corner pocket near me. "She's just cooling off. You wait. Everything will be fine."

It practically floats in, leaving just the one and six balls.

My youngest brother stands up and shakes his head. "I'm going to tell you what you told me when it seemed like I was making a mistake with Kate. You're blowing it, dude. That woman is not going to just suddenly come back to you simply because everyone knows you guys are together now. She's hurt, and she's pissed. Think what you want, but everything is not going to be fine. And on that note, I'm going."

He walks out of the game room before I can say anything to all of that, but the truth is, I have nothing to say. Matthias stays with me, and it doesn't take him long to pick up where Ronan left off.

"Seriously, Marius. You can't believe just giving Eden time alone is your best idea. Even worse, Ava's been with her for the past three hours. How do you think that conversation has gone? Because if you're not realizing it, they've called you every name in the book and are likely devising some way for her to feel better by starting over. You know, with someone else?"

That wasn't what I was thinking about at all. Dammit, Matthias better be wrong about what those two are doing at the penthouse.

I point at the table and say, "One ball in the right center pocket." The balls goes in beautifully, followed by the six ball, which leaves only the eight ball since Matthias hasn't even sunk a single high ball yet. As he stands on the opposite end of the table practically sneering at me, I say, "Eight ball, corner pocket."

When it goes in, I set my pool cue down and ask, "Do you really think Ava would do me dirty like that? You don't think there's any brother-in-law love for me coming from her?"

Matthias levels a disbelieving gaze on me. "Marius, you've known Ava all your life, just like I have. She's the sweetest person in the world, until you hurt someone she loves. She's best friends with Eden, and I can promise you, she loves her like a sister. On top of that, she slapped you across the face when she found out what happened. I know my wife, and I'm telling you if Eden is saying it's over, Ava is working on coming up with a list of guys she plans to start setting her up with this week."

So she would do me dirty. Damn. Why can't life be as easy as a game of pool?

"She loves me, Matthias. I know she does. And I'm madly in love with her. This will work out. I just have to figure out what to do now to make her see that."

He smiles and lets out a sigh. "I believe you. I do. I just don't know if you understand your own wife. I mean, what did you think would happen when you insisted on keeping your relationship secret for two years? I get why you wanted that, but seriously? I think you should be counting your lucky stars she let it go that long."

My brothers don't understand. Maybe if any of them were like me they would.

I watch him toss his cue onto the pool table as the memory of my time with Eden in Vegas slowly fills my mind. I know she loves me as much as I love her.

"You know, I knew one of your girlfriends in high school. She used to say after being with you, she walked funny."

For a moment, I consider asking how well she knew Maia since I assume that's the ex she's talking about, but I don't. Leaning forward, I kiss her neck and feel her body melt into mine.

"I promise to do my best to make sure you can say that too."

When I sit back and look at this stunning woman sitting on my lap, she has a very knowing expression on her face. I'm guessing she heard a lot more than that little nugget from that ex of mine.

Neither of us says anything for a long moment, but then Eden surprises me by jumping up off me. For a few seconds, I stare up at her in shock.

"Was it something I said?" I ask, hoping a joke will bring her back.

Instead, she shakes her head and smiles. "No. I just thought we should head for the bedroom. I mean, this couch is nice, but I'm guessing it's not too comfortable, and those windows don't offer much privacy."

I turn my head to look at the floor-to-ceiling windows that give us a phenomenal view of Vegas but don't offer much in the form of privacy. Not that I care. I've had sex in public places before, and I doubt anyone can see much from street level.

But if having the world see us fucking makes her

193

uncomfortable, I'm game for the bedroom. Or anything else, for that matter.

"Well, lead the way, Duck."

She narrows her eyes and seems to glare at me before turning and walking away. I follow her, assuming what's about to happen is angry sex, which is just fine with me. Some of the best sex I've ever had was after a fight. Eden and I haven't truly disagreed about much, but that look she just gave me says she still hasn't come around to loving my nickname for her.

"So should I assume this is going to be hate sex?" I ask with a chuckle.

Eden stops and turns around to face me with that same narrowed-eye look. "I don't hate you, Marius. I don't even hate that nickname. Much."

"Then what's with the glaring?"

Her expression instantly softens, and she shrugs. "Sorry. I have one of those faces that shows every emotion I ever have. I didn't mean to glare. I'm just not super crazy about Duck."

I step forward and wrap my arms around her waist to pull her to me. She feels incredible against me, like she was made to be mine.

"I wish you liked it. I think it's cute."

She twists her expression into one of pure disgust. "I think you can guess this, but nobody has ever called me cute."

Dipping my head, I press a soft kiss to her lips and whisper against them, "You're not cute. You're gorgeous. My nickname for you is cute."

Again, her look softens, and this time I get a smile. "Well, gorgeous I like. So, no hate sex today."

"Oh, well. I'm sure I'm going to aggravate you at some point, so the chance for some great angry sex will be there."

Even before I finish speaking, I'm surprised I'm already

talking about a future for Eden and me. Not that I have an aversion to staying with one woman, especially one like her. It's just that I don't remember ever thinking of anything but the moment with any woman.

Not since Maia.

"I can't decide if you're serious or not, so let's forget the hate sex and see how we do with the we-actually-want-to-sleep-with-each-other sex," she says with a giggle.

This woman with her glaring looks and black eye is nothing short of charming. I've always known she was beautiful, but now that I've gotten to know a little about her today, I want to know everything about her.

I kiss her, teasing her tongue with mine, and it's as if she transforms into a different person right in front of me. I've been with enough beautiful women to expect them to be selfish and self-involved, but she's open and sensual in a way I didn't expect.

When she pulls away, she smiles up at me with a wicked twinkle in her eye. "I have to say you're a great kisser, Marius. I guess I should have thought you would be with that mouth of yours, but I was worried you might be one of those egotistical guys who only cares about your own pleasure. I'm glad you're not."

How interesting. We were thinking pretty much the same thing. I am curious about how she knows I'm not some self-absorbed dickbag, though.

"How can you be sure I'm not that kind of guy?"

Eden thinks about the question for a moment or two and then smiles. "It's all in the kiss. If a man doesn't seem to give a damn if his kiss does anything for a woman, then he's a selfish lover. If his kiss shows he wants to please the woman, he's probably going to be good in bed. And even if he isn't, if he has the goods and his kissing is great, then a woman can work with possible subpar moves in bed."

She stops for a moment and adds, "Not that I think you're going to have any issues in that area."

"Because of what my ex told you?"

Eden shakes her head as she gives me the sexiest grin I've ever seen. Then she slides her hand down the front of my pants and says, "No. Because of this."

I do love a woman who isn't afraid to admit she likes sex.

The feel of her hand on my rock hard dick makes my eyes roll back into my head. If we don't get to the bedroom very soon, I'm going to fuck her right here in the hallway.

Sliding my hands down her back, I cup her ass and pull her against me so she has no doubt how hard I am and how ready I am. I kiss her long and deep, and when she lets out a tiny moan, I swear it feels like I'm in heaven.

And we're not even naked yet.

She unzips my pants, a clear sign we're ready to roll, so I push them down my legs and kick them off to the side. I slip out of my dress shirt and toss it onto my pants, leaving me in just a pair of boxer briefs that won't be on for much longer.

But now that I'm nearly nude, what she's wearing needs to change, so I pull that dress I liked so much off over her head and leave it on top of my clothes. She's only got underwear on now, and fuck, does she look incredible. Eden doesn't have a lot on top, but I'm liking what I see.

Nearly breathlessly, she whispers in my ear, "We better get to the bed, or we're going to end up doing it right here in this hallway."

"That's fine with me," I answer as I tug her panties down her legs.

When she's finally fully naked standing in front of me, it's *all I can do to not take her right here I'm so fucking excited. I don't know what this woman has about her, but whatever it is, I'm into it big time.*

She hooks her thumbs in my waistband and pushes my boxer briefs off, so now there's nothing between us. When she palms my cock and strokes it as she kisses me, I have to stop myself from bending her over and fucking her hard.

I don't want her that way, though. Sure, a rough fuck every so often is nice, but that's for women you never plan to see again. Although I didn't plan on us getting together here in Vegas, now that it's happening, I know she's definitely not one of those women I don't give a damn about seeing again.

Lifting her by the waist, I position her over my cock and slowly let her down onto it, filling her tight cunt completely. Jesus, she feels fucking fantastic. Like the kind of feeling you're afraid to believe exists because you might find out it's all a damn dream.

She stares at me, her green eyes wide and filled with need, as I begin to slowly pump into her. Her heels press into the small of my back, but all I can feel is that incredible cunt of hers with each time I drive my cock into her. She's wet and open and perfect in every way.

Her mouth delivers even more wonderful sensations that go straight to my dick. I thrust into her, and she makes a noise that's a mixture of need and surrender that might be the best sound I've ever heard in my life.

I move us over to the wall and set my left hand against it as I hold her up with my right hand. She clings to my neck, her fingernails digging into the skin just above my shoulders. I swear it's as if Eden knows every tiny thing that gets me going.

For a fleeting second, I can't help but think that Maia told her much more than how sex with me made her walk funny, but then Eden begins to buck against me, and thinking becomes almost impossible. My body shifts into overdrive, and all I can focus on is coming and making her come. My mind loses all ability to pay attention to anything but how fucking her makes me feel.

My heart pounds in my ears as we race toward that finish line, but I have to admit I wish this first time would last longer. Eden teases me by biting my earlobe, and the combination of pleasure and pain I feel at this very moment is exquisite. With each moan, she makes me want her more and more.

I feel her cunt squeeze even more around me, and I know she's almost there. I close my fingers in her hair, tightening until I have a fistful and pull hard. She cries out, sinking her teeth into my neck. It's rough and raw, and I swear I've never been this turned on in my life.

Her orgasm starts, and she moans, "Oh, God…Marius, don't stop…I'm there!"

I watch her come and think she's perfect in every way. Over and over, she cries out before she buries her face in my shoulder and the final waves of her release roll over her.

I'm not quite there yet, so I keep fucking her, and she doesn't stop rolling her hips and taking every last inch of me. My thighs ache and my body craves release, but if I could stay here for the rest of time fucking her, I would.

When I finally come, it's so powerful that I nearly drop her. "Hang onto my neck," I grunt out as I press my right palm to the wall to brace myself.

I'm like a man lost, but I don't care. Being with Eden feels too fucking good to ever be wrong.

Sagging against the wall, I press a kiss against her ear and sigh. I don't think I've ever come like that. Not even with the only woman I've ever loved.

I finally lift my head to look at her and see her smiling. That's a good sign. "That was fucking amazing."

Not exactly my smoothest line, but I am honest. At least sometimes I am.

"I think we can safely say that the reports are true about you," she says with a giggle. "I think I might need some time to recover."

"I aim to please," I say as I gently set her on her feet.

Eden stands on her tiptoes and kisses me sweetly on the lips. "You succeed."

I don't say this to her, but I think I might be falling for her. That's not possible, right? I'm a man who loves being single. Then why do I feel like I don't want to live without her after today?

Best to keep that to myself. For now, at least.

I OPEN MY EYES AND SEE EDEN'S BLACK HAIR SPREAD OUT across my chest. I touch it and marvel at how soft it is.

She lifts her head and pushes her hair back off her face so she can see me. "Hey. Good morning."

Her black eye is even worse this morning, but somehow, she looks even more beautiful than usual. "Sorry. I didn't mean to wake you."

"It's okay. I felt something touching my head. Was that you?"

I smile at how she doesn't pull any punches. I do love a woman who speaks her mind. I'd bet most women I've been with wouldn't have been that direct at this moment, but it's quintessential Eden.

"Yeah. I don't know why I wanted to touch it. Your hair's really soft."

She sits up and smiles down at me. "Thanks. I use this special stuff that has actual vanilla bean in it."

Now that she mentions that, her hair does smell like vanilla. I've always loved that scent.

"So, we slept together."

The way she says that sounds ominous, like something terrible is going to happen now. I thought we had a good time. If the soreness in my legs is any indication, we had a damn good time.

"Uh-huh."

Eden leans down and presses a soft kiss to my lips. "By the way, I had to get up in the middle of the night to go to the bathroom, and I can tell you your ex wasn't wrong."

I smile at how cute she sounds right now. "Walking funny?"

Just as I think she couldn't be more incredible, she blushes and looks down at the sheets. "Yeah."

Unsure if that means no sex this morning, I sit up, propping the pillows behind me against the headboard. "I don't know if I'm supposed to say I'm sorry for that."

She smiles and shakes her head. "Not at all. You did say you would do all you could to make sure I walked funny after sex with you, and you definitely did that. I just think I might need a little time to recuperate."

Okay. No sex this morning.

We fall into an awkward silence until she runs her hand over my stomach, instantly making me even harder than my morning erection already had. She looks at it and then up at me.

"Are you always ready to go?"

I shrug and answer, "It's a guy thing. We're always ready to go."

Eden blushes again, charming me even more. "I wish I could. Really, I do. It's just that we had a lot of sex last night, Marius.

I'm going to need a day to recover. You should take that as a compliment, though, since if you weren't the size you are, I'd be raring to go right now."

Talk about a double-edged sword.

Pulling her down onto me, I kiss her long and deep and whisper against her lips, "Then we'll just have to pick up tomorrow where we left off."

She snuggles up against me, and in a quiet voice says, "I'm supposed to leave to go back home tomorrow."

Even though I haven't thought about anything past how incredible sex with Eden was, I say, "You should change your plans."

Eden doesn't respond to my suggestion, but a few seconds later, sits up and looks at me like she's surprised I said that. "Are you saying you want me to stay longer? With you? Here?"

Honestly, I'm as shocked I said that as she is. I can't remember the last time I wanted more than one night with a woman.

"Yeah. I think we can have a good time."

"You mean like sex? That kind of good time?"

I smile at how cute she can be. "Sure, when you recuperate, of course. We can also do other stuff like gamble. I hear there are some good shows in Vegas. We could go see one or two of them."

"Don't you have to go back to work?" she asks.

Throwing my head back, I laugh. "No. I don't have a shoot scheduled for another week or so. At least I don't think I do. I should probably check in with my assistant on that."

"Well, I guess I could stay longer. My boss is always after me to take my vacation time. I usually just let it accumulate, but I could use it this week. I'm sure it'll be fine."

"Then it's settled. Marius and Eden are doing Vegas this week."

She leans down to kiss me and then says, "And each other. Don't forget that."

God, I do love the way this woman thinks.

I know what I have to do. I have to see her. I know if we can talk, we can figure this out.

We're crazy in love. We have been since that first day.

That has to count for something, right?

CHAPTER EIGHTEEN

den

After hours of talking about how Marius and I got together, I give in on the ice cream idea, so Ava orders some to be delivered while I get cleaned up. I think I got all my crying out, but as I stand in the shower, memories come rushing back that make my eyes fill with tears.

What good is it to remember the time we had great shower sex or the time he found me taking a bath and climbed in clothes and all to join me and we laughed until our sides hurt? Yes, those are great memories, but do they fix the problem at hand?

No. In fact, they only serve to make me even more miserable because I can look back at the time I've been with Marius and honestly say I was happy. Happier than

I've ever been in my life. And now it's crashed and burned, ended with some stranger serving him divorce papers.

My attorney told me it would be fine if I had a friend or colleague deliver them to him, but I was too embarrassed to ask anyone I know. Thank God in this state it's illegal for the spouse to do it because if I had to be the one to serve him, it would have never happened. I know myself. When Marius decides he wants to be charming, I can't deny him anything.

Two years of lying about us to everyone I know and love proves that.

I turn the water to hot so it practically attacks my back as I stand here thinking about how it all went wrong. How is it that two people can love one another and this happens?

No doubt some would question if Marius loves me since he wanted us to be a secret all this time. There are many things I'm not sure of in this world, but his love isn't one of them.

So why am I divorcing him?

As soon as that question forms in my brain, I start crying. I bury my face in my hands and sob like a baby, already missing everything we had together. The laughs. The way no matter how bad I felt after a hard day at work Marius knew how to make me smile. How we'd watch movies together, sometimes never saying a word for hours but then talking all night about what we loved and hated about the story. The way he'd surprise me with breakfast in bed. And a million other things that made me love him.

Make me love him.

See, that's the problem. I still love him.

After another ten minutes sobbing in the shower, I get out and throw on some clothes before heading downstairs. I hoped the ice cream would have been here by now, but maybe the delivery company is running behind tonight.

"Ava, I wonder what's taking them so long."

The words are barely out of my mouth before Marius steps out from the pantry. Ava looks at me sheepishly, but I can't be angry with her. She's a romantic who loves the idea of love, so naturally, she made sure not tell me he was here.

"Duck, I thought we should talk."

Of course, he had to come around when I look like something the cat dragged in. My hair is soaking wet, I'm dressed in ratty black yoga pants and an old t-shirt from college, and I don't have a stitch of makeup on.

For a moment, I consider saying I don't want to talk, but that's not the truth. I love talking to Marius. In addition to being incredibly funny, he's smart, so our conversations are always interesting.

The man is everything I've ever wanted in a husband, so how can I not take the chance to talk to him?

Just then, the phone rings. I answer it and hear the doorman downstairs telling me the delivery guy is here with our ice cream.

"Okay. Thanks, Conrad."

Ava walks across the kitchen to stand with me. "How about I go downstairs to get the ice cream? Just text me when you want me to come back up with the goodies."

I shake my head at that idea. "No. Just go down and get it and then come back up and hang out here. Marius and I will talk upstairs so you don't have to stay down in the lobby with melted ice cream."

She smiles and gives my hand a sympathetic squeeze. Leaning in toward me, she whispers, "I think it's a good start that he came to talk, don't you?"

Rolling my eyes, I shrug. "I guess."

When Ava begins walking toward the hallway to get on to the elevator, she turns to Marius. "I'll be right down here, so my warning from before stands."

He nods and says, "Got it. No funny stuff or the best friend slaps me across the face again."

She gives me one last glance before walking out to the elevator and leaving us alone. For a few moments, neither of us say a word. To be honest, I don't know what to say. What exactly are you supposed to talk about with the man who was just served divorce papers from you not four hours ago?

Finally, he speaks first. "Thanks for not throwing me down the elevator shaft as soon as you saw me."

Marius still looks like he hasn't slept all week, but at least his sense of humor hasn't disappeared.

"Let's take this upstairs. I don't want Ava hearing what we have to say."

I start walking toward the stairs as he follows me, but he stops me by touching my hand before I reach them. When I turn around, I see hurt filling his eyes. I hate seeing him look like this. I don't want him to be unhappy. That was never my goal.

"Eden, I know you want us to talk upstairs, but before we head up, I have something I need to say. I'm sorry. This whole thing is my fault. I never meant to make you feel like I wasn't the proudest man in the world to have you as my wife."

Well, he's definitely come armed with the big guns. An apology and taking responsibility for this mess on top of a lovely compliment? Who would dislike that?

"I appreciate you saying that."

We don't say another word until we get upstairs. I'd wanted to talk away from Ava without having to make her sit in the damn lobby, but now I'm wondering if this was a good idea. Talking in the bedroom will probably give him the wrong idea.

So instead, I stop at the top of the stairs in that area on the second floor that the realtor called a mezzanine. It's partially open to the downstairs, but I don't think Ava will be able to hear what we're saying.

Like in the much of the penthouse, this area only has those minimalist chairs Marius hates. I don't like them much either, which I guess begs the question why neither one of us has bought new ones. Then again, he spends more time at Ava's home than here, so that explains why Marius hasn't done anything about them. As for me, I barely notice these ugly chairs when I come upstairs.

He realizes we aren't going into the bedroom and looks around as I stop next to one of the chairs. "Oh, we're talking here? Why not in the bedroom?"

"Because I thought a more neutral ground would be better."

The real reason is I know what will happen if we're near a bed for any amount of time. While a bout of lovemaking is always great, I'll never be able to have a real conversation with him if sex is looming over our heads.

Marius looks down at the barely there chair and sighs. "Mental note to self: get some new fucking furniture for this house."

I smile as I think about how much effort we put into buying bedroom furniture but nothing else in the rest of the penthouse. I guess you wouldn't have to be a genius to figure out where we spend most of our time.

"That's assuming I still live here," he says in a low voice.

"You barely ever lived here, Marius. You sleep in your old room at Matthias and Ava's house more than you do here."

He winces before saying, "Fair enough. In my defense, though, I wanted to keep an eye on Ronan for the past few months. That won't be much of an issue anymore, though, so I can be here every night from now on."

"I know you were concerned about Ronan, but why couldn't you stay here and go out to the house every day? It's not like you have a job that forces you to be chained to a desk from nine-to-five, Monday through Friday."

As much as I understand his concern for the youngest King, I'm not ready to let him off the hook as easily as he'd like.

Marius opens his mouth to respond to me but closes it again. Sitting down on the chair closest to him, he sighs. "Again, fair enough. I wasn't thinking the right way about things when it came to Ronan."

He doesn't say it, but I know finding Ronan bleeding

out was devastating for him. He's always been very protective of that brother in particular, and going to his apartment and seeing him barely hanging onto life must have been terrible.

"I know, Marius, and I don't want to fault you for anything you've done with Ronan."

"I'm sorry that I got sidetracked with him and neglected you. I never meant to. It's just that after finding him like…"

His sentence trails off, but I understand. I also know he's been struggling with what happened.

I touch his hand, and he looks at me. God, his eyes are filled with so much sadness.

"Marius, I think you need to see someone about what you've gone through with Ronan."

He looks at me oddly and shakes his head. "I'm fine. Really. He's the one who went through something. Not me."

Clearly, my husband doesn't see what I'm seeing. "Baby, you found your brother bleeding to death when he tried to take his own life. That's bound to affect a person. I know you want me to think you haven't been sleeping because you miss me, but that's not it. Not entirely. You have to deal with what happened."

"I am. I promise. Right now, I need to make sure you know how sorry I am for everything that I did. I never meant to hurt you, Eden. I love you. You're my entire world. I'm lost without you."

Hanging my head, I sigh as the weight of missing him presses down on me. "I love you, too."

We fall into an awkward silence until he says, "So, Matthias thinks Ava's been giving you a list of guys she's interested in setting you up with. Is that what you guys have been doing all this time?"

I can't help but smile at how little Matthias and Marius understand us. Shaking my head, I answer, "No, that's not what we've been doing. We watched Air Disasters, and then I told her how we got together. Between you and me, I think Ava is hoping you'll do something incredible to fix things between us. I know she slapped you, but she's still one of your biggest fans."

"Air Disasters, huh? I bet it was an episode with that guy you like in it, wasn't it?" he asks, and I swear I hear jealousy in his voice.

"If you must know, it was."

"I get it. I'm not around enough, so you watch that guy. I'm a little confused since he looks nothing like me, though."

As I sit down in the chair next to him, I ask, "Do you only fantasize about women who have long black hair and green eyes?"

Marius shakes his head. "I don't fantasize about anyone but you, Duck." He stops for a moment before adding, "Eden."

For the longest time, I secretly hated that nickname he gave me, but now that he seems to not want to call me that, I'm sad. Still, I don't believe him when he says he doesn't fantasize about women who don't look like me.

Leveling my gaze on him, I say, "You watch porn, Marius. Don't tell me you don't fantasize about those women, and let me remind you, they rarely look like me. They're mostly blondes with giant racks and big asses, three traits I don't possess."

"I don't make the decisions regarding who stars in

pornos. Personally, I'd like more women who look like you to star in them, but that isn't up to me."

We're clearly getting lost in the minutiae.

"Is this what you wanted to come to talk to me about tonight, Marius?"

His mouth turns down in the frown, and he shakes his head. "No."

"Then why don't you say what's on your mind, and then I'll do the same."

Even as I say that, I'm terrified to hear what he has to say. What if he's decided my serving him with divorce papers was a step too far? What if he actually plans on signing those papers? I knew when I said yes to my attorney that it was a risk Marius might just agree to divorcing me, but until this very moment, I didn't know how crushed I'd be if that's what he wants to do.

"Fine," he says nodding his head, almost like he's trying to convince himself we're okay.

We aren't.

Staring into my eyes, he looks so sweet when he says, "I meant what I said before, Eden. Everything that's happened is my fault. I just want you to know that I've never been ashamed of being with you. I'm proud you're my wife, and I hope I can continue to say that."

Relief washes over me at hearing those words. He doesn't want to divorce me. Good because I don't want to divorce him. Now if we can figure out how to right this ship, we'll be okay.

"You can call me, Duck, Marius."

He reaches out for my hand and smiles. "I wasn't sure you wanted me to use that nickname anymore."

"What I don't want is to be the last thing you think of

in your life. And I don't want to wonder if we'll ever have a marriage where I mean more to you than everyone else. I've gotten used to that nickname and actually like it. It's all the other stuff I can't do anymore."

In his dark eyes, I see genuine fear as I say those things. It's almost as if he isn't understanding me. Does he truly believe I don't want to be married to him?

"Duck, you were never less important to me, but I see now that's what you felt. I'm sorry. You mean more to me than anything in this world. Do you really want a divorce?"

I don't answer for a long moment. No, I don't a divorce, but we can't continue like we were.

Looking down at where our hands are joined, I shake my head. "I never wanted a divorce, Marius. I just couldn't keep lying to everyone I love."

He slides his forefinger under my chin to lift my head. With a smile, he says, "No more lying. I promise. If you want, I'll buy a billboard in Times Square to let the world know. Or dozens of them so we can tell everyone we're together."

My husband loves the big gesture. It's his signature thing. I've always loved that about him. He's generous to a fault.

"You don't have to do that. All I want is to know my husband isn't ashamed to be married to me."

"I've never been ashamed of you, Duck. You're gorgeous, smart as hell, accomplished…everything any man would kill for. I've never been happier than when I've been with you. God, I hate that you think I was embarrassed by you."

Fighting back tears, I say, "I didn't know why you

didn't want to tell the world we were together. My mind came up with dozens of scenarios to explain it, and none of them felt good. Then you brought that beautiful girl to Ava's party, and I couldn't do it anymore. I couldn't wonder why you were fine with showing her off but not me."

"Aww, Duck. Sam is just my assistant. She means nothing to me. I thought I was proving a point, but I know now I was just being an asshole. I never meant to hurt you. I swear. Will you ever be able to forgive me?"

The pain of that night at Ava's rushes through me, and suddenly, I'm angry again. "I know who the hell she is, Marius. It's the fact that you thought it was okay for you to bring her to the party that was the problem."

"I know. I get it. Honestly, I do. Just tell me you think you can forgive me. That's all I need to hear."

"And what if I can't?"

Until this very moment, I wasn't able to entertain the thought that I wouldn't forgive him, but what if I can't? What if all that's happened is too much?

As soon as I ask him that question, I'm met with the saddest expression I've ever seen on anyone's face. "Duck, you have to forgive me. You just have to. This can't be the end of us."

"I don't know, Marius."

"You love me, right?"

My eyes fill with tears at hearing him ask me that. "I do love you. I wouldn't have married you if I didn't love you."

His face lights up. "I've loved you since that first day, Duck. You knocked me off my feet, and I've never been the same again. I know I've screwed up, but please remember all the good times we've had. There have been some, haven't there?"

I laugh at the memory of the two of us eating Chinese food and Marius utterly failing at using chopsticks. He was so frustrated by his inability to handle those two pieces of wood.

"What? What's so funny?"

"I was thinking about us eating Chinese that one night and you practically throwing the chopsticks across the room when you couldn't figure out how to use them."

"Yeah, I'm more of a fork kind of guy, but you walked over and stood by my side to help me learn how to use them. I'm still not good at chopsticks, but I'm better because you helped me."

He stops and then adds, "I'm a better man and a better person because of you, Duck. Losing you would mean losing the best thing in my life."

My heart breaks hearing him like this. I love this man. I'm crazy about him. I don't want to lose him any more than he wants to lose me.

Marius takes both of my hands in his and holds them, almost as if he's afraid if he doesn't that I'll run away. "I just need to hear you think you can forgive me. That's it, Eden. If you can't, I don't know what I'll do."

As much as I wish I could simply walk away from him and never forgive what he's done, that's simply not possible. Not with how I feel about him. Even sitting here in this neutral space in our home and in these horrible chairs we both hate makes me want to take him into my arms and never let him go again.

"I think I can forgive you," I say in a quiet voice.

His eyes get big, and his face lights up with pure joy.

"That's all I needed to hear. You're going to see being married to me is a good thing from now on."

"It wasn't bad before, Marius. It wasn't enough of a marriage. That's all."

He stands up and then leans down to kiss me. "Now I know what I have to do. I think I heard Ava come back, so go enjoy your ice cream together. I have to go."

What?

Now I'm confused. He came here to apologize for all that he did and to find out if I can forgive him for being such an absent husband, and the first thing he thinks to do to prove his love is leave me again?

"Where are you going?" I ask as he starts down the stairs.

Marius looks back at me and gives me a big smile. "To make you see why you should forgive me. I love you, Duck! Never doubt that."

And with those lovely words, he bolts downstairs, leaving me unsure what the hell just happened.

When I get downstairs, Ava is waiting with bowls of mint chocolate chip ice cream for us. "Hey, Marius looked happy when he left. He even apologized to me and said he deserved me smacking him. What happened?"

I sit down at the island and dig my spoon into a big scoop of ice cream. After I let it melt in my mouth, I answer her as truthfully as I can. "I have no idea. He said he was sorry. He told me he loved me. He asked me if I could ever forgive him, and when I said I think so, he jumped up and said he had to go."

Ava stops eating and shakes her head. "Where?"

"I have no idea. He said he knows what he has to do

now to make him forgive me, and then he practically ran down the stairs. Should I be afraid he thinks everything is better and he doesn't have to do anything else?"

My friend smiles and scoops up a spoonful of ice cream from her bowl. "I think you should be ready for him to do something ridiculously big. Matthias does that when we have fights. One time, after we had a huge argument about him working every day, he bought me my car. I would have been fine with some flowers and an apology, but he thought saying sorry and handing me the keys to a brand new car was what I needed."

As I dip my spoon into my melting ice cream, I smile and joke, "I like the car I have already. I don't need a car."

Ava levels her gaze on my face. "Eden, he bought you this penthouse when you said you didn't want to go to hotels anymore. Marius is obviously a man who likes to go big."

"I guess he took go big or go home literally, although I guess it should be go big and go back home for him."

"This ice cream is delicious, Duck. Am I allowed to call you that? It's cute, and I've never though of you as cute."

Shaking my head, I smile. "No, that's a Marius King thing. I'm still regular old Eden to you and the rest of the world."

I don't tell her the truth why she can't call me by his nickname for me. She'd understand, but I want to keep that private.

The reason no one but Marius can call me Duck is that's his unique name for me. It's a special thing only between us.

So what is that man going to do to convince me to forgive him? I don't need a car or a house, and we've taken vacations around the world so I can't imagine where he might think of us going now. He'll probably go with jewelry.

Maybe I'll get an engagement ring finally.

CHAPTER NINETEEN

*M*arius

NOW THAT I KNOW MY DUCK CAN FORGIVE ME, I'VE got to make some plans. This can't be some lame forgiveness tour we go on. No way. My wife deserves the best.

Believe it or not, this is one of the few times I've thought of her like that. Most of the time, I think of her as Duck. I did call her my wife the night we got married, but since then, not much.

That's about to change.

As I drive along the very road that nearly took my youngest brother from me last New Year's, I think back to that night she and I stopped in at that little chapel in Vegas. I hadn't planned on asking her to marry me that day, but something about how much fun we had that week made me think Eden should be my wife.

I roll over and open my eyes, but I'm alone in bed. I can't believe Duck's up already. What time is it?

So much for me having a hollow leg and handling my liquor. My head is pounding, and I feel like a bus hit me. And then backed up over me again.

What I need is water. Gallons of water.

I swing my legs off the bed and practically throw myself off the mattress to get up. No dizziness. Well, that's good. Maybe I'm not hungover.

The moment I stand up I know that's a lie. I'm so fucking hungover. Just standing up makes my head feel like it wants to explode.

Where is the water? Not that I would know the answer to that question. I haven't had a sip of the damn stuff in the past five days. Perhaps subsisting on room service and whiskey isn't the best way to live life.

But what a way it is, I think with a smile.

I take a few steps across the room and consider where I can find water to cure the cottonmouth I'm currently sporting. There's water in the bathroom sink. No, thanks. Bathroom water always tastes awful.

A few more steps lead me out to the living room where I know I saw some bottles of water this week. Where, though? Maybe the bar? That seems as good a place as any to check.

I thankfully find two bottles and proceed to down them like a man who just crawled in from the damn desert. Wide awake, I look around for Eden but don't see her anywhere. Then again, this suite is pretty big, so she could be here and I just can't see her.

"Duck!" I call out. "Where are you?"

No response.

Did she leave me? I thought we were having a good time. The four orgasms she had last night would usually mean she'd be here when I woke up. Maybe I needed to give her five.

Just then, the door opens and she comes walking in looking incredible. That's probably because she hasn't been drinking all week. Maybe I should try going on the wagon too.

"Where have you been, Duck?"

She holds up two shopping bags and grins. "I didn't want to wake you up, but I thought since I've got a couple more days here and nothing good to wear that I should get some clothes. The boutique on the main floor has the cutest dresses! Here, look!"

I sit down on the sofa as she pulls out a white dress with pale pink flowers along the hem. Or maybe those are hearts. I don't know. All I do know is she loves it and will look incredible in it since she always looks good no matter what she wears. The second dress is a longer one and black with a huge slit up the side. A little more formal but it'll still look great.

She sets the bag down without showing me the rest of what she bought. "I won't bore you with the other things I got. Are you okay? You don't look right."

Running my hand over the top of my head, I mumble, "Hung way over. I'll be okay after a shower, though."

We fall into a strange silence considering we've spent every day having sex for hours on end all week. My excuse for being quiet is I'm hungry. What's hers?

"Everything okay?" I ask, wondering why she's still standing so far away.

She lets out a heavy sigh. "Ava texted me."

"Oh, yeah? What's new back at the old King place?" I ask, attempting a joke but sort of failing in my condition.

"I don't know. I'm too bothered by the fact that I had to lie to her."

"What did you tell her?"

Duck's shoulders sag like she's carrying the weight of the world on them. "I told her I was having a good time."

"And that was a lie?" I ask, trying not to let my feelings get hurt since they're about the only damn things about me that don't ache.

Eden stares at me and twists her face into a grimace that's sort of cute. I don't tell her that since my experience with women has shown they like to think they're really terrifying when they're upset.

"No, that wasn't a lie. The lie was not telling her I'm here with you instead of Justin."

I open my arms and smile. "Come here, Duck. We can be miserable together."

She reluctantly walks over to the sofa and collapses onto the cushion next to me. "I'm not miserable, Marius. I just don't like lying to my best friend."

Pulling her into me, I hug her. She feels so good against my body that in no time I feel much better than I did just a few minutes ago.

"Let's focus on the positive. Your black eye is almost gone. Whatever that stuff was that the woman sold you in that store we went to Sunday night is doing the job. We've had a good time all week, and we still have a couple days more."

Eden leans back on the sofa and sighs again. "I guess. I just hate lying."

I sense she needs something more, so I wrap my arms around her as I think of how to make her happy again. Suddenly, it comes to me.

"What do you think about us getting married at one of those chapels we've seen around town?"

Her response is deafening silence. Since I've never proposed to anyone before, I'm not sure how this is supposed to work, but I don't think not saying a single word is good.

"I'm guessing you didn't hear me?"

Finally, she sits up and looks at me like I've grown two heads next to the one I was born with. I wait for her to say something, but she seems stunned or unwilling to speak.

"So is that a yes or no to getting married?"

"Are you seriously asking me to marry you? To become Eden King? Seriously?"

Now I'm not an expert, but I don't think her use of seriously twice is a good sign.

"Yeah."

"Do you love me, Marius?"

I see in her beautiful green eyes she thinks that's going to put an end to this marriage talk, but if she believes that, she's mistaken. I've been in love with her since that first night she stayed here with me. That I haven't told her that yet is only because I didn't find a good time to say it.

"Well, yeah."

"Pro tip, dear. When you want a woman to marry you, you tell her you love her first. Making her ask is just poor manners."

See that right there? I love when she's like that. She basically just called me a thoughtless jackass but in a way that sort of cushions the blow for me. How could I not love her?

I sit up, and thankfully, my head doesn't begin to pound when I lower myself to the floor. I don't have a ring, but we can remedy that after I get a shower.

"Are you seriously going down on one knee to propose we get married in some drive-thru chapel?" she asks wide-eyed.

Looking up at her, I smile. "I don't feel like renting a car, but if you're really into a drive-thru wedding, I can get one. In the meantime, Eden, will you marry me?"

Her mouth drops open like she's surprised, which seems odd since I've already asked her to marry me not two minutes ago. It's probably the down-on-one-knee thing. It's a little old fashioned, but I like it.

"Marius, you still haven't told me you love me."

I'm really not great at this. Maybe if I had done it a few times before I'd be more practiced, but this is my first time asking anyone to marry me.

"Duck, I love you. I've never had a week like this. I haven't laughed this much in my entire life. I've been wearing a smile every day since we got together."

She rolls her eyes at me. "That's the sex, baby."

Again, how could I not love her?

"You make me happy, Duck, so I want you to marry me. Will you marry me?"

"You're crazy."

Not exactly the response I was looking for.

"So that's a no?" I ask, not even trying to hide how hurt I am right now.

She shakes her head and sighs. "I think I must be crazy, but I love you too, Marius. Yes, I will marry you."

I stand up feeling like the king of the world. Pulling her up off the sofa, I take her in my arms and kiss her. I've never wanted to marry any of the women I've dated. I don't know what it is about this one, but I'm enchanted by her. I want to spend the rest of my life with her.

"So we're getting married. You can wear that white dress."

Eden leans away from me and smiles. "It sounds like you have this all figured out."

I wish that was the case, but I'm pretty much flying blind here. All I know is when this week ends, I don't want to live without my Duck.

Remembering that day makes me smile. I've never regretted for even a single moment marrying my wife. I know it doesn't seem that way, but I don't and never have. I'm not sure we have the perfect love you read about in books and see in movies. I don't care if we do. What I know is I love her and she loves me.

Now to figure out how to show her that so she sees I'd be lost without her.

By the time I get back to the house, I'm still unsure how I'm going to prove my love. Matthias is sitting in the kitchen with Matty asleep in his arms, and my brother looks like he's about to pass out too.

When I sit down at the table, he straightens up and looks around like he expects Ava to walk through the door any minute. The baby remains fast asleep, thankfully.

"Hey, what happened?" Matthias whispers sleepily. "Did you get the girl?" he jokes.

I'd be pissed if he didn't sound exactly like I would in this very instance. "I will. Not to worry. What's going on here?" I ask, pointing at his younger son.

He looks down and smiles at his namesake. "Lynn has Theo upstairs, but this little guy was making it impossible for his big brother to sleep, so I brought him down here."

"Have you guys considered the idea that they need two separate rooms?" I ask, wondering why with all the bedrooms in this house they haven't tried that solution to the no-sleeping problem plaguing them.

Matthias blows the air out of his lungs and shrugs.

"We wanted to keep them together like Mom and Dad did with Theo and me."

Ah, that explains it. My brother isn't remembering the past as clearly as he thinks.

"Dude, Mom and Dad didn't put you guys into a room together until I came along. Dad used to talk about how they had all these rooms, but he thought young boys should share a room. You two had separate nurseries, and when I was born, I went into yours and you and Theo were moved into his room to share."

My brother stares at me for a long moment and then shakes his head. "Holy shit! You're right. We've been torturing ourselves the whole time for something that never happened. I have to tell Ava this little guy needs to move into my old room."

"Sounds good. Hey, how is Eleanor tonight? I feel like with everything that's been happening that I haven't been paying enough attention to her."

Finally, my brother has something to smile about. "She's good. It's been impossible trying to keep her from cooking, but she promised she won't overexert herself. Her doctor has her on some new medication, and he's happy with the way things are working out so far. He still wants her to relax, so I'm thinking about hiring a cook."

I shake my head, unhappy with that idea and sure Eleanor will hate it too. "Matthias, you can't take that away from her. Eleanor loves to cook. You bring someone new in, and she's going to be crushed. Don't do it. If she needs to take it easy for more time, then I'll help in any way I can and I'm sure Ronan and Kellen feel the same way. Just don't take that away from her."

All the while I'm speaking, he nods his head, and I see his expression grow sad. "I should have realized that. What the hell is wrong with me?"

With a smile, I point to the ten pound bundle of joy wearing a blue sleeper with a dump truck on his belly. "You're running on too little sleep, man. Get that kid into your old bedroom and stat!"

"You know that room is close to the room you stay in."

I shrug, knowing I won't be there for much longer. "Not to worry. I'm making plans to sweep Eden off her feet so I won't be needing to stay here anymore. You and Ava can finally have your house back."

"We like having you here. I know her slapping you across the face doesn't seem like we do, but we enjoy when you stay with us."

"I know, and when I was worried about Ronan, it made sense. I have a place to live, though, and it's with my wife. It's time I start living there full-time."

A slow smile spreads across my brother's face. "Look at you being all responsible. So what's your plan to get her back?"

I don't answer for a few seconds because I'm not really sure. I think my older brother can help me out, though.

"Not exactly settled on a plan yet, but if you're willing to give me a hand with a few things, I think I have something that will work. You game?"

Matthias nods as he stands up from the table. "Let me put this little guy down in his crib, and I'll be right back. I'm curious to know what you're planning."

He leaves me wondering if what I've got in mind is

enough. I need this to work so my Duck sees that we belong together.

I smile as I remember that's sort of how I felt the day we got married at that cute little wedding chapel in Vegas.

Eden stops at the end of the sidewalk leading to The Little Wedding Chapel of Las Vegas and lets go of my hand. I turn around to see if she's having second thoughts and notice she's looking down at her dress.

"You look incredible, like always, Duck."

She doesn't look up at me for a long moment, but finally she lifts her head, and I see worry in her eyes. Is it that she doesn't want to marry me, or is it that she's having second thoughts about us getting married here in Vegas?

"Are you doing this for some reason I don't know about, Marius?" she asks in a hushed voice.

I don't have to think about the answer to that question for more than a second, so I shake my head and say, "No reason other than I'm crazy about you. Are you getting cold feet?"

Eden steps forward so she's right in front of me and stares up into my eyes. "No. It's just that this all happened so fast. What if we're making a mistake?"

"Then you'll be a very wealthy woman when you divorce me and take half of everything I have?" I say as a joke.

A joke that lands like a lead balloon.

Her expression grows dark, and once more, she can't seem to look at me and instead prefers the concrete sidewalk. "I never wanted to be with you because of your money."

I slip my finger under her chin and lift it so she sees my face when I say, "I wasn't serious there. I don't think you wanted to be with me for my money."

"You said it, though, so some part of you must think that."

Fuck. I swore to myself I wouldn't let my insecurities from Maia get in the way when and if I met someone I fell for, and here I am doing just that.

Another couple stops behind us, so I smile and wave them ahead since I have a feeling Eden and I are going to need a few minutes. I take her by the hand and walk a few feet away so we can have some privacy.

Alone, or as alone as two people can be in a city that never seems to sleep, I cradle her face and kiss her before I confess the truth about how I feel. She looks into my eyes, and I swear I see fear in them. That can't be good.

"Duck...Eden, I'm crazy about you. I've had the best week of my life, and it's all because of you. I don't know how it happened, but at some point this week in between the gambling and the laughing and the sex, I fell in love with you. I've only loved one other woman in my life, and that went south pretty bad. So I swore off love and dedicated myself to being single and having a good time. I don't know how, but just being with you this week changed all of that."

"Marius, what happened with Maia? She's the other woman you loved, isn't she?"

I nod and let out a heavy sigh. Nothing like your wedding day to drudge up the worst feelings you've ever experienced.

Hanging my head, I answer, "I heard she was with me because of my family's money. When I asked her if that was true, I saw by the look on her face that it was. She tried to say it wasn't, but I knew the truth."

If you think that part was hard, you have no idea how fucking impossible the next part is to say.

Eden nudges my arm, so I look up, knowing I can't escape telling her everything that happened. "I'm sorry you had to deal with that. For what it's worth, she never said anything like that to me. I thought she was crazy about you."

I blow the air out of my lungs. "Yeah, so crazy that she slept with Theo not two weeks after we broke up. That's some great love there, huh?"

She kisses me softly and whispers, "I'm sorry, Marius. You deserved better than that from her and your brother. Between you and me and the rest of Las Vegas, I always thought Theo was a dick. He took advantage of Ava's good heart. She wouldn't even hear a bad word against him, and trust me, I had some to say."

Her defense of me makes me smile. "Well, that's another thing we have in common. That means we definitely should get married."

With a smile, Eden giggles. "I guess we should. I just want you to know I would never do that to you."

"Well, I don't have any more single brothers, so I don't think you can."

She rolls her eyes at my attempt to be funny. "Even if you did have some single brothers, I still wouldn't do that to you."

"I knew I loved you for a good reason. Beautiful, smart, sexy, and kind. You've got it all, Duck."

She smiles and takes a deep breath in, letting it out slowly before she says, "I guess we better go in. We've got some I do's to say."

I take her hand in mine and walk up the sidewalk to the front door of The Little Wedding Chapel of Las Vegas. We step inside, and I swear I've never seen so much white in my life. White walls. White church pews. White carpeting. Hanging from the ceiling, which is also painted white, are two crystal chandeliers. At the altar, white flowers complete the all-white look with just a little greenery.

Leaning over toward Eden, I whisper, "I don't know why, but I wasn't expecting this to be so white."

She giggles and whispers back to me, "Especially since this is Las Vegas, Sin City. I'm surprised it's not a lot more red."

The couple ahead of us says their I do's and kiss, so now it's our turn. I squeeze Eden's hand and take a deep breath because my heart is racing a mile a minute. If ever I wanted to back out, now's the time.

But as I look at her in that white dress with pink flowers, all I can think is I'm the luckiest man in the world to have the chance to marry this woman.

"Ready?"

My Duck smiles and nods. "I am. Let's do this."

Fifteen minutes later, she and I walked out of The Little Wedding Chapel of Las Vegas as Mr. and Mrs. Marius King, and although it may seem otherwise, I've been happier than I ever thought possible being her husband.

Now to show Eden how much I want to make her happy.

CHAPTER TWENTY

den

ALONE NOW THAT AVA HAS GONE BACK HOME TO HER husband and babies, I wander around the penthouse wondering what to do with myself. I don't understand why Marius left like he did, but then again, Ava was still here and she did slap his face. She didn't mean anything by that, though. She was just upset and worried about me. If he heard her talking about him earlier, he'd know she's still one of his biggest fans.

I want to believe he'll be coming back here tonight, but something in the way he was acting makes me think this will be another night of me sleeping alone. That might be for the best, though, since I never have the kind of strength to oppose him when it comes to sex, and he knows it. The problem is, though, that great sex will only confuse the entire situation between us.

The phone connected to the lobby desk downstairs rings, so I pick it up. It's not Marius wanting to come up. He wouldn't need Conrad to ask permission.

"Mrs. King, there's a young woman down here who's asking to come up. She says her name is Samantha McCann. May I send her up?" he asks in his very stuffy yet kind way.

I could ask him what she looks like, but even though I don't know Sam's last name, I'm sure it's her since I remember Marius mentioning her name in passing a few times. I don't know what she wants, but she's likely to be disappointed when she finds it's just me here.

"Thank you, Conrad. Please send her up."

Sam and I have never actually spoken. I've heard about her working with Marius, but we've spent exactly zero minutes together in the two years I've been married to him.

Nothing like two perfect strangers having a first meeting on what's been the worst day of one of their lives.

The elevator doors open, and I watch her step out, her blond head swiveling back and forth as she takes in the impressive penthouse he bought me. Dressed in a cute pair of black Bermuda shorts, a pale green t-shirt, and adorable black sandals, she looks cute.

As much as I may not be in the mood to play hostess, I guess I have to. "Hello, Sam. I'm Eden."

I could have tacked on the fact that I'm her boss's wife, but that seems unnecessary. She must know who I am by now.

She turns to look at me, and I see instant recognition in her eyes. "Oh, hi. I'm Sam, Marius's assistant. Well, I guess you know that since you called me by my name. Is he here?"

"No. Would you like something to drink?" I ask, unsure what she's doing here but desperately needing a glass of something right about now.

I turn on my heel and head toward the bar in the living room. Sam follows me, neither one of us attempting to make small talk.

When I stop in front of the bar and begin to pour myself a glass of bourbon, I turn to look at Sam and ask, "What can I get you?"

Instead of answering me, she practically collapses onto the new oversized ottoman I bought, the only comfortable piece of furniture in the entire room since I haven't gotten around to replacing all of this minimalist stuff. I watch in confusion as she covers her face with her hands and begins to cry.

Terrific. Now the woman my husband brought to the party is sobbing in front of me. This day just keeps getting better and better.

I pour her a glass of bourbon and walk over to sit on the ottoman with her. As she continues to cry, I nudge her and say, "Here. Drink some of this. You'll feel better."

She sniffles and turns to look at me. Her mascara runs in streaks down her cheeks, and her nose is bright red from crying. I recognize that look all too well. How many times have I cried over some guy? I may be nearly a decade older than her, but I have a feeling I know what's going on with Sam.

"I don't really drink," she says as she takes the glass from me. "Will I get drunk?"

Chuckling, I nod and lift my glass to take a drink of bourbon. "If you're lucky. Cheers!"

Now that I've gotten her to stop crying, I wait until she takes a few sips of her drink before handing her a tissue. "Here, clean your face. Sam, what are you doing here, and why are you crying?"

She hesitates and then answers as she rubs the mascara off her skin, "Marius texted me that he's letting me go because he can't be around me anymore. I just don't understand."

That makes her start crying again, so while I wait for her to calm down, I take another drink. Why am I not surprised he sent her that text? Men can be such idiots sometimes.

"It's okay. I'll talk to him. Wives have a way of getting through where others can't."

As I say that, she stares at me with her mouth hanging open. When I finish, she stammers out, "Wi-wi-wife? What?"

"Yeah. I'm Mrs. King. Marius and I have been married for two years. Don't feel bad that he never mentioned it to you. My best friend Ava, the woman whose house the party was at, just found out today."

That causes another bout of crying that lasts a few minutes. That husband of mine is having a wonderful effect on people today. I served him with divorce papers. Ava slapped him across the face. And Sam is bawling her eyes out over him.

It's been a hell of a day for Marius.

When Sam finally regains her composure, she turns her body to face me and frowns. "I'm so sorry. That's why you left the party so early. I had no idea he was married. I would have never gone with him to that party if I knew. I'm so embarrassed."

I set my glass down on the coffee table nearby and take hers to join it before opening my arms to hug her. "Please, don't worry. I know Marius wasn't looking to cheat on me. He was trying, in his stupid man way, to prove a point. That he involved you in that was wrong. I'm sorry. Come here."

She isn't sure at first, but I suspect her desire to feel better wins over everything else she's feeling, and she practically collapses into my hold. As I thought would happen, she begins to cry again, so I gently pat her back.

"It's okay. I'll talk to him about your job. As for the two of us, we're good. I don't blame you, Sam. My husband is like most men. He means well, but sometimes he misses the mark."

"He's always been the best boss I've ever had," she says in between sobs against my shoulder. "I didn't know all those times I thought he was flirting with me that he was married. I'm so sorry."

"Oh, it's okay. I'm sure he was flirting. That's Marius for you."

Sam leans back away from me and wipes under her eyes. "I swear we never did anything. He never made any moves. He didn't even want to kiss me when I was leaving that day after the party. I swear."

"I believe you. Marius isn't a bad man. I'm sure he never meant to make you cry. As I said, he thinks he's doing good things, and most of the time he does. Like this penthouse he bought me."

Looking around at the beautiful home he gave me, I smile. "I mentioned once that I wanted somewhere better than where we were, and a week later, he brought me here and said it was mine."

Sam practically gawks as she looks at my home. "You're very lucky then. I'd love to have someone buy me a place like this. You should see my apartment. It's a two bedroom with one bathroom I share with two other girls just so I can afford my junky car, although Marius said he was going to give me a year's salary as severance pay."

That sounds like him. The man knows how to spend money. That's for sure.

"I think he's going to want to keep you as his assistant, Sam. Whether you want to stay working for a man who lied to you is entirely your choice."

She's quiet, and I think I know why, so I continue. "You care about him, don't you?"

Nodding, she looks down at her lap. "Yes," she answers barely above a whisper.

"You love him, don't you?" I ask, seeing in her what I've seen in my own reflection many times before.

Still avoiding my gaze, she says in a tiny voice, "I thought so, but now I feel terrible. Is that how love is supposed to feel?"

Oh, to be twenty years old again.

"Pretty much. Love is basically the highest highs and the lowest lows. Somewhere in between those, you hope you find some happiness. You don't have to be uncomfortable about being in love with Marius. It's something we have in common."

That finally gets her to look up, and she gives me a tentative smile. "You don't hate me?"

"How could I? You care about someone who means

the world to me. In truth, I completely understand that you'd fall in love with him. He's funny and sexy and sweet in a way most men can't even hope to be. I fell for him, and I'm supposed to be older and wiser, so how could I think you wouldn't do the same?"

She gives me a big smile and lets out a heavy sigh. "Thank you for not hating me. I bet most wives wouldn't have even let me come up. I can see why Marius married you. You're gorgeous and smart, but most of all, you're really nice."

"I have my moments. The truth is I had a choice when I heard you were downstairs. I could have chosen the path that included me turning you away, but I needed to make sure you knew I didn't blame you for that night at the party. Here's a little more truth too. I can be a huge bitch, but I'm proud to say I'm never a woman who attacks another woman over a man. That's high school bullshit, and as you can clearly see, I'm a long time away from high school."

Sam leans over and grabs her glass of bourbon, downing the rest of it in one gulp. "This may be the drink talking, but I think you're beautiful and sweet. I'm pretty sure most women wouldn't have wanted to talk to me at all after what happened."

"I know. Far too often, women go after other women instead of the men who are doing the wrong. We're good, Sam. I'll talk to Marius and remind him of how much he likes your help. It won't take much for him to realize he should keep you as his assistant, but it's entirely up to you if you stay."

She doesn't say anything for a long moment before

she asks, "Did you two have a fight or something? I thought he'd be here."

I debate with myself how much of the truth I should tell my new friend and choose very little. Sam doesn't need to know much of what happened today.

"Let's just say I'm forcing Marius to take a good look at what he's been doing lately and leave it at that."

"I hope I can be as strong as you someday. I always end up brokenhearted with guys. I do exactly what they want, make sure to like the things they like, and I never give them a hard time, and it always turns out bad."

Ah, Sam's a pick-me girl. They always think the guys are crazy about them when they abandon their entire personality to be just like their boyfriends, but it never works out. Men, especially those like Marius, want a challenge, not a lapdog with no opinions of her own.

Standing from the ottoman, I grab my glass of bourbon. "My strength is the kind that comes from years of hating even the idea of being weak. Do you know the day Marius and I first got together it was after my then boyfriend pulled me by my hair and punched me in the eye because he thought my dress was too slutty? Don't beat yourself up too much. That was only two years ago. You'll get stronger. You either get stronger, or you get hurt all the time. Just remember that even when you become someone's girlfriend, you're still you."

I've never had a younger sister to say things like that to. Spending this time with Sam, I wish I had.

As we walk out to the kitchen, she says, "Thank you for being so great about everything, Eden."

I shrug, secretly pleased as punch that she thinks I'm cool. I would have been a great big sister.

"I'll tell you what. Give me your number, and I'll give you mine. We can do coffee sometime, okay?"

Her face lights up with happiness, and she quickly tells me her number. I put it into my phone, and then she does the same with mine. I didn't plan on making a new friend tonight, but it seems like I have.

Sam smiles and steps forward to give me a hug. "Marius is lucky to have you. I hope he knows that."

"Well, if he doesn't, I'll be sure to remind him," I say with a chuckle.

She looks at me and nods. "Me too. Thanks, Eden. I guess I better go."

"Don't worry, Sam. I'll talk to Marius. If you decide you don't want to keep working for him, that's his loss. Remember that."

She smiles before walking to the elevator and pressing the button to go downstairs. The doors immediately open, and after she steps inside, she turns around to look at me.

"I hope we can have coffee soon," I say and mean it.

"Oh, I'd like that. Have a great night!" she says as the doors close and she disappears.

I stand in my kitchen wondering how many times a wife in this city has had to console another woman because of her husband. I'd bet a lot. The difference is this man is my husband.

Sam meant no harm. I don't blame her for falling in love with Marius. How could I?

CHAPTER TWENTY-ONE

 arius

Noise from the kitchen wakes me, so I throw on some clothes and head downstairs. Matthias and I talked a lot about what I should do to win Eden back. Now I just have to convince Ava to go along with it.

Assuming she doesn't want to slap me again.

I chuckle at the idea of my sister-in-law, a woman who's half my size, getting rough with me. I deserved it, though. Ava's always been very kind to me, and I hurt someone she loves.

Let's hope she isn't interested in round two this morning. That'll make my winning back Eden difficult.

Walking into the kitchen, I see Matthias with the boys and Eleanor but no Ava. Did she spend the night at the penthouse with Eden?

"Good morning, Marius," Eleanor says as she opens a cabinet to get a plate for my breakfast.

I stop dead and give her my best disapproving look. Since I'm pretty much a hedonist, I don't disapprove of much in this world, but her overworking is one of the big things I'm not a fan of these days.

"Why are you up and around doing work? We're supposed to be helping you, not vice versa," I say as I walk over to her and give her a hug.

When I step back, she looks at me strangely. "You seem different today, Marius. Is something changed?"

Behind me, Matthias says with a laugh, "I'm not sure Eleanor has heard the news that you're a married man, Marius."

The shock written all over her face followed by her mouth hanging open tells me that she and the boys are the only ones who didn't know. "I guess the cat's out of the bag now."

"You're married? Who is your wife? Where is she?"

I look back at Matthias to see him grinning from ear to ear. "Are you happy? You've upset Eleanor."

He throws his head back in laughter. "Nobody upset her. She just can't believe you're married and still sleeping here. Want to explain it to her? It's quite the story, Eleanor."

The woman who's been my only mother figure since I was a young teenager dries her hands on the yellow towel beside the sink and waits for me to say something. I really don't want to tell her the story about how Eden and I got together, but since Matthias has already mentioned my being married, I'm going to have to come up with a shortened version.

I look into Eleanor's pale blue eyes and see real concern in them. It's nice to know that while the rest of my family thinks I'm a fool who fucked up royally, at least one person who knows me all my life is worried about me.

"Eden, Ava's friend. I married her two years ago. We kept it quiet until the other day."

I stop there, but my brother says what I was hoping to keep out of the story for today. "Yeah, when she served him with divorce papers."

After throwing Matthias a dirty look, I turn back to see Eleanor's eyes are full of even more worry now. "It's okay. We're not getting divorced. I'm going to fix things."

She doesn't say anything for a while, but finally she smiles. "I've always loved her eyes. She has the most unique green eyes I've ever seen in my life. And I know she's a lovely girl since Ava thinks the world of her."

Leave it to Eleanor to be positive about the mess my life has become.

"But what's this about divorce? Are you getting divorced?" she asks as she reaches for my hand.

She gives it a tiny squeeze while I explain things as much as I can. "No, there's not going to be a divorce. Things are going to be good from now on."

Then a darkness comes over Eleanor, and she asks, "Wait, didn't I see her with that man Ava set her up with at the party?"

Looks like there's no escaping this explanation.

"Yes, but don't worry. That was all my fault because I didn't want her to tell anyone about us getting married, so she had to lie to Ava. That's why she was with that guy."

Matthias stands up from the table and takes both boys in his arms. "I'm going to leave on that note since I'm pretty sure I've heard this story before."

Alone with Eleanor, I sit down at the table in the seat Matthias just vacated while Eleanor sits across from me. I see by the confusion on her face that she doesn't understand.

"It's really okay. Honest. We're going to be fine. I promise."

She shakes her head and sighs. "I've always hoped you would find someone like your brothers have, Marius. I know it would make your parents thrilled beyond belief to know you've settled down with someone you love. Do you love her, though?"

I smile, unable to keep how I feel about my Duck a secret anymore. "I do. More than you can imagine. I made a mistake by not wanting to let the world know, but that's all over. I bought her a penthouse when she said she wanted a place for us. I'd do anything to see her happy, Eleanor."

Even that doesn't make her smile, though. "Money doesn't buy happiness, honey. I hope you know that."

Max and Elizabeth King gave us a lot growing up, but the one thing they drilled into our heads day after day was the fact that even though money could do a great deal, it couldn't replace the important things in life like friends and family and love. I know Eleanor was there when our parents would say things like that. My guess is she thinks the lesson didn't sink in with me.

"I do know that."

"Why didn't you want the world to know you married that beautiful girl, Marius? I'm sitting here trying to imagine any reason, but I can't come up with a single one."

I hang my head and answer, "I was being stupid. I wanted her all to myself. I didn't want to risk having to share her with anyone else. It was wrong."

"Ahhh. This is what happened with Theo coming back to haunt you, isn't it?"

When I lift my head, I see Eleanor knows the truth about Theo, Maia, and me. "How do you know about that?"

Finally, she smiles. "I've lived here all your life. I've lived here since before any of you boys were born. I may not say much about the things that you all do, but I notice what happens around here. I was upstairs cleaning when you and Theo had your conversation in the game room that day."

Reluctantly, I have to admit the truth. "Then you know what he did and how I never forgave him for it."

Eleanor reaches across the table to softly touch the top of my hand. "Oh, honey, you can't keep carrying that around with you forever. Theo wasn't like the rest of you boys. He was more like your great-grandfather."

"The one who almost went to jail for swindling people out of all their money during the Depression?"

Nodding, she answers, "The very one. Your mother fell in love with the name Theodore and thought it would be a nice nod to your great-grandfather. She had no idea he was a bastard who cheated people when they needed to be treated with kindness the most. When it all came out, both your parents were mortified. Your father was embarrassed to share a last name with him. But that's why they never called your brother Theodore. From the moment they learned all about how awful Theodore King was, they always called him Theo. I guess now we know that didn't change the fact that of the two men named Theodore in the King family, neither one of them was a good man."

For a moment, I wonder if I should ask her if she knows what Theo did to Matthias and Ava, but I'm sure she does. Eleanor likely knows about most of the things that have gone on in this house.

"I guess I've been living with what he did for all this time, but you're right. I can't keep carrying it around with me forever. Not if it's going to hurt Eden."

"No, you can't. I've always thought you would find someone perfect for you. I just worried you wouldn't want to let them in. You've always played your cards very close to the vest, so I guess I'm not surprised you kept your marriage a secret for so long."

"Well, no more. That's in the past. Future Marius and Eden will be fine. I just have to win her back."

She smiles and says, "I noticed you didn't say easy peasy like you do about most things."

"No, but not to worry. I've got a plan."

I have a lot of faults, but lying to myself isn't one of them. Getting Eden back won't be easy. Yes, she said she can forgive me, but now I have to make sure I don't blow it when I do what I have planned.

Eleanor gives my hand another gentle squeeze. "Oh yeah? Well, honey, I hope it works because I want to see you happy."

"Thanks. Between you, me, and the lamppost, if my plan works, you'll be one of the first to know."

With nothing short of sly grin, she says, "I've never doubted you could charm the birds out of the trees, Marius. You've been like this since you were a little boy."

"I thought Kellen was the charming one. That's why he's your favorite."

That comment gets me an odd look, and then Eleanor cranes her neck to check if anyone is nearby in the hallway. When she's sure we're alone, she leans forward toward me.

"Kellen always needed someone to champion him. I promised your mother when she was dying that I'd be here for all you boys, but she made me swear I'd do two additional things. She wanted me to make sure that Kellen always had a fan in me. She didn't have to since I've always loved all of you, but she was worried because Matthias would be getting the job Kellen should have had. She was concerned he'd lose his way."

That brother always could get the women in this house to do what he wanted.

"The second thing she made me promise had to do with you."

"Really?"

It's not that I'm completely shocked my mother may have mentioned me to Eleanor on her death bed. I was one of her children, and she seems to have had worries about all of us. It's just that hearing it today sort of surprises me.

Eleanor nods, smiling. "Yes. Your mother so wanted to be around to see you all grow up, Marius. I've always felt it was incredibly cruel to let her see you five get so far and then rob her of watching you grow into men. When it came to you, she made me promise that I'd make sure you didn't get lost in the shuffle. You were always the one who kept so much to yourself, and in a group of five, that can mean being forgotten. Your mother knew what that was like because she was like that."

Hearing that stuns me. In my memories, my mother is always sweet and kind and completely open.

"I don't remember that."

"That's because you only saw her as she had to be. Elizabeth King had to play a lot of roles as the mother of five boys. Guidance counselor, nurse, referee, and those were just the ones she fulfilled on a daily basis. She put aside her nature to make sure you boys had a mother who was there for you."

For a moment, Eleanor stops and then she lets out a heavy sigh. "I wish she had lived long enough for you boys to know her as adults. You would have seen that she was very much like you. She opened up for her children because she knew that's what you needed, but your mother, like you, preferred to play her cards close to the vest. In fact, I think that's what made your father fall in love with her. She wasn't like other women he knew. That mystery was very appealing. You know how that is."

I smile at her compliment. "I wish she was around now. I know Ronan needed her this year."

"He's thankfully going to be fine. Now all we have to worry about is you," Eleanor says with more than a hint of apprehension in her voice.

Waving away any concern she has, I say, "It'll work out. I know it will."

Just as Eleanor begins to ask exactly how I'm going to make things work out with Eden, the kitchen door opens and Ava walks in. Her arms are filled with grocery bags, and she barely makes it to the counter to drop them off.

"What is this? I told the store we'd be getting things delivered for the next few months while I'm not going shopping," Eleanor says as she hurries across the room to where Ava has dropped off the overfilled plastic bags.

"Matthias told me we're going to need a lot more food for the next couple days, so I stopped at the store to get some things."

I look over at the ten bags she set on the counter and then at Ava. "Is the fifth army coming to stay?"

My sister-in-law doesn't respond, which could mean she didn't hear me or she's still upset with me. I'm hoping it's the former since I need to talk to her, and if I can't convince her to help me with my plan, I might be shit out of luck.

As the two of them start to put the haul away, I clear my throat and say, "Ava, can we talk?"

While she puts three gallons of milk in the refrigerator, she glances over at me. "I'm pretty busy."

Okay, she's still pissed at me.

"It's important."

Ava doesn't respond, so I add, "It has to do with Eden."

Just as I thought, she stops what she's doing and turns to face me. "Okay. Give me a minute."

"Do you want my help?"

Eleanor smiles at me, but Ava shuts me down. "We're fine."

I can't remember Ava ever being this icy with me. I didn't think she had it in her. Guess I was wrong.

Five minutes later, she and Eleanor finish putting away what looks like eight hundred dollars' worth of groceries, and Ava finally walks over to where I'm sitting. "Do you want to talk here or somewhere else?"

Suddenly, the thought of having this discussion around Eleanor seems like a bad idea. The last thing she needs is to see the two of us fighting, and I have a feeling Ava might not be a huge fan of my plan.

"How about we go outside?" I suggest.

"Back to the scene of the crime? Okay."

She marches out of the kitchen, and as I walk behind her, I look back and see Eleanor give me the crossed fingers sign. I have the sense I'm going to need more than luck in the next few minutes.

I follow Ava out to the patio, and when she sits down at the table, I take a seat across from her. She folds her arms across her chest, a distinctly bad sign. I don't have a choice, so I ignore her body language and launch into what I have to say.

"You're still angry with me, and I get that, but I need your help to get Eden back."

That seems like a good start, doesn't it? You'd think so, but the stony look on Ava's face says no.

When she doesn't say anything, I continue. "I'd like you to have a party here tomorrow night. Just the family. Matthias told me he thinks Kellen and Ronan are free, and you guys are always here, so—"

That's as far as I get.

Sitting up straight in her chair, she glares at me as

she says, "What would make you think I want to help you get my best friend back?"

Damn. I wasn't expecting that response. I don't exactly know what to say to that.

Ava doesn't wait for me to answer before she adds, "I spent hours with her, and I'll tell you what. I don't like seeing my friend sad, hiding under the covers, and watching that show she loves just hoping to see a guy she has to have a crush on since her husband isn't taking care of business."

Ouch.

My first instinct is to defend myself, but I get the feeling that would only irritate Ava more, so I focus on what's important for the moment.

"I want to make things up to her. I promise. I hate the idea that Eden is sad and I'm the reason for it. I swear, Ava, I'm going to make things right. I love her. I can't imagine my life without her."

Those aren't merely nice words, but my sister-in-law isn't impressed. Her arms still crossed, she says, "If you loved her so much, why did you hide her like someone you're ashamed of for two years?"

Okay, that's harsh. True, but harsh.

"I know I was wrong for what I did, Ava. I didn't want to hide Eden or anything like that, and I wasn't ashamed of her. I just loved having her to myself. I didn't have to share her with anyone, and you have no idea after being one of five all my life how great that was."

"So you got what you wanted while she was left sneaking around like some mistress nobody can know about. Do you have any idea what that must have felt like for her?"

Hanging my head, I nod. "I didn't, but I know now." I look up at her and add, "That's why I want to make things right."

Ava doesn't say anything to that, but I see by the serious look on her face that she's thinking of how she wants to respond. I know what I did was shitty. All I want to do is fix it.

"I remember Theo telling me that you did something like this to that Maia girl you were dating. He couldn't figure out why you pushed her away when she was so crazy about you. Have you considered the idea this is a problem you have, Marius?"

She could have mentioned anyone else's opinion, and I'd be fine, but that brother's? No fucking way.

Before I can stop myself, I snap, "Oh, Theo told you that? Did he happen to tell you that he knew I was still in love with her and he made a point of sleeping with her? Probably not. That would have ruined your opinion that he was perfect. Well, he wasn't. Maybe the problem I have is the last time I thought I was in love, one of my damn brothers thought it would be a good idea to fucking sleep with her, even though he knew I still was crazy about her."

All those words come out like some kind of manic train of thought, and when I finish talking, all I see is a look of horror on Ava's face. Fucking terrific. I guess I'm going to need a plan B.

Slowly, she slumps in her chair, shaking her head. "He wouldn't do that."

The words coming out of her mouth should sound defiant as she defends him, but there's doubt in her voice.

Maybe Ava does know that her best friend Theo wasn't the person she thought he was.

"Yes, he would. You know it. You don't want to admit it, but Theo was always like that."

Sadness fills her expression, making me wish I didn't say anything. I just couldn't stand her thinking that the reason I did what I did is because of a reason so meaningless like I just want my freedom.

Ava stays silent for a long time, but finally in a low voice like she doesn't want anyone to hear her admit it, she says, "I had no idea, Marius. Theo never told me anything about going with Maia. When did that happen?"

"Less than two weeks after we had our fight and broke up. He knew I was still crazy about her. That's what hurt the most."

"But he's gone. Matthias, Kellen, and Ronan would never do anything like Theo did."

I have to smile at how she doesn't understand. I'm not even sure I do. All I know is the first thing I thought about when Eden and I got together was how I needed to make sure to keep her to myself.

"He's gone, but the memory of how that felt isn't." I pause, and even though I know I shouldn't say what's on my mind, I don't stop myself. "Your buddy Theo wasn't the person he made himself out to be."

Ava blows the air out of her lungs and nods. "I know more than you think. Remember, I was the one he refused to talk to after he left. He never answered any of my texts or my calls. You have no idea how devastated I was that he could cut me out like that."

It's been years since that happened with Matthias,

Theo, and Ava, and still she tears up talking about him. He never did deserve Ava.

"Probably about as devastated as when I found out he slept with the girl I loved. There's no deep answer to why he did what he did to you and me. It's simple. Theo was selfish."

Again she nods. After another minute or so of silence, she smiles and says, "Well, I wasn't expecting this today. I guess we better start talking about that party you want us to have."

My mind races with all the ideas I have for getting Eden back, but before I start asking Ava to help with them, I say, "Thank you for being in my corner on this. I know it isn't easy, but I only want to make sure Eden knows how much I love her. I hope you believe that."

Ava reaches across the table and tenderly touches my hand. "She loves you. I know that. I want her to be happy, so whatever it takes, let's do it!"

I rub my hands together as I start telling her what I want to do. This is going to work. I know it.

This plan has to work.

CHAPTER TWENTY-TWO

den

MY DAY AT WORK INCLUDED ENOUGH FRUSTRATION for me to want to scream, so I'm happy to be back home by just before six. I barely have enough time to shower and change for Ava's little get-together that I suspect is some effort by Marius to make me forgive him. She wouldn't tell me what the party is about, so I figure she's hiding the real reason we're getting together on a Monday night.

It's so typical of Ava to want to play Cupid this one last time.

So Marius has convinced my best friend to help him. He really is quite the charmer. Not that Ava is a tough customer. She's a pushover when it comes to those King men. She has to be to let them crash at her house whenever they feel like it.

I pour myself a glass of wine and head up to the bedroom to get ready. It's nearly October, but Mother Nature still thinks it's summer. Ava should have put off that end-of-year party for a few weeks.

Setting my glass down on the dresser, I wonder if I should bring a bathing suit tonight. It will certainly be hot enough to swim, but I don't think I want to. If the party moves outside, I'll hang out on the patio while everyone else takes a dip.

I wish I knew what Marius had planned so I could know what to wear. Since I don't, I walk over to my closet and start choosing from my favorite outfits. I should probably just go with a sundress since in warm weather they're always a good choice, but I decide to check with Ava just in case what's going to happen tonight doesn't call for a dress.

Grabbing my phone out of my purse, I call her, and she answers almost immediately. "Eden, you're coming, aren't you?"

"Yeah, of course. I wouldn't miss one of your parties for my life. It's just that I'm unsure what I should wear. I'm not going to be doing anything strenuous, am I?"

She laughs at my question, which I guess gives me my answer. "Strenuous? Not that I know of, but if you and Marius make up, then what happens after might be considered strenuous."

As she giggles at her comment, I think about sex with Marius. I should correct her about that description. Strenuous would be the least of what happens with us. Exhausting, mind-blowing, and intense would be better descriptions.

I don't tell her that, though. I might not want to hide

my marriage to Marius King, but I guess I'm a little like him in that I don't want to share everything about us, even with my best friend. That's the reason I can forgive him.

"Okay, so if I wear a sundress, that will be okay? This isn't a formal to-do, is it?" I ask as I lift my teal blue dress with the cute black bows where the skinny straps meet the dress off the hanger.

"Yeah, that will be great. Wear the diamond necklace. I love that on you. You'll be here in time, won't you?" Ava asks, and I have the sense she's hiding something big from me.

"You know that was a gift from Marius."

She chuckles and says, "Now that I know you've been together for two years, I could guess that."

As I hold the dress up in front of me and look in the full-length mirror, I ask, "Hey, you don't have anything you want to tell me, do you? Ava, you know as well as anyone else in the world that I'm not a fan of people springing things on me. Marius isn't going to do anything like that, is he?"

"You mean like jumping out of a cake and surprising you?"

"No, like he's going to do something that scares me. I can handle a person surprising me, but I don't want to feel like I'm blindsided."

She doesn't answer for a few moments, which makes me worry even more, but then she says, "Oh, Eden, it's not anything like that. Marius just wants to make you see he loves you. That's all."

"So now you're a big fan of that King? What

happened to the woman who slapped him across the face?"

Again, she hesitates to answer, so I add, "It's okay, Ava. The man is very persuasive."

"I was going to stay mad at him, but then he told me about how Theo slept with his girlfriend right after they broke up. He was heartbroken because he still loved Maia. He made me see why he was so insistent about keeping you a secret."

I toss the dress on the bed and head for the bathroom to freshen up my makeup. "No worries. As I said, Marius is very persuasive."

"That really happened, though. Eleanor told me she heard the two of them in the game room the day Marius found out what Theo did, and she told me Marius sounded devastated."

Normally, I'd ask Ava how hearing something like that about Theo makes her feel, but I can hear in her voice how sad she sounds simply telling me about it. She always did have a huge blind spot when it came to that particular King brother.

"Okay. I'm not angry you're being nice to the man I love, Ava. He's not a bad man. He just made some mistakes. In fact, I'm happy you're back to being one of his biggest fans. I don't know what I'd do if my best friend hated my husband."

"Oh, good! So you'll be leaving soon to come up here? I want to make sure the food we're making will be nice and hot."

I check the time on my phone. 6:22. I'm going to have to leave in the next few minutes if I want to reach the King estate on time.

"Let me go so I'll be there by just after seven, assuming I don't hit traffic. I'm sorry I might be late. Work was a bear, and it took forever to get back home. I swear everyone and their brother was in the city today."

"It's okay. Just get here as soon as you can. I'll keep everything waiting for you. See you soon, Eden!"

The call ends, so I set my phone on the vanity and get busy redoing my makeup. When I finish, I tip my head down and then stand up to give my hair some body. Just about ready for whatever awaits me tonight, I smile at myself in the mirror.

"Ready to forgive that husband of yours?" I ask my reflection, but I've known the answer for days.

Of course, I am.

After getting my dress and my favorite necklace on, I look in the mirror one last time and grab my purse before walking downstairs. As much as I love this penthouse apartment, I wish we lived closer to Ava and Matthias. Maybe I'll mention that to Marius after the party tonight.

Just as I reach the kitchen, the doorman calls from the main floor. I answer it, even though I really don't have time to spare right now.

"Mrs. King, a woman named Samantha is down here. She said you'd know her. She'd like to come up and see you."

He drops his voice to barely a whisper and continues. "She seems upset. I think she may have been crying. May I send her up?"

For a few seconds, I silently debate whether or not I should make time for Sam. I'm in a hurry, but she was sweet and I'd hate to abandon her if something happened. I haven't had a chance to mention the whole situation to Marius yet, so I should talk to her.

I'm sure Ava and everyone else will be fine with me being a few minutes late.

"Sure, Ernest. Send her up. Thank you."

"My pleasure, ma'am."

I don't have to wait long before the elevator doors open and Sam steps out. I can immediately see her eyes are red rimmed like she's been crying for a while. I don't know how I might be able to help, but the least I can do is listen if she wants to talk.

Sam hurries over to me, sniffling. "Thank you for letting me come up." When she notices I'm dressed and ready to leave, she adds, "I'm interrupting. I'll leave. I shouldn't have come here. You're a busy woman. I'm sorry for bothering you."

She turns to walk back toward the elevator before I can say a word, so I reach out and grab her hand to stop her. "No, it's fine. My friends know I'll be a little late. I can talk for a few minutes. What's wrong?"

Without turning around, she says in the saddest voice I've ever heard, "I texted Marius about if I have a job or not, and he never got back to me. I think he's ghosting me, and I don't know why."

The poor thing. That husband of mine can be such a piece of work. What is he doing that he's too busy to answer a text from this girl?

"Oh, honey, I'm sure he's just being his absentminded self again. He gets like that sometimes. You know how he is."

Every word of that is a lie. Marius King never forgets anything. It's actually one of his most impressive personality traits. He's attentive to details occasionally to a fault, almost as if he's single-minded. If he's not answering her texts, she's right. He's avoiding her.

Sam turns around and sniffles again, wiping her tears away. "Do you really think so? He's never been like this. Every other time I've texted him about a shoot or anything else, he's always answered within a few minutes. I was sure he was ghosting me."

I slip my arm around her shoulders and gently guide her into the kitchen. "Men do silly things. You just have to roll with the punches. At least that's how I handle things like this. I didn't get a chance to speak to Marius yet, but when I do, I know you'll hear from him and things will be back to normal. I'm sure of it."

"Thank you so much for being willing to listen. I'm just so worried. I can't afford my rent if I lose my job, and when I talked to my roommates last night about what's going on, they were nice but they said they can't give me any extra time. I'm barely hanging on."

After giving her a sisterly squeeze to show I sympathize with her, I walk over to the refrigerator. "How about a drink? I have iced tea, soda, and water."

"Is it sweet tea?" she asks, and I swear I hear the hint of a southern twang when she says the words sweet tea.

I shake my head. "No, just regular unsweetened. I have sugar, though, so you can make it sweet."

"Okay. Thanks!" she says, and although I listen for the twang again, it's gone. Odd.

As I pour her a glass of iced tea, I ask, "Are you originally from here, or did you move here from somewhere? I ask because when you said sweet tea, I was reminded how my grandmother says that. She's from Virginia, down near Richmond."

She smiles, but it's half-hearted. "I grew up in South Carolina, but we moved up here when I was sixteen. I guess when I'm upset, my southern comes out."

I nod as she explains why I heard a twang, wondering why I didn't hear it when she was really upset earlier. It doesn't matter. People can't control a lot about themselves when they're crying over their life falling apart.

"Well, you don't have to worry. Everything's going to work out. I know it."

My attempt to be a supportive big sister type seems to work, and as Sam drinks her tea, she says, "Where are you going? Do you need to leave?"

I wave away her concern with a smile. "My friend's house. Ava's, the house you were at for that party. She's having another one, and I think the whole thing has been set up for Marius to convince me I should forgive him. Between you and me, it's going to work."

"Oh, that's nice."

Instantly, I feel bad for rubbing my impending happiness in her face. "I'm sorry. I didn't mean anything by that."

"It's okay," Sam says with a smile, but I see tears in her eyes. "You and Marius make a great couple. I hope I can find someone like him."

God, I could use a drink. Then I remember I left my wine glass upstairs.

"I'll be right back. I just want to get my drink from the bedroom."

"Sure!" Sam says, suddenly less weepy than before.

My grandmother always says a nice glass of iced tea can make anyone feel better. She usually means sweet tea with enough sugar to rot a person's teeth out of their head, but I guess regular unsweetened tea works too.

I hurry upstairs so I don't leave Sam alone for very long. On my way, I glance at the clock in the mezzanine area. 6:35. I should get leaving in the next few minutes so I'm not too late for the party, but it feels wrong to make Sam leave when she's so sad.

Then again, she sounded like she was fine right before I came up here. Maybe she'd be okay with my having to go.

A noise makes me spin around, and I see Sam walking toward me. What the hell is she doing up here?

Holding up my glass like I need to prove I had a reason for coming up here, I say, "Found it! I was just coming back downstairs."

She doesn't say anything, and a second later, she pulls a gun out from behind her and aims it at me. "You're not going anywhere. Sit on the bed and don't do anything stupid, or I'll shoot you."

I notice the twang is back, but my fear makes that detail suddenly unimportant. My hands shake as I sit down like she ordered me to, and I spill the last few sips of my wine on the floor next to the bed. Terrified, I set the glass down on the floor and sit up to see her pointing the gun directly at the center of my forehead.

"Why are you doing this, Sam? I thought we were friends. I welcomed you into my home."

She paces back and forth across the bedroom, her focus and the gun pointed at me the whole time. "Why is it okay that you have everything and I have nothing? It's not! Why should you get a man like Marius?"

Oh, God! She's lost her mind. She's going to kill me because she's obsessed with Marius.

I don't know what to say, but I have to try something, so I settle on the truth or some nice version of it. "Sam, you deserve a great man. You do. I hope you know that. It's just that Marius is with me. It was pure luck that we got together. Nothing more. Not that I deserve him and you don't. Please let me go. You don't have to do this."

"He'd want me if you weren't around. You know that, don't you? That's why you want him back. Because you know that he would be with me if he was free."

With every word she utters, her voice cracks and inches higher and higher. I need to keep her calm, but if we keep talking, she's only going to get more upset.

If I want to get out of this alive, I need to find a way to make her see I'm not the bad guy here. I just don't know how.

"I knew that night he called me and said he wanted me to come to that party with him that he finally realized how he felt about me. I've waited for so long, but that night I knew. All I had to do was be my bubbly self, and we'd finally sleep together and he'd be mine. Then you ran out of the party upset, and he suddenly felt sick. I knew right then and there that if Marius and I are ever to be together, you have to go."

My heart slams into my chest as my stomach roils, nearly making me sick. Nobody is going to come to save me because they don't know I'm in danger. Even if Marius left Ava's right now, he'd take too long to get here.

I'm not going to make it out of this alive.

CHAPTER TWENTY-THREE

*M*arius

I LOOK OUT AT THE LONG DRIVEWAY UP TO THE HOUSE and don't see Eden's car. Ava told me she'd be here right after seven, but it's already nearly seven-thirty.

Behind me, Ronan says, "I'm sure she's on her way. Don't worry. Your Juliet will arrive, Romeo."

Turning around, I throw my youngest brother a nasty look. "I think this version of you irritates me."

"Which version?" he asks with a chuckle.

"Ever since you and Kate got back together, you've been practically insufferable."

Ronan rolls his eyes. "God forbid I should be happy. Would you like me to go back to being miserable?"

"Hell no! How about you find a happy medium between miserable bastard and insufferably happy? That could work."

He looks out the door and then at me. "This isn't your routine for tonight, is it? If it is, I think you need to change it up. You're never going to get anyone back acting like a cranky shit."

"Don't worry about me," I say as I stare out the door looking for Eden's car. "It's in the bag. She loves me."

My brother chucks me on the shoulder as he walks away. "I'm off to find someone to explain to me how the hell a woman like her ends up with you."

"Good! I don't need your nonsense right now anyway."

Leave it to one of my brothers to bust my balls when I'm stressed out. The woman I love is half an hour late, and I'm starting to worry she's not coming.

My Duck wouldn't do that. At least I don't think she would.

For ten minutes more, I watch for her like a child on Christmas Eve looking for Santa Claus. She never shows. By quarter to eight, I'm worried. I wish I could say I'm scared she got into an accident, but my gut is telling me something else.

She changed her mind. She doesn't want us to get back together. I fucked up too much, and she can't forgive me.

"Don't worry. She'll be here."

I turn around and see Ava smiling at me. "Eden's never late. You know that. She hates when people are late. It's one of her biggest pet peeves."

Taking my hand, my sister-in-law gives it a supportive squeeze. "I do know her. She's been my best friend for most of my life, so I know her as well as she knows herself. She'll be here, Marius. She's crazy about you. She's just giving you a hard time because her feelings got hurt when you brought Sam to the party. You watch. Eden will be here any moment."

"Thanks, Ava."

When I turn back toward the road, I still don't see any cars. Where could she be?

"Want to hear a story?"

I shrug, understanding what Ava's trying to do but not sure it's going to work. Looking back at her, I nod. "Sure."

"When we were fifteen, I slept over at Eden's house one Saturday night. We stayed up until the wee hours of the morning, gossiping and eating so much pizza and junk food that we both had stomach aches. She ended up feeling like she was going to be sick, so she ran to the bathroom, but her brother Adam wouldn't let her in. He was a bust ass, always teasing her, so he kept blocking the door. She threw up right outside the bathroom door and was furious with him for that. She wouldn't talk to Adam for three months, even when her parents told her she had to. Nope. She refused. No matter what they said, she wouldn't talk to him. The only reason she finally forgave him is he convinced her he was sorry. When Eden is upset with someone, she doesn't care who says she should forgive them. So you see, the very fact that she said she'd come here tonight means she's okay with what's happened and forgives you."

"Then where is she?" I ask, growing more worried by the moment.

Ava steps closer and wraps her arms around me. "She'll be here. I know her. Just give her a few more minutes."

As if I have a choice.

My phone vibrates in my pocket, so I fish it out of my pants and see it's a text from Eden. My spirits soar at seeing her name. Quickly, I read it, but I don't understand.

decided to stay in tonight why don't you come here instead of me coming there

I read it twice and shake my head. "This doesn't make sense."

"What is it?" Ava asks, now her voice full of concern.

Turning my phone, I show her the message. As she reads it, I say, "Something's off about this text."

Ava looks up at me with pure worry in her eyes and points at my phone. "Eden would never send a text like that. You know her. She punctuates everything and correctly too. And she'd never write anything that sounds like this. I had to read it three times to figure out what it was trying to say. And no capitalization? No way. This wasn't the person I've known for most of my life texting this. What could be happening, Marius?"

My blood runs cold as Ava says that. If Eden didn't write that message, then who did? Something is very wrong.

"I don't know what's happening, but I need to get back to the penthouse right now."

Before Ava can say another word, I race up the stairs to grab my keys and bolt back downstairs as my heart races. I can't imagine what's wrong, but the woman I love would never send me a text like that.

I nearly run into Matthias at the bottom of the stairs. "Whoa! What's the matter? You look like you just saw a ghost."

"Something's wrong with Eden. I'm driving to the penthouse to see what's going on," I answer as I push past him.

"Do you want me to come with you?" he asks as Ava joins us.

When I don't answer, she nods and kisses him. "Yes, go with Marius. He'll tell you about the text on the way. Bring Eden back here so I can know she's safe, okay?"

My brother promises her he will, but he looks baffled, like he isn't sure what he's getting himself into. After they say their goodbyes, he walks over to where I'm waiting at the door.

"Okay, let's do this! I have no idea what this is, but it'll be like old times when you, Theo, and me used to cause trouble."

I smile at the memory of those days. "Let's hope it is. I'm driving, so get ready because we're going to be getting there as fast as possible."

The two of us look back at Ava and then head out to my car. My stomach's in knots, and my chest hurts just thinking of Eden in trouble.

She better be okay when I find her, or I swear to God someone's going to pay dearly.

MATTHIAS AND I PRACTICALLY RUN THROUGH THE lobby of my building, but then I remember the doorman would have to let someone upstairs if they wanted to see Eden. I stop my brother and point at the desk just inside the front door.

"Hang on. I need to talk to him for a second."

The doorman on tonight is Conrad, the one I like the

most. An older man with white hair and a mouth full of the nicest teeth I've ever seen, he never fails to smile and say something nice whenever he sees me.

"Conrad, I need to know if anyone is upstairs with my wife," I say nearly breathlessly.

He shakes his head immediately. "I didn't let anyone upstairs, but I just came on, Mr. King. Are you expecting someone?"

I crane my neck to scan his desk for any hint about what may be happening to Eden. "No, but my wife sent me a very strange text, and she didn't show up at my brother's house like she was supposed to. Is there any way of knowing if she's still up there?"

Again, he shakes his head. "No, we don't track tenants that way here. I can check the logbook to see if Ernest let anyone up. Give me a second."

My patience is practically null right now as I watch him flip through pages. Matthias pats me on the shoulder and quietly whispers, "It's going to be okay. I'm sure we'll find her upstairs and fine."

Conrad looks up from his logbook and nods. "Yes, there was someone who asked to be let up. Ernest wrote down that a young woman named Samantha McCann requested permission to be allowed up to the penthouse at just before half past six tonight. Mrs. King approved her, and the young woman rode up in the elevator. He doesn't note anything about the woman leaving, and since we do track visitors, he would have written down when she left if it occurred on his shift. I haven't seen anyone leave since I got on."

Samantha? My assistant? My mind races for a few

moments as I try to imagine why she would have come here for anything. Then I remember Eden's text.

"Okay, thanks, Conrad. I appreciate it."

I hurry over to the elevator and punch in my code. As I wait, I pull out my phone and search through my messages to find the last one Sam sent me.

"What's going on? Is Samantha the same girl you brought to the party?" Matthias asks as the elevator doors open.

We hurry inside, and I press the button for the penthouse as I search through my messages. I finally find the last one Sam sent me and turn my phone toward my brother.

"Same thing. No punctuation. No capitalization like Eden always uses. But if Sam used my wife's phone to send me a text, the question is why?"

"My guess is we're about to find out."

Just as he utters that ominous sentence, we stop on the top floor and the elevator doors open. We step out into the entryway and look around, but nothing seems out of the ordinary. The wrought iron table with the glass top and huge flower arrangement with those white calla lilies Eden loves still sits right in front of the elevator as we walk out, and those two fake trees she claims give the place some life are still flanking that table.

I look down at the floor, not really sure what I'm looking for, but it seems fine. Same white marble as usual. The entire entry with the white walls Eden always corrects me about look the same as always (they're not white—they're white smoke, although I'd bet you wouldn't know the difference either).

The place is deathly quiet, but that's nothing

abnormal for this place. We can be watching TV upstairs in the bedroom, and if I come down to the kitchen to get a snack, I can't hear a sound from up there.

Matthias and I walk into the kitchen, and my brother stops dead as he looks around. "Damn, Marius. This place is nice."

"Yeah, yeah. Compliment me later. For now, let's separate and search the entire apartment. You take down here. I'll handle upstairs. Call me if you find anything."

He gives me a strange look and asks, "Why can't I just yell out that I found something?"

"Because I can't hear you. It's a big place, okay? Just call my damn phone, all right?" I say, my patience completely gone now.

"Jeez, okay. I'll call."

I race upstairs and stop at the area Eden calls the mezzanine where we talked the other day. Everything here looks normal.

To be honest, I'm looking for blood. Thankfully, I guess, this penthouse hasn't been redone, so it's all bare bones furniture that's incredibly fucking uncomfortable to sit in and white (sorry, white smoke) walls that would show blood splatter if someone had...

I don't let my mind go where it wants to. Shaking my head, I repeat over and over in my head, "Eden is okay. She's fine, and when she sees me, she's going to explain what the fuck that message was all about."

When I finish thinking that a third time, I turn and start walking down the hallway, stopping at each room to look for her. I'd call out for her, but since that's the same thing every person in the movies does just before they find who they're looking for dead in a pool of blood, I'm not going to do that.

After checking the second bedroom and finding nothing, I walk into the upstairs living room, or what I've been secretly referring to as my future mancave. Eden would roll her eyes if she heard me say that. I can hear her already. "Mancave? What the hell does a grown man need a cave for? It's the twenty-first century, Marius. The world has decided. We aren't doing immature men anymore."

That's my Duck. She doesn't put up with any nonsense. It's one of the million reasons why I love her.

I walk back out to the hallway and a noise hits my ears that makes my heart skip a beat. Eden's muffled voice is coming from our bedroom.

Quickly, I walk down the hall and stop in front of the closed door. Something is very wrong. Eden never closes the door. She told me one time that whoever built this penthouse didn't understand it's so big that it gets cold when you shut the doors to the rooms. So she leaves them open all the time.

Christ. She's in there. But is she alone? Is Sam still here, or did the doorman make a mistake?

I touch the doorknob and look down to see my hand shaking. I've never been this fucking terrified in my life. If I walk in there and she's bleeding out like Ronan was when I found him, I'm going to lose my fucking mind.

Slowly, I push the door open and hear Eden sobbing. As soon as I step into the room, I see her sitting on the bed with a gag in her mouth. Her wrists and ankles are bound, so she doesn't move when she sees me.

"Duck, what the hell is going on? Are you okay?" I ask her as my emotions threaten to overwhelm me.

Whatever's happened, at least she's alive and safe.

And then, out of the corner of my eye, I see something move. I turn to find out what it is, and I see my assistant standing there with a gun.

"Sam, what's going on? Put that gun down. What the fuck are you thinking?"

She frowns and walks around the bed behind Eden, pointing the gun at the back of her head. "No, Marius. I wanted you to come here for me, and you did. Now I want you to do something else."

I have no idea what the hell is happening right now. Has my assistant lost her mind? Do she and Eden know one another?

Raising my hands so I seem to be surrendering, I calmly say, "It's okay, Sam. You can ask me to do anything. You know that. You've always been a great assistant. I tell you that all the time, don't I? Tell me what you need me to do, and I'll do it. Just put the gun down."

"Tell her you don't love her. Tell her you love me. That's why you asked me to come to that party. Tell her."

I could say those words. I wouldn't mean them, but I could say them. The problem with that is people who are out of their minds are never logical. No matter how much I tell Sam what she wants to hear, it won't matter.

"Come on, Sam. Put the gun down. You don't want to hurt Eden. She's never done anything to you. If anyone deserves to have you hold a gun to their head, it's me. You know that, so let her go."

Sam's expression twists into a distorted grimace, and she shakes her head wildly as I try to calm her down.

"No! She's the problem, not me. I'm not the problem. I've done everything you ever wanted me to do. Tell her! I have, and you know it."

I take a step toward where Eden sits on the bed, but Sam screams, "Stop! You can't be with her! You're supposed to be with me."

Eden looks up at me with eyes filled with dread for the person behind her with the gun. I wish I could tell her everything will be okay, but I have the feeling if I speak to Eden at all, that will only enrage Sam more.

So I keep my focus on the person who could make or break my entire future right now and give the woman I love a tiny smile to let her know I won't let her get hurt.

I force myself to give Sam a big smile and say, "You don't want me. You know that. I'm terrible with remembering what I have to do. You have to remind me constantly. I drink too much, and how many times have you complained that I smell like cigars and liquor when you've seen me at a shoot? Think about it, Sam. Being with me would be like working twenty-four seven with me, and that sounds awful, now doesn't it?"

Tears fill her eyes, and she continues to shake her head as I attempt to be as self-effacing as possible. "We had a good time on the shoots you took me on. Remember Fiji? I bought that pink bikini especially for that trip. You said it looked great and that I looked as good as the models you were shooting."

If I tell her the truth—that we've never been more than employer and employee—she's going to lose it and probably shoot Eden. If I lie, though, that might backfire too.

Then an idea pops into my head, and I go with it. If

she shoots me, at least I can pray Matthias will come running in and save Eden. That's all I'm hoping.

I sneak one more glance at Eden and pray to God she understands what I'm trying to do before I start walking around to the other side of the bed. I'm betting on Sam regretting shooting me and not being able to hurt Eden before Matthias can come rushing in.

"Sam, listen to me. You're a great girl, but I'm too old for you. I'm nearly thirty. What would a beautiful twenty-year-old want with me when you can have guys your own age? Think about it. I'm old, a pain in the ass to deal with, and I have terrible habits like drinking and smoking. You don't want me."

As I talk, I make it halfway around the bed before she screams, "Stop! You're just saying that because you don't want to hurt her feelings!"

Shaking my head, I keep walking toward her. "I'm not lying. You know me as well as anyone does. How many times have I been late for a shoot because I was having too good a time the night before? And that's saying nothing about how I often don't work for months at a time. Who wants someone like that?"

Sam winces like what I'm saying bothers her. "You take time off because you have your family to worry about. I know that. I understand the kind of man you are. Anyway, what does it matter since you're a billionaire?" she says, her voice filled with sadness.

I take another few steps toward her, and finally, she turns the gun on me. Tears roll down Sam's cheeks, and I sense she's about to have a breakdown at any moment. Now's the moment when Eden has to escape.

"Duck, now!" I scream before lunging at Sam.

We fall to the floor as I try to wrestle the gun away from her. I don't know if Eden got away, but as long as Sam is busy with me, she's not aiming her gun at my Duck. That's all that matters.

As small as my assistant is, she's got a hold of that gun like it's stitched to her hand, and I can't wrestle it away. I hear Matthias bark out something, and then a second later, the gun goes off.

"Marius! Oh, God! Marius!"

Between Sam's crying and screaming my name, I'm not sure what's happening. My brother grabs her by the back of her shirt and lifts her off me, but when I try to stand up, I see blood.

My blood.

CHAPTER TWENTY-FOUR

den

MATTHIAS UNTIES MY HANDS AND FEET, AND I FINALLY spit that goddamned gag out of my mouth. I want to smack the hell out of Sam, but I've got other concerns right now.

Immediately after hearing the gun go off, I scream, "Marius! Are you okay?"

I begin to cry before running around the bed to see the man I love on the floor with blood pouring out of his left arm. Oh, God! That crazy woman shot him!

Dropping to my knees, I cradle his face in my hands. "Oh, baby. You're going to be okay. I promise."

Behind me, Matthias holds Sam who can't stop sobbing. "I'm calling 911. Marius, don't worry. The paramedics will be here in no time."

He takes her out of the bedroom, leaving just Marius

and me. The gunshot wound doesn't look too bad, but I can't tell with all the blood.

"Duck, she didn't hurt you, did she?" Marius asks in that sweet way of his.

I shake my head and smile even as I fight back tears. "I'm fine. All she did was hit me on the back of the head with the gun. It's you I'm worried about. She shot you. I wasn't even sure she had bullets in that gun, but she shot you. Are you in pain?"

Marius looks down at his arm and winces. "I think I'm in shock. I don't feel much of anything right now. I'm just happy you're safe."

Looking into his dark eyes, I smile at how much I love this man. "You saved my life, honey. You're a hero."

He frowns and shakes his head. "I'm not a hero, Duck. Sam would have never been here holding you hostage with a gun if I hadn't invited her to Ava's party. I was trying to make you jealous, and look what it did. You nearly got killed because of me."

I lean in and kiss him softly on the lips. "You're my hero, Marius. I'm so sorry I ever went to see that divorce attorney. I never wanted us to break up. I was so stupid."

Even sitting here after being shot, he's willing to blame himself for all that's happened. "You had every right to. I was the stupid one. I wasn't ashamed of you, though. I hope you know that. I'm prouder than any man alive to have you as my wife."

"Well, no more talk of divorce or leaving. We're together now, and I forgive you. Do you forgive me?" I ask, worried that if I don't say these things and the paramedics don't get here soon that I won't have time to tell him all I have in my heart.

He smiles in that way that reminds me of a pirate and shakes his head. "There's nothing to forgive. I was never angry with you for serving me with those papers. I had it coming. I was acting like a selfish jackass for way too long, and you had every right to put your foot down."

I throw my arms around him, not caring if I get covered in blood too. "I'm so sorry. I never should have let Sam come over the other day, but she was so sad about you saying you were going to fire her. I guess I thought I was helping, you know, like a big sister, and look what happened. The crazy pick-me bitch pulled a gun on me."

When I sit back, he looks at me strangely. "Duck, I never told Sam I was firing her."

Suddenly, it all dawns on me. She was planning this the whole time. That first visit to see me was to get on my good side so I'd let her up when she really intended to do me harm. And to think all this time I thought she just needed a friend to talk to. So much for my being a big sister to her.

This is why women don't try to make friends as adults. Everyone's goddamned out of their minds.

"She told me you did. That's why I let her into our home today. I told her I'd talk to you and tell you not to fire her."

Marius sighs. "That's my fault too. I honestly never meant to lead her on, but I can't say I never flirted with her. You know me. I'm all about the good time."

He stops and takes my hand in his right hand. "But I swear I never slept with her. I promise you that, Eden."

"I believe you, baby. And for the record, I love when you call me by your nickname for me. Don't stop, okay?"

"Okay, Duck. I love you. I hope you know that. I'd be lost without you."

I kiss him again and whisper against his lips, "Then you should know I plan to stick around as Mrs. King for a long time."

Relief washes over me when I hear the sound of the paramedics' footsteps coming down the hallway. "By the way, Ava's going to be furious at you for missing her party," I say to him as help arrives.

"And just as I was getting her back on my side."

The paramedics need me out of the way, so I kiss him one more time and say, "I love you, Marius."

When I step back to let them work on him, his first words are, "Please check my wife. Sam hit her on the head with a gun, and I worry she may be hurt."

The female paramedic looks back at me and smiles. "I'll check you out at soon as we're done with your husband, ma'am. Are you feeling dizzy? If so, please be sure to sit down."

I wave off her concern for me. "I'm fine. Please, there's no need to worry. My husband is the one who needs your attention."

Matthias stands off to the side still holding Sam who hasn't stopped crying after shooting my husband. I want to walk over and slap her across the face like Ava did with Marius, but I know my focus needs to be on him and not his crazy assistant.

"The cops are on their way, Eden," Matthias says in his cool, steady way. "How are you doing over there, Marius?"

Always the joker, he looks over the bed, and as the paramedics work on him, he answers, "A bullet went through my arm, Matthias. So, on the whole, not great."

Leave it to my husband to make light of being shot.

I PARK THE CAR BEHIND AVA'S AND TURN TO LOOK AT Marius in the passenger seat. "Are you sure you're up to this? You just got shot four days ago."

He lifts his left arm and pretends to try to flex his bicep. "I'm great! Just a flesh wound. Isn't that what they always say in war movies? No worries. I'll be fine."

"You're sure? I can tell Ava you're not up to this, and we can go right back home. You just give the word."

Marius waves away that suggestion. "No way. I need to celebrate something good after all that's happened. Tonight we eat, drink, and be merry."

Thankfully, he doesn't say the rest of that because if he mentioned anything about dying, I might burst into tears. I'm not usually a woman who's prone to crying, but this whole thing has made me far more emotional than usual.

And the last thing either of us needs right now is me sobbing like a baby over the thought of him dying.

"Then I guess we better get inside. Your family is waiting."

Marius covers my hand resting on the console with his. "Our family, Duck. You're married to a King, so that makes them your family too."

All week, Ava hasn't stopped talking about how thrilled she is that we're sisters-in-law. She's got a million ideas of things we should do together, and to be honest, I love every single one as much as I love being married to this King.

"Okay, Then we better get inside. *Our* family is waiting."

He leans in and kisses me sweetly. "Better. Don't worry. Being a King has its perks."

I can't help but smile at how cute he can be. "Do you mean to say marrying into a family of billionaires comes with bonuses?"

Marius winks at me before nuzzling my neck. "Quite a few, actually. I'll be sure to show you a few tonight."

Entirely too cute. No wonder I can't deny him anything.

"All right Mr. Big Perks, let's get going before Ava comes out and drags us inside."

We don't even make it to the door before all three of his brothers come out of the house to greet us. Matthias makes a beeline to where we are and gives me a big hug while Kellen and Ronan joke around with Marius about having the dubious distinction of being the first King shot since some great-great-uncle who got gunned down in some saloon in Wyoming back in the nineteenth century.

Ava stands in the doorway, which seems strange, so after I thank her husband once more for being there that night when all the madness with Sam happened, I hurry up the sidewalk to see her. We haven't talked much about that night, so I'm sure she wants to know every little detail.

"I know, you want all the dirt, and trust me, I've got it. One thing, though. My mother was right. Making friends as an adult is a nightmare!" I say with a laugh.

But Ava doesn't say a word. Instead, she throws her arms around my neck and hugs me tighter than I've ever been hugged before. When I start to ask her what's up, she begins to cry.

"I could have lost you, Eden. That crazy girl could have killed you. I don't know what I would have done if she did that. I've been beside myself all week. Ask Matthias. If I'm not crying, I'm yelling about the dumbest stuff."

When she takes a breath, I gently ease out of the hug to see tears rolling down my best friend's face. "Aww, you didn't think you were going to get rid of me that easily, did you? It was horrible, but I'm fine. Promise."

Ava wipes her tears away and smiles. "You better be. We can finally enjoy being sisters-in-law, so you better not go anywhere. We've got a future of kids and grandkids and vacations and holidays and all that great stuff families do together when they don't hate one another."

"It's you and me, kid. Together forever. The world better watch out."

This time, I hug her and let my serious side come out. "It was horrible, but I never doubted Marius would save me."

"Me neither."

Behind me, he says, "So many people who believe in me here. I'm going to start to think I can leap tall buildings in a single bound."

We look at him and shake our heads. "Well, Superman, today is all about you two, so get in there so we can get this party started," Ava says.

As Marius passes me, he leans in and whispers,

"Does this mean you're Lois Lane? Because if you are, I'm feeling some role play coming on later."

Typical Marius.

We all head inside to the dining room where Eleanor is waiting with a dinner of all his and my favorites. "Everyone sit down because we've got a meal for you. Marius, we've got steak, chicken kabobs, and that pasta salad you've loved since you were a little boy. For you, Eden, we made shrimp scampi and coq au vin, and we got cheesecake from that place in Brooklyn whose name I can never remember."

I look at Marius and smile. "That's a pretty diverse meal they made for us."

"We're two very different people, Duck."

Everyone takes their seat, and Eleanor begins to walk out, but Marius quickly stands up to stop her. "You're a part of this family as much as I am, so pull up a chair, Eleanor. It wouldn't be a celebration without you here."

The older woman tears up at his kindness and nods. "Thank you, Marius. I'm so happy you're safe and sound." She hugs him and looks over at me. "You too, Eden. I'm just thrilled everything turned out okay."

The entire family settles in to eat, but at the head of the table, Matthias taps his fork on his plate to get our attention. Standing up, he raises his glass and says, "Before we all start, I want to make a toast. To my brothers, who never fail to keep life exciting for the rest of us, and to the women we love, who must wonder sometimes if they should have chosen differently, thank you for being here to celebrate Marius and Eden tonight. And to Eleanor, whose motherly love has seen us through all the ups and downs since we lost our mother, we don't know what we'd do without you. Thank you for always being here for us."

We all raise our glasses to toast the people we love and begin to eat a delicious meal. It's the family I know Ava has always dreamed of having. Now that I'm officially a part of it too, I can understand why.

By the time we finish, I swear I've eaten an ocean of shrimp and all the cheesecake to come out of Brooklyn. Stuffed, we all head to the living room. I notice Ava doesn't stray far from me, so I pull her aside to talk to her.

"Hey, I'm okay, you know?"

She nods and seems to be fighting back tears. "I know. I was just really scared. The thought of someone pointing a gun at you freaks me out."

I chuckle at that since I can't agree more. "Me too. It's something I never want to do again."

"No more trying to make adult friends. As your mother always told us, it's a nightmare," Ava says with a smile.

I shrug, not really caring about new friends tonight. "I've got all the friends I need right here."

All those years ago when I told Ava I was interested in Marius, I could have never guessed this would be my life. Married to the man himself, sister-in-law to my best friend, and surrounded by people who've welcomed me with open arms into their family.

From across the room, I see Marius walking toward me. He looks off, like he doesn't feel well.

"Hey, are you okay?" I ask him when he gently

guides me over near the fireplace. "Do you want to leave?"

He shakes his head and points at the chair he's led me to. "No. Sit."

Marius has me worried, but he appears intent on something, so I don't fight him. "Okay, I'm sitting. Would you like to tell me why you look like you're going to throw up?"

Instead of answering me, he turns around and says to Matthias, "Ready?"

I don't understand what's happening, but a moment later, I hear music. As I listen, I realize it's a song I know and love.

With a smile, Marius slowly eases himself down on one knee and pulls out a little robin's egg blue box. I stare at him and then at it in shock as he begins to speak.

"Duck, I thought Willie could say it better than I ever could, but I need you to know you were always on my mind, even if I didn't show it."

I couldn't stop the tears if I wanted to now. "Oh, Marius. This is so sweet."

"You deserve this and so much more. I'm sorry I never realized I was hurting you. I thought because I bought you anything you wanted that I was showing you how much I love you, but now I know I wasn't. I love you, Eden. I'm so sorry."

Barely able to get the words out, I sniffle and say, "I love you, Marius. And I know you weren't trying to be hurtful."

"Well, I know this is probably a little backwards, but that's okay. We don't follow rules anyway, do we?"

I smile and shake my head. "Never have."

"Well, in the spirit of not following the rules, will you marry me even though we're already married?"

He tilts back the top of the box to reveal a gorgeous round cut diamond nestled in a bed of black velvet. I'm not sure, but by the size of it, I'm thinking it has to be at least three or four carats.

And it's perfect.

I look down into his eyes and sigh at how wonderful he is for this. Even though we're already married, this week has felt like a new start with a fresh slate. I never mentioned to him that I wish we had a traditional wedding, but I have longed for that. I just figured I'd have to wait until we renewed our vows years from now.

"Of course, I'll marry you, Marius. I love you."

He leans forward and presses a kiss to my lips that makes my stomach flip. "Thank you for giving me another chance. I promise you won't regret it."

As he moves to stand up, I stop him. "Wait. I've got some conditions."

Marius smiles and shakes his head. "That's my Duck. Okay. Hit me with them. I'm ready."

I wipe the tears away and say, "First, I want us to move."

He looks confused for a second but nods. "Okay. You don't like the penthouse?"

Cradling his face, I lean over and kiss him softly on the lips. "I love it, but if we're going to be a family, I'd like a house out here. I loved growing up in this area, and I want our kids to have that too."

My mention of children makes his eyes get big. "Is there something you want to tell me, Duck?"

I chuckle at how worried he looks. "No. It's just that

I want to have children, and I want to be in a house before they come."

"Okay. I'll contact the realtor tomorrow. We can start house hunting this weekend. Sound good?"

"Yes. Onto condition number two. You have to promise me you're going to talk to someone about everything that happened this year. You've had a lot to deal with, not the least of which is having me held hostage by a crazy woman and you getting shot."

He nods and says, "I can do that."

I don't know if he's struggling as much as I think he may be. If he is, I want him to get the help he needs.

"Are there any more?" he asks, probably hoping I'm done with my conditions.

Smiling, I answer, "One more. I want a big, traditional wedding. I'm my parents' only daughter, and it will break their hearts if they don't get to see me get married. They couldn't be there the first time, so I want them to see our wedding this time."

"Traditional? Like me in a tux traditional?"

I nod. "Yes. Don't worry. I'm sure you'll look great. And I'm going to have a white wedding dress with a long train and a veil."

Marius leans forward and kisses me before whispering against my lips, "Whatever you want, Duck. I love you."

"I love you too, Marius. I guess we better not keep everyone in suspense any longer."

He stands up and turns around to everyone waiting to hear my answer. "She said yes. We're having another wedding in the King family!"

Ava rushes over and throws her arms around me. "I

was so worried I'd miss this because Lynn told me Matty woke up and was warm. He was just dressed a little too snugly for his new room, so I made it back down just in time to see Marius break out the ring! Let me see!"

I wiggle the fingers on my left hand to show off the stunning rock that amazing and wonderful man got me. Ava's mouth drops open at how beautiful it looks.

"Oh, he told me I was going to be impressed, but I have to say I think he undersold it. It's gorgeous! I love it!"

Marius comes up behind Ava and rests his chin on her shoulder. Smiling, he asks, "Did my biggest fan who was my biggest hater for a while there see the ring?"

She turns around and throws her arms around him. "I did, and it's perfect! Congratulations, Marius!"

"So when is the wedding?" Ronan asks when he and Kate stop in front of me to check out my ring.

Everybody's attention turns to me, so I shrug and shake my head. "No idea. I'll have to talk to Marius about that. To be honest, I'm a little surprised by all of this, so we're going to need a few days to get things planned."

"I know I say this to everyone, but if you want to have the wedding here, we'd love it," Ava says with so much hopefulness in her voice that I can't say no.

Not that I want to say no. I love this house and the estate. It's the home of my best friend and her husband, and even more than that, it's my husband's childhood home that I know he still loves.

Marius looks at me and then says to everyone, "We'll have to see if our plans conflict with Ronan and Kate's. If not, then if my wife is okay with it, I'm fine with our wedding being here."

One by one, each person comes over to see my ring, and as we all sit around laughing and celebrating, I know this is the part of being married that I missed the most. I never doubted Marius and I loved each other, and I never needed to be with him every day and every night. That's not who we are.

But being with the people you love and having the chance to be who you really are without lies and pretending is the part I missed out on for the past two years. Now that all changes, and I couldn't be happier.

Eden King is marrying Marius King again, and they're going to live happily ever after.

CHAPTER TWENTY-FIVE

den

I STARE AT THE BEAUTIFUL ENGAGEMENT RING ON MY left hand, wiggling my fingers to watch the light as it shines off the diamond. That husband of mine certainly does know how to make up to a woman.

Marius walks into the bedroom and stops dead just inside the door. He seems odd, like something's wrong, so I hurry over to where he's standing.

"Baby, what's wrong? Is your arm hurting? The doctor said that it might throb a little. You did have a bullet go through your body, after all."

He shakes his head and kisses me. "No, I'm fine. I was just thinking about the first time I brought you here and told you it was yours. You were so thrilled, and I loved seeing you like that."

"I love that you did this for me, honey. I hope you

don't think because I want to move out to where we grew up that I don't appreciate this beautiful penthouse."

With a shrug, he smiles. "It's not a problem. This was for the old Marius and Eden. The new version of us belongs somewhere else."

Wrapping my arms around him, I look up into his dark eyes and ask, "Are you ready to become a full-time husband and owner of a suburban home?"

"Yeah, I am. It's time the world knew me as your husband, Duck."

Marius King really is the most wonderful man I've ever met. I don't know how I've been so blessed, but I thank my lucky stars for him. I'm so happy right now that I might even thank Justin and Maia, if I saw them tonight.

With a sly grin, he cradles my face with his right hand and says, "I think as a farewell we need to have some mind-blowing sex in this bedroom. You know, to celebrate our leaving here and finding a new house."

In truth, we've been having mind-blowing sex all week. Much of it has been me on top since he's nursing a gunshot wound in his left arm, but it's been a hell of a week for us. I'm thinking of something slightly different for tonight, though.

"I'm way ahead of you, baby. You just sit down on the bed and let me take care of everything."

Marius looks at me in disbelief, like he isn't sure what's about to happen. "Okay. I'm wondering what you have planned, Duck."

I lead him over to the bed and stand in front of him when he sits down. Smiling, I say, "Well, all week you've had a hard time in bed because of your arm, so I thought for the man who bought me such a gorgeous ring and made me the happiest woman in the world, that I'd make this night all about you. So sit back and relax because tonight is all about Marius."

He doesn't have time to say another word before I unzip his pants and lower myself to the floor. Like usual, he's ready to have a good time, so I slip his hard cock out and wrap my fingers around it. Since I'm left-handed, I use that hand, but tonight it looks a little different.

Marius notices it too and smiles down at me. "I like the way that ring looks with your hand around me. It's fucking sexy."

"It is. Now relax and enjoy, baby."

Taking the head into my mouth, I give it a few sucks before sliding down as far as I can. My husband is a man who's been blessed in many ways, including what's in his pants, so there's no chance of deep throating with him. I have figured out ways to compensate for that, including that thing I do with my tongue he loves.

"Jesus, Duck...I don't know if it's getting shot or what you're doing with your mouth, but I think I'm getting lightheaded."

Although I shouldn't tease him, I let his cock fall out of my mouth and ask, "Do you want me to stop then?"

His eyes get big, and he shakes his head. "Fuck no! I'd be a fool to say no to my beautiful wife going down on me."

I wrap my fingers around him again and flick my tongue over the tip of his cock, knowing that drives him crazy. "Good. Now lean back and enjoy the ride, so to speak."

The thing he loves the most is when I jerk him off

and flick my tongue over the vein that runs on the underside of his cock, so after giving him a little taste of the good stuff, I get down to business. Above me, he moans softly before stuffing his hand into my hair. When he starts to pull, I'll know he's close.

See, that's how well I know him. We may have had some tough times lately, but what's never changed is how much I love him and want to see him happy. Thankfully, he feels the same about me.

That's what makes me a lucky woman.

The smell of his skin—a mixture of his natural scent and the coconut soap he loves—fills my nose as I run my tongue over that vein. I've always loved how he reacts when I do this for him.

His fist tightens around my hair, and I brace myself for him to come, but instead he eases me off him. I look up in confusion, sure he's in pain from his injury.

"Marius, are you okay?"

He nods but waves me up to him. "I'm fine. I just want to do something else."

I can't deny I'm a little disappointed to hear him say that, but I stand up as he wants. "Okay. You're the one who got shot. I guess you should call the shots on this."

"Duck, you know how much I love when you go down on me. Trust me. It's fucking fantastic. I just thought I'd like you to get off too. So take your clothes off and come sit on my lap."

I get it now. I can't blame a man for wanting to make me happy too. So I strip out of my clothes in front of him and straddle his hips.

He looks up into my eyes and says in a low voice, "I wanted to make sure you felt good too tonight, and even though I want to say I'm up for anything, how I've felt this week says I might not be up for as many rounds as usual."

Lifting myself up, I slowly sit down on his cock, loving how he fills me up so completely. "I'd be crazy to say this isn't exactly what I want tonight."

He lifts his right hand and pulls me down to kiss me long and deep. It's one of those kisses that tells me everything he's feeling that he may not be able to say. I don't need him to tell me he loves me right now or that he always wants to be with me. I know. I've always known because unlike so many men, Marius makes sure to let a woman know how he feels about her.

I ride him with abandon, reveling in how incredible he feels with every time I lower myself down on him. His size stretches me as it always has, and every movement brings me closer to release.

When I'm almost there, I slow down because I want to make this last, but he has other ideas. Surprising me, he rolls us over so he's on top. When he looks down at me, I see such love in his eyes.

"I love you, Duck. You made me the happiest man on earth when you said yes today."

I open my legs wide so he can slide in and kiss him. "I'd be crazy to say no to you, baby."

Even though he probably thinks I'm referring to how much I love sex with him, it's not just that. It's everything else. It's the way he makes me feel like I'm the most beautiful creature he's ever seen. It's the way he bought me this penthouse after I mentioned not liking hotels anymore one single time. It's the way I know he'd do anything to make me happy.

Most of all, it's the way he didn't let his hurt at my even thinking about divorce affect us. There aren't enough men in the world who understand when they mess up and actually do something about it.

But at this very moment as he fucks me better than no man has ever done before, it's his cock and how it makes me feel better than I ever have that I'm crazy about.

With one final drive into me, he stills. I feel him come, and something about how sexy he looks above me sends me over the edge. My orgasm roars through every inch of my body, making me feel like I'm flying.

Mind-blowing is the least of what we're like together.

Marius collapses on top of me, his heavy breathing in my ear telling me he enjoyed himself as much as I did. I stroke the back of his neck, feeling the beads of sweat that have formed there.

"Duck, that was fucking incredible," he says when he lifts his head to look at me.

"It always is with us, isn't it?"

He smiles, and I swear he lights up the entire room. "It is. Promise me when we move to the burbs and have kids that we'll still be us."

I hear the worry beneath his words and hurry to reassure him. Caressing his cheek, I smile and say, "I promise I'll always be the same woman you fell in love with."

He kisses me and says, "My Duck. And I promise to never let you even think for a second I'm not madly, crazy in love with you."

As we lie there in each other's arms, I can't wait for the rest of our lives together. We'll make mistakes, but as long as we remember we love each other, we're going to be fine.

And even though I haven't told him yet because of all the mania over Sam holding me hostage and him getting shot, we're going to need to get moving on buying that house in the suburbs so we can be settled when the baby comes.

"Um, Marius, I wanted to talk to you about something," I say quietly, not even sure he's awake.

He doesn't answer for a long moment but finally moves his arm so he can roll over onto his side to face me. "Okay. What's up?"

I don't know why I'm suddenly nervous. It's not like we've never thought about having children. I've mentioned it more than once, so what I have to say shouldn't come as a complete surprise.

Taking a deep breath in, I let it out slowly and say, "I'm glad we're going to be looking for a new house."

He nods. "If that makes you happy, it makes me happy, Duck."

"Well, it's not just that we'll be closer to Ava and Matthias. I'll be happy to have somewhere we can decorate."

That makes him smile. "Definitely! And the first thing we're going to do is get real furniture and not that minimalist nonsense we have here."

"Yes, we absolutely need furniture that's comfortable for when people come to visit. We'll have other rooms to decorate too, though. Like bedrooms."

As he talks about us taking our current bedroom furniture to the new house we hope to find soon, I know

I can't drag this out anymore. When he finishes, I take another deep breath and blurt out my news.

"Marius, I'm pregnant. I found out the other day. I wanted to tell you before this, but everything with Sam happened, so I didn't want to just announce it. I guess that's what I just did, though."

He stares at me wide-eyed for a long moment that feels like forever before a smile lights up his face. "You're pregnant? Really?"

"Really. Just a few weeks."

I feel his hand slide over my belly until it rests against my skin. "A baby. We're having a baby. Wow."

His reaction confuses me. I thought he'd be more animated about the news.

"Are you happy? You're strangely subdued right now."

Marius kisses me softly on the lips and sighs. "I'm thrilled we're having a baby, Duck. One question, though. You knew tonight when I asked you at the house? Why didn't you tell me then?"

"Because I didn't want to tell our entire family before I told you in private. I know you Kings love to share all the good and bad things with one another, but I wanted this to be just for us at first."

He smiles and kisses me again. "Thank you for that. You know I'll be telling everyone the good news tomorrow, though, right?"

"Then you are happy?"

Taking me into his arms, he hugs me to him and says, "I couldn't be happier, Duck."

Eden and Marius are not only getting married again.

They're having a baby. Just wait until Ava finds out. I see many trips to shop for baby clothes in my future.

CHAPTER TWENTY-SIX

arius

I STEP OUT OF THE ELEVATOR TO SEE DUCK LIFTING that enormous floral arrangement of lilies and some other flower I can't remember. Immediately, I hurry over and take it out of her hands.

"You can't be doing this kind of stuff, Eden. You're pregnant."

She levels a very stern look on my face. "Marius, I'm maybe a month along, honey. I can do anything any other normal person can do. Wait until I'm as big as a house and in danger of toppling over for this kind of worry."

"Fine, but I still don't want you lifting this huge thing. Where do you want me to put it?" I ask as I try to see around the white flowers filling my vision.

Behind me, she says, "On the island. I'm trying to get

things situated for the movers when they come on Friday."

I set the giant flower arrangement down in the kitchen and turn around to see her smiling at me. "What's that grin for?"

She walks over to me and slides her hands around my waist before giving me a kiss. "I'm just so happy we found a house so quickly. I can't believe it's only been like three weeks since we started looking and we're moving in next week!"

"That's what paying cash and overbidding by twenty grand will do for you," I say with a chuckle.

I should be more responsible with money now that we have a baby coming early next year and a wedding in a few months, but when Eden saw that house with the big yard, a swimming pool, and what she called the "cutest little greenhouse she'd ever seen," I knew that was the place for us. I couldn't risk not getting it for her, so that meant pulling out all the stops since we were competing with at least four other bids.

"Ava and I can't believe we're going to be living a stone's throw away from one another. It's like a dream come true."

I love seeing my Duck like this. When I can do things that make her smile, I feel like my fuck ups earlier in our marriage might not be anything she remembers. I want to make her forget how selfish I was, and what better way than to give her whatever she wants?

Cupping her almost non-existent belly, I say, "I woke up early to go to my appointment. Any morning sickness today?"

She makes a face that tells me it's bad today. "Yeah. I

threw up three times, so I settled for a little tea and saltines. Eleanor told me last week that your mother suffered terribly with morning sickness with every one of you, so I'm guessing it's a boy."

I know that's what she thinks I want, but every time she says that, all I can think of is the King family doesn't need any more boys. I've never told her how I feel, though. Maybe today's a good day to do that.

As I push her black hair back behind her ear, I say, "Duck, I'll be happy with whatever our baby is, but if you're thinking I want a son, you're wrong. I think I'd like a little girl I can spoil like her mother."

"Really? I just assumed all of you King men wanted sons like Matthias."

I shake my head and shrug. "No. I'd be happier than anything if we have a daughter. Not that a son would be bad, but I think I'd make a hell of a girl dad."

That makes her smile, and she kisses me softly. "I think you'd make a great girl dad. Actually, I'm sure you're going to be a great dad no matter what our child is. Now if only I could believe I'll be as great as you."

She's been worried from the moment she told me that she might not be as good a mom as Ava is. She shouldn't be concerned, but I've told her every time she mentions her fears that my brother and Ava didn't know what they were doing in the beginning, so we're going to be fine.

And if things get bad, we know where to turn since those two have been through it before us.

I cradle her beautiful face in my hands and kiss her. "You are going to be a great mom, Duck. You're sweet and kind and when people step out of line, you have that look you give them that makes them get right back in. I can't wait for you to see how great you're going to be."

She covers my hands with hers and asks, "How did your doctor's appointment go?"

I've been seeing a therapist for two weeks now, twice a week, and it's been okay. I'm not used to telling strangers about my deepest, darkest thoughts, but that was one of her conditions so she'd marry me all over again, so I kept up my side of the bargain and found a doctor a week after.

"It was okay. The therapist said she thinks I'm making good progress. I've got a lot to deal with, but I feel good about it."

"Oh, baby. You've lost a lot in your life, and then when you almost lost Ronan, I knew you should talk to someone about it. I'm so proud of you for doing this. You know that, right?"

"I know, and I owe this all to you. I wouldn't have gone to see anyone without you lighting a fire under me, but now that I am, I think it's good. I guess I have some unresolved issues around Theo and Maia, along with issues that stem from losing my mother so early in my life."

For a moment, I stop because I'm getting choked up. "Then there's what happened with Ronan. Eden, I don't want to drag these things into my life with you and our baby. I want to be able to be there for you and her. Or him. Old Marius was good, but I want to be better for you two."

"Well, I love old Marius and this new Marius. I love all the versions of you, baby."

When the word baby comes out of her mouth, her

eyes get very big, and I'm instantly worried. She quickly reassures me she's fine and then says, "I want to show you something I bought this morning. Wait here."

She runs away, so I call after her, "Slow down! You're pregnant!"

A minute later, she returns with a white and gold bag and sets it down on the island already crowded with that enormous floral arrangement and a dozen other decorations from around the penthouse. Before she shows me what's in the bag, she gives me one of her trademark Eden looks of disapproval.

"Marius, you do know there are women who run marathons while they're pregnant, so I can jog through our house. Just because I'm expecting a baby doesn't mean I can't do the same things I've always done. Well, at least in the first two trimesters."

I don't want to ask what happens in the last trimester. Matthias has already told me those last three months were hard on Ava, especially with Matty. I can only hope my Duck has an easier time of it.

"Fair enough, but I worry about you. I'm allowed to do that, right?"

That gets me a smile. "Yes, you can worry. Just don't worry too much. This baby is like the size of a walnut right now. It can handle me trotting into the living room to get a bag."

Appropriately scolded, I glance at the bag. "Did you want to show me something, or is the bag what you wanted to show me?"

Duck rolls her eyes and gives me a tender jab to the solar plexus. "You're silly. No, I didn't want to show you the bag. What I want you to see is in the bag, so look inside."

I do as she says and see white fabric inside the white and gold bag. It doesn't look like enough to be something for a fully grown person, so I have to assume it's something for the baby.

"You bought cotton," I say, teasing her.

She rolls her eyes again and takes the bag off the island to pull out a little outfit. Holding it up in front of her, she points at something in the center of her chest.

"Look! It has a little duck on it. Isn't that cute?"

I lean in and see a little yellow duck with an orange bill on the onesie. "A little duck for my Duck."

Instantly, I realize what I said and smile as I look at Eden. "That's it! I don't know why I didn't think of this before. I've got the kid's nickname already. Little Duck. Duck and Little Duck. It's perfect!"

Eden folds the outfit and slides it back into the bag. "You are too cute. Do you know that? I love that you're as thrilled as I am about us having a baby."

I take her in my arms and hold her to me before kissing her. "Whatever makes you happy, Duck, makes me happy. What is it they say? Happy wife, happy life."

For some reason, that makes her frown. I want to ask why, but Matthias warned me about pregnant women's hormones. The last thing I want to do is make her cry.

"Marius, I want you to be happy all on your own. I love that you want me to be happy, but it's important you're happy too. Tell me. Are you really happy?"

Now I understand. She misunderstood. Okay, I can fix this.

I pull her to me and say, "Duck, I've never been

happier in my life. Seeing you happy makes me happy. I don't know how else to explain it. I've had everything anyone could want in this world, except what you give me."

"And what's that?"

"Your love. I don't need anything but that. I have everything else. But without it, I'd have nothing."

Now she starts crying for real. First come the sniffles, and then a second later, tears fill her eyes.

"That's so beautiful, Marius. How did I get so lucky to find a man like you?" she asks, wrapping her arms around me in a hug.

I kiss the top of her head and whisper against her soft hair, "Well, you see, there was this guy, and he was a real jackass. I saw this gorgeous woman and decided I wanted her for my own. Luckily for me, he made it easy."

She lifts her head and wipes the tears from under her eyes. "So if it was hard, would you have still wanted me?"

I lightly tap the tip of her nose. "I would always want you, Duck."

Eden begins talking about how much we have to get ready for the movers and how she's so glad Matthias and Ava are willing to let us crash at their house until our new place is ready in a couple weeks. I'm not really listening, though, because all I can think about is at this time next year, it'll be three of us.

My Duck and my Little Duck. And me.

EPILOGUE

den

LILY FINISHES HER MINT CHOCOLATE CHIP ICE CREAM and proudly sits up in her chair to show me she's done. Pointing at her empty dish, she smiles broadly.

"All done, Mommy."

"I see, honey. Good job. You didn't get brain freeze either. I'm impressed."

Whenever my five-year-old daughter gets around ice cream, she gobbles it up like a starving soul who hasn't seen food in a week. Invariably, that results in her getting brain freeze, which then is followed by crying. Thankfully, that didn't happen today.

I clean her face and pull her chair out for us to leave just as I see a familiar face walk into the ice cream shop. It's been years since I saw Maia, possibly high school, and she hasn't changed a bit.

Not that I've changed that much. My hair still looks the same, although it's a little shorter now that I'm a mother. I don't have the time I used to have to take care of it with Lily around. Still, I'm not surprised when she recognizes me and starts to walk over to where my daughter and I are sitting.

"Eden? Is that you?" she asks with a big smile.

"Maia? What a blast from the past! How are you?" I ask as Lily stands up from her chair and takes my hand.

"I'm great! How are you?"

For a quick moment, I study how she looks and have to admit she's as beautiful as she was all those years ago. She still has great hair. I always loved how her warm brown hair hung so perfectly. There are still some days I can barely get my hair to behave well enough to put it up in a pony tail.

I look at her brown eyes and see she still can wear makeup like few other women I've encountered in this world. She always did know how to accentuate the positive. I wish I could learn how to use eyeshadow like she does. I never did get the hang of contouring and highlighting like she did.

"You look fantastic, Maia. Whatever you're doing, it's working."

That may sound a bit over the top, but I mean it. She looks great.

She looks down at Lily standing by my side and smiles at her. "And who's this?"

Lily has been practicing for when she goes to kindergarten in a few weeks, so she's ready with an answer. Still holding my hand, she answers, "I'm Lily King. I'm five years old. I can count to one hundred, and

I know my ABCs. I know my address too! Do you want to hear me count?"

As much as I love her being so enthusiastic about school, I'm sure Maia and everyone else in this ice cream shop on this August afternoon aren't interested in hearing all that Lily knows right now. "It's okay, honey. We can count and do your ABCs when we get to the car."

Disappointed she doesn't get to regale strangers with her newfound knowledge, she nods and lets out a heavy sigh. I never want to curtail her learning, but there's a time and a place for everything.

I return my focus to Maia and see a look of confusion. "Is this your daughter? She's lovely," she says.

Beaming my pride in my little girl, I nod and say, "Yes, this is Lily. Lily, say hello to Maia."

My daughter is happy to once more be involved in the conversation and smiles at her. "Hi, Maia!"

"She looks so much like you, Eden. She has the same gorgeous black hair as you."

"Oh, thank you. She's got a lot of me in her, but she's got her father's eyes."

"Did she say her last name is King? Did you marry one of the Kings?" Maia asks, and I sense something in her tone has changed.

I know all too well the history she has with the King brothers. She dated Marius, and then right after they broke up, she slept with Theo.

"Yes, I did. Marius."

Before she can say anything, Lily looks up at us and announces, "My father's name is Marius, and my mother's name is Eden."

317

But Maia isn't listening to my daughter anymore.

"Really?" she asks in a strange voice. Is she jealous?

"Oh, yes. Marius and I have been married for nearly eight years now. I'm sure you remember Ava, my best friend. She married his older brother Matthias, so we're one big happy family."

I watch her reaction carefully, and my suspicions are proven correct when she frowns and says, "Oh. That's nice. Is he still playing at photography?"

Normally, I'd let a comment like that slide since it means nothing to me what anyone thinks of Marius or our life together. What do I care about other people's opinions on what we do?

However, this is Maia, and there's no way I'm letting her get away with making a snide comment like that about the man I love and in front of his daughter, no less. Oh, no. Not happening.

Tilting my chin up ever so slightly so it seems like I'm looking down my nose at her, I answer, "He's a billionaire, Maia. It's not like he sells insurance for a living or anything like that. He doesn't have to work at all. We travel and enjoy life, and I tell him all the time he has my blessing to play around at doing whatever he wants."

Before she can say anything in response, I lean in close to her ear and say in a low voice, "Thankfully, most of the time that's me. You remember how that was, don't you?"

When I lean back away from her, I can see by the flustered expression that's she's upset. Now to go in for the kill.

"Time to go, baby. Say goodbye to Maia."

Lily gives her a cute wave, and as we turn to walk out of the ice cream shop, I say to Maia, "Eat your heart out. You had two Kings and still didn't grab the brass ring you so desperately wanted. Enjoy your ice cream."

I leave her looking absolutely furious and love it! On our way out of the shop, Lily tugs on my hand. I look down at her to see she wants to ask me something.

"Yes, honey. What's up?"

"Don't you like that lady?" she asks with all the innocence of a child.

"I like her well enough. Why?"

"You said you wanted to eat her heart. That doesn't sound like you like her."

Throwing my head back in laughter, I open the door for us to walk out into the hot August afternoon. "Not exactly, but you pick up quickly. Good girl."

I BARELY GET LILY OUT OF HER BOOSTER SEAT BEFORE she's tearing up the driveway to the house. Ava and Matthias are having one of their parties, and we're a little late due to us stopping for ice cream.

"No running in the house!" I call after her, but she's already through the kitchen door by the time I finish.

When I get inside, I find Ava with her daughter Elizabeth sitting at the kitchen table. Dressed in her bathing suit, she's eager to get outside to swim.

"Come on, Mommy! Matty and Theo are already outside with Daddy," she says as she tugs on Ava's arm.

"I'm afraid we got impatient. Where were you? Everyone else is here," Ava says.

I smile as the thought of Maia's upset expression fills

my mind. "I promised Lily we'd go for i-c-e-c-r-e-a-m, so that's why we're late."

Both little girls stare up at us wondering what I spelled, but neither Ava nor I are going to tell them. We still have a little more time to enjoy being able to keep our daughters in the dark about what we're talking about, and neither one of us is going to ruin that.

"Can we go, Mommy?" Lily asks me just as Marius walks into the room.

He opens his arms, and when she sees him, she runs to him and throws her arms around his neck. "Daddy!"

"How's my Little Duck? Did you enjoy your time with Mommy?" he asks as he lifts her up into his arms.

"Daddy, why does Mommy want to eat people's hearts?"

Confused, he shakes his head before glancing over at me. "I'm not sure."

Like most five year olds, our daughter's attention quickly shifts from one topic to the next. "I want to go swimming with Elizabeth. Can we go swimming? Mommy and Aunt Ava are talking, so can you take me and Elizabeth outside to the pool?"

Marius looks over her head toward me for an answer, so I say, "I want to talk to Daddy for a minute, so we have to wait."

The two girls start complaining, so Ava says, "I'll take them. You two talk."

I see by the look on my husband's face that he's sure what I'm about to say isn't good, so I quickly move to show him that he's mistaken. Wrapping my arms around his neck, I kiss him sweetly on the lips and whisper, "I've got a story to tell you."

His expression changes from unease to confusion. "Oh? Something happen at the ice cream shop? And what's this about you wanting to eat people's hearts?"

I stare into his dark eyes and smile. "We met up with someone from the past today when we were getting ready to leave the ice cream shop."

"Really? Your past or my past?"

I answer with a single word, knowing that's all that's necessary. "Maia."

He doesn't say anything, but he still looks confused so I continue. "When she asked Lily her name, our daughter gave her full name. That piqued Maia's curiosity, and she asked me if I had married one of you King boys. I loved telling her I married you."

"I can't believe she even remembers me."

I roll my eyes at his fake modesty. "Baby, you were the best thing she ever had in her life. Trust me. She remembers. From how she asked about if you were still playing around with photography, I'd say she's kept up with what you've been doing."

"Imagine that."

He tightens his hold on me and kisses me long and deep, but I've got a little more to tell him. Knowing how things happened between the two of them, this last part is really what I want to share with him.

"So I didn't get to the good part yet. The part Lily was referring to. So after she made that crack about you playing around with photography, I made sure to remind her that you're a billionaire and can play at anything you want since you're not an insurance agent or anything like that."

A tiny smile lifts the corners of his mouth. "You do know her husband is an insurance agent, right?"

"Of course, I do. I wouldn't have mentioned that job if he wasn't."

Now his smile grows bigger. "I do love when you're sassy, Duck."

"Maia always had a bit of the snob in her. You know I don't look down on any job, but if our places were reversed, she would have made sure I knew she thought she was better than me."

Marius smiles. "She was never better than you at anything."

"Well, I didn't stop with that little slam on her. As we were leaving, I told her to eat her heart out because she had two of you Kings and still didn't get the brass ring."

His eyes fill with love, and he hugs me tightly against him. "I love you for saying that. Thank you, Eden."

I stroke the back of his neck thinking he needs a haircut. "I wasn't going to let her get away with saying anything about you, baby. It's been over a decade, but it was time for her to know she messed up when it came to you."

He leans back and sighs, smiling at me. "You're one of a kind, Duck. I love you. Don't ever doubt that."

"And I love you, Marius. I'm very protective of the people I love. There was no way I was going to let her say anything about you, especially in front of our daughter. Let her go back to her husband and be miserable because she knows she could have had you."

Marius shakes his head as his expression turns serious. "I thought I loved her when all that happened with her and Theo. From the moment you and I got together, I realized whatever I felt for her wasn't love. Not love like I feel for you. You and I were meant for one another."

"I made sure to mention that Ava married Matthias, so we're one big happy family. Trust me. She's eating her heart out right now."

He cradles my face in his strong hands and softly kisses me. "Duck, how did I get so lucky?"

Pretending to think about that question, I look up at the ceiling and answer, "Hmmm. Well, I was with a jackass who thought it would be good to pull my hair and punch me in the eye. The rest, as they say, is history."

"I'm just glad I was there that day. I hate the idea of another man being the person to help you."

He sounds genuinely concerned, like I would have just gone with any old guy who showed up in that hotel lobby. "Marius, I don't know if it was meant to be or a happy circumstance, but I'd wanted you for years. Why do you think Ava tried to set us up all that time?"

"Really?"

I nod, smiling as I think back to the first time I told Ava I was interested in him. "Oh, yeah. In fact, you could say we have Maia to thank for us getting together."

"How's that?" he asks, clearly not believing she could have any part in our happiness, other than today, of course.

I look around to see if anyone is nearby and then slide my hand down the front of his shorts. Palming his already hard cock, I answer, "I didn't lie when I told you

Maia always said she walked funny after she was with you. That was too tempting for me not to find out if she was telling the truth."

His eyelids slowly flutter shut as I slowly stroke him up and down. "Well, thank you to my ex-girlfriend."

When I stop, his eyes open and he looks disappointed. "You know, I have to go out to the pool like this now."

"You better go somewhere and handle this situation because that's nothing short of creepy with little kids around."

Suddenly, he gets a twinkle in his eye. "I've got an idea. We can go to the powder room off the living room. I'm game if you are."

I roll my eyes at his suggestion. "The kids use that bathroom when they come in from swimming. Do you really want to risk any of them, including our daughter, walking in on us?"

His shoulders sag, and he sighs heavily. "Well, when you put it like that, I guess not. Too bad Ava and Matthias gave my old room to Matty."

"Yeah, too bad." I hesitate for a moment before confessing something that's been on my mind for a while. "Marius, I was thinking that I'd like to have another baby."

I watch his eyes grow big in utter shock. "Really? I thought having Lily put that thought right out of your head. You said it was pretty bad."

"It wasn't bad. That was just me talking in the moment."

"Morning sickness for the first three months, back

pain, high blood pressure brought on by pregnancy. Am I forgetting anything?" he asks.

I know what he's trying to do. I haven't forgotten how being pregnant made me feel. I just think I can handle it again.

"Yes, you forgot my ankles swelling up so I had to walk around with cankles for the last trimester."

He levels his gaze on me and nods. "Yeah. That too. Are you sure you want to go through all of that again?"

"Honey, I know how hard it was with Lily, but maybe it won't be with a second baby. Or if it's worse, then I guess we'll stop at two. I'm just thinking I'd like to have another child. What do you think?"

Marius smiles and kisses me. "I am always the man for that job, Duck. We can start right now. I'll run out and tell Matthias and Ava they're watching Lily for the day. They'll be fine with it. We can be back at the house in less than five minutes, assuming I drive fast, ten if I get stuck behind some slowpoke."

"We can wait for tonight. I think that would be okay, right?"

He pouts and lets out a heavy sigh. "I guess that would work too. Are you sure you don't want to get freaky in the powder room?"

I take his hand and start to lead him toward the kitchen door. "I think we shouldn't, but since you're already raring to go, maybe we should take the long way out to the pool. That'll give you time to get yourself in order."

"You have this effect on me, Duck. I can't help it. This is what happens when a man is crazy in love with his wife."

I look back at him and smile. I know how lucky I am to have a man like Marius King.

Look for Forever King (King Brothers #5 coming soon!

ABOUT THE AUTHOR

K.M. Scott writes contemporary romance stories of sexy, intense, and unforgettable love and edge-of-your-seat thrillers. A New York Times and USA Today bestselling author, she's been in love with romance since reading her first romance novel in junior high (she was a very curious girl!). Under her Gabrielle Bisset name, she writes paranormal and historical romance, and under the Anina Collins name, she writes cozy mysteries. She lives in Pennsylvania with a herd of animals and when she's not writing can be found reading or feeding her TV addiction.

Be sure to visit K.M.'s Facebook page at **https://www.facebook.com/kmscottauthor** for all the latest on her books, along with giveaways and other goodies! And to hear all the news on K.M. Scott books first, sign up for her newsletter today and be sure to visit her website at **https://www.kmscottbooks.com**

ALSO BY K.M. SCOTT

Addicted To You Series Box Set

PROJECT ARTEMIS SERIES

In The Darkness (Project Artemis #1)

After The Storm (Project Artemis #2)

Behind The Scenes (Project Artemis #3)

Project Artemis Box Set

FINDING THE ONE SERIES

Hard Work (Finding The One #1)

Big Love (Finding The One #2)

DIRTY BOSS SERIES

Sweet Things (Dirty Boss #1)

Private Secretary (Dirty Boss #2)

Play Date (Dirty Boss #3)

Dirty Boss Volume One

THRILLERS

Now You Know How It Feels

The Neighbor

The Cult

K.M.'S BOOKS ARE IN AUDIOBOOK TOO!

BOOKS BY K.M. SCOTT WRITING AS ANINA COLLINS